THE KING OF THE JUNGLE
IN THE LAND OF THE NOONDAY SUN

When word came from the inner world that David Innes, Emperor of Pellucidar, was imprisoned in a Korsar dungeon, Jason Gridley sped to the jungles of Africa to seek aid from the one man capable of besting the terrors of savage Pellucidar. And Tarzan, true to his reputation, organized an expedition, supervised construction of a giant dirigible, and set off at once for the polar entrance to the hidden land.

But having arrived, Tarzan realized the worst was yet before them. For almost immediately, Tarzan, Jason, Captain Zuppner and the ten Waziri warriors became separated—each forced to face the terrors of the unknown alone.

The thrills of man against prehistoric monster are at fever pitch in TARZAN AT THE EARTH'S CORE.

EDGAR RICE BURROUGHS (1875–1950)

Edgar Rice Burroughs is one of the world's most popular authors. Although not fully recognized by some critics and libraries, he remains one of the best known American fiction writers of the 20th century. With no previous experience as an author, he wrote the renown classic TARZAN OF THE APES, first published in 1912. In the ensuing forty-two years, he wrote over 100 stories and articles, nearly all of which were published during his lifetime. Although best known for creating TARZAN, his worlds of adventure and romance ranged from the American West to the jungles of Asia, from inside the earth on to the moon, Mars, Venus and even beyond the farthest star.

No one knows how many copies of ERB's 68 books have been published throughout the world. It is conservative to say, however, that of the translations into 31 languages in addition to the artifical languages of Esperanto and Braille, the total number must run into the hundreds of millions. When one considers the additional world-wide following of the Tarzan newspaper feature, radio programs, comic magazines, motion pictures and television series, Burroughs must be known by a thousand million people.

Whether you are about to read an adventure on Mars, a romance of the jungle, or a fantasy of the future, the magic of the prolific imagination of Edgar Rice Burroughs will hold you spellbound for a long time to come.

* * *

Attesting to the unparalleled following of Edgar Rice Burroughs, a club and several magazines are managed by dedicated ERB admirers, who publish information, discussions and art on Burroughs and his creations. Interested readers are invited to inquire for further information from:

The Burroughs Bibliophiles (club), 6657 Locust St., Kansas City, Mo. 64131

ERB-dom (magazine), P.O. Box 550, Evergreen, Colo. 80439

The Barsoomian (magazine), 84 Charlton Road, Rochester, N.Y. 14617

ERBANIA (magazine), 8001 Fernview Lane, Tampa, Fla. 33615

EDGAR RICE BURROUGHS
TARZAN
AT THE EARTH'S CORE

AN ACE BOOK
Ace Publishing Corporation
1120 Avenue of the Americas
New York, N.Y. 10036

FOREWORD

PELLUCIDAR, as as every schoolboy knows, is a world within a world, lying, as it does, upon the inner surface of the hollow sphere, which is the Earth.

It was discovered by David Innes and Abner Perry upon the occasion when they made the trial trip upon the mechanical prospector invented by Perry, wherewith they hoped to locate new beds of anthracite coal. Owing, however, to their inability to deflect the nose of the prospector, after it had started downward into the Earth's crust, they bored straight through for five hundred miles, and upon the third day, when Perry was already unconscious owing to the consumption of their stock of oxygen, and David was fast losing consciousness, the nose of the prospector broke through the crust of the inner world and the cabin was filled with fresh air.

In the years that have intervened, weird adventures have befallen these two explorers. Perry has never returned to the outer crust, and Innes but once—upon that occasion when he made the difficult and dangerous return trip in the prospector for the purpose of bringing back to the empire he had founded in the inner world the means to bestow upon his primitive people of the stone age the civilization of the twentieth century.

But what with battles with primitive men and still more primitive beasts and reptiles, the advance of the empire of Pellucidar toward civilization has been small; and in so far as the great area of the inner world is concerned, or the countless millions of its teeming life of another age than ours, David Innes and Abner Perry might never have existed.

5

When one considers that these land and water areas upon the surface of Pellucidar are in opposite relationship to the same areas upon the outer crust, some slight conception of the vast extent of this mighty world within a world may be dreamed.

The land area of the outer world comprises some fifty-three million square miles, or one-quarter of the total area of the earth's surface; while within Pellucidar three-quarters of the surface is land, so that jungle, mountain, forest and plain stretch interminably over 124,110,000 square miles; nor are the oceans with their area of 41,370,000 square miles of any mean or niggardly extent.

Thus, considering the land area only, we have the strange anomaly of a larger world within a smaller one, but then Pellucidar is a world of deviation from what we of the outer crust have come to accept as unalterable laws of nature.

In the exact center of the earth hangs Pellucidar's sun, a tiny orb compared with ours, but sufficient to illuminate Pellucidar and flood her teeming jungles with warmth and life-giving rays. Her sun hanging thus perpetually at zenith, there is no night upon Pellucidar, but always an endless eternity of noon.

There being no stars and no apparent movement of the sun, Pellucidar has no points of compass; nor has she any horizon since her surface curves always upward in all directions from the observer, so that far above one's line of vision, plain or sea or distant mountain range go onward and upward until lost in the haze of the distance. And again, in a world where there is no sun, no stars and no moon, such as we know, there can be no such thing as time, as we know it. And so, in Pellucidar, we have a timeless world which must necessarily be free from those pests who are constantly calling our attention to "the busy little bee" and to the fact that "time is money." While time may be "the soul of this world" and the "essence of contracts," in the beatific existence of Pellucidar it is nothing and less than nothing.

Thrice in the past have we of the outer world received communication from Pellucidar. We know that Perry's first great gift of civilization to the stone age was gunpowder.

We know that he followed this with repeating rifles, small ships of war upon which were mounted guns of no great caliber, and finally we know that he perfected a radio.

Knowing Perry as something of an empiric, we were not surprised to learn that his radio could not be tuned in upon any known wave or wave length of the outer world, and it remained for young Jason Gridley of Tarzana, experimenting with his newly discovered Gridley Wave, to pick up the first message from Pellucidar.

The last word that we received from Perry before his messages faltered and died out was to the effect that David Innes, first Emperor of Pellucidar, was languishing in a dark dungeon in the land of the Korsars, far across continent and ocean from his beloved land of Sari, which lies upon a great plateau not far inland from the Lural Az.

I

THE O-220

Tarzan of the apes paused to listen and to sniff the air. Had you been there you could not have heard what he heard, or had you you could not have interpreted it. You could have smelled nothing but the mustiness of decaying vegetation, which blended with the aroma of growing things.

The sounds that Tarzan heard came from a great distance and were faint even to his ears; nor at first could he definitely ascribe them to their true source, though he conceived the impression that they heralded the coming of a party of men.

Buto the rhinoceros, Tantor the elephant or Numa the lion might come and go through the forest without arousing more than the indifferent interest of the Lord of the Jungle, but when man came Tarzan investigated, for man alone of all creatures brings change and dissension and strife wheresoever he first sets foot.

Reared to manhood among the great apes without knowledge of the existence of any other creatures like himself, Tarzan had since learned to anticipate with concern each fresh invasion of his jungle by these two-footed harbingers of strife. Among many races of men he had found friends, but this did not prevent him from questioning the purposes and the motives of whosoever entered his domain. And so today he moved silently through the middle terrace of his leafy way in the direction of the sounds that he had heard.

As the distance closed between him and those he went to investigate, his keen ears cataloged the sound of padding, naked feet and the song of native carriers as they swung along beneath their heavy burdens. And then to his nostrils came the scent spoor of black men and with it, faintly, the suggestion of another scent, and Tarzan knew that a white man was on safari before the head of the column came in view along the wide, well marked game trail, above which the Lord of the Jungle waited.

Near the head of the column marched a young white man, and when Tarzan's eyes had rested upon him for a moment as he swung along the trail they impressed their stamp of approval of the stranger within the ape-man's brain, for in common with many savage beasts and primitive men Tarzan possessed an uncanny instinct in judging aright the characters of strangers whom he met.

Turning about, Tarzan moved swiftly and silently through the trees until he was some little distance ahead of the marching safari, then he dropped down into the trail and awaited its coming.

Rounding a curve in the trail the leading askari came in sight of him and when they saw him they halted and commenced to jabber excitedly, for these were men recruited in another district—men who did not know Tarzan of the Apes by sight.

"I am Tarzan," announced the ape-man. "What do you in Tarzan's country?"

Immediately the young man, who had halted abreast of his askari, advanced toward the ape-man. There was a smile upon his eager face. "You are Lord Greystoke?" he asked.

"Here, I am Tarzan of the Apes," replied the foster son of Kala.

"Then luck is certainly with me," said the young man, "for I have come all the way from Southern California to find you."

"Who are you," demanded the ape-man, "and what do you want of Tarzan of the Apes?"

"My name is Jason Gridley," replied the other. "And what I have come to talk to you about will make a long story. I hope that you can find the time to accompany me to our next camp and the patience to listen to me there until I have explained my mission."

9

Tarzan nodded. "In the jungle," he said, "we are not often pressed for time. Where do you intend making camp?"

"The guide that I obtained in the last village complained of being ill and turned back an hour ago, and as none of my own men is familiar with this country we do not know whether there is a suitable camp-site within one mile or ten."

"There is one within half a mile," replied Tarzan, "and with good water."

"Good," said Gridley; and the safari resumed its way, the porters laughing and singing at the prospect of an early camp.

It was not until Jason and Tarzan were enjoying their coffee that evening that the ape-man reverted to the subject of the American's visit.

"And now," he said, "what has brought you all the way from Southern California to the heart of Africa?"

Gridley smiled. "Now that I am actually here," he said, "and face to face with you, I am suddenly confronted with the conviction that after you have heard my story it is going to be difficult to convince you that I am not crazy, and yet in my own mind I am so thoroughly convinced of the truth of what I am going to tell you that I have already invested a considerable amount of money and time to place my plan beore you for the purpose of enlisting your personal and financial support, and I am ready and willing to invest still more money and all of my time. Unfortunately I cannot wholly finance the expedition that I have in mind from my personal resources, but that is not primarily my reason for coming to you. Doubtless I could have raised the necessary money elsewhere, but I believe that you are peculiarly fitted to lead such a venture as I have in mind."

"Whatever the expedition may be that you are contemplating," said Tarzan, "the potential profits must be great indeed if you are willing to risk so much of your own money."

"On the contrary," replied Gridley, "there will be no financial profit for anyone concerned in so far as I now know."

"And you are an American?" asked Tarzan, smiling.

"We are not all money mad," replied Gridley.

"Then what is the incentive? Explain the whole proposition to me."

"Have you ever heard of the theory that the earth is a hollow sphere, containing a habitable world within its interior?"

"The theory that has been definitely refuted by scientific investigation," replied the ape-man.

"But has it been refuted satisfactorily?" asked Gridley.

"To the satisfaction of the scientists," replied Tarzan.

"And to my satisfaction, too," replied the American, "until I recently received a message direct from the inner world."

"You surprise me," said the ape-man.

"And I, too, was surprised, but the fact remains that I have been in radio communication with Abner Perry in the inner world of Pellucidar and I have brought a copy of that message with me and also an affidavit of its authenticity from a man with whose name you are familiar and who was with me when I received the message; in fact, he was listening in at the same time with me. Here they are."

From a portfolio he took a letter which he handed to Tarzan and a bulky manuscript bound in board covers.

"I shall not take the time to read you all of the story of Tanar of Pellucidar," said Gridley, "because there is a great deal in it that is not essential to the exposition of my plan."

"As you will," said Tarzan. "I am listening."

For half an hour Jason Gridley read excerpts from the manuscript before him. "This," he said, when he had completed the reading, "is what convinced me of the existence of Pellucidar, and it is the unfortunate situation of David Innes that impelled me to come to you with the proposal that we undertake an expedition whose first purpose shall be to rescue him from the dungeon of the Korsars."

"And how do you think this may be done?" asked the ape-man. "Are you convinced of the correctness of Innes' theory that there is an entrance to the inner world at each pole?"

"I am free to confess that I do not know what to believe," replied the American. "But after I received this message from Perry I commenced to investigate and I discovered that the theory of an inhabitable world at the center of the earth with openings leading into it at the north and south poles is no new one and that there is much evidence to support it. I found a very complete exposition of the theory in a book written about 1830 and in another work of more recent time. Therein I found what seemed to be a reasonable explanation of many well known phenomena that have not been satisfactorily explained by any hypothesis endorsed by science."

"What, for example?" asked Tarzan.

"Well, for example, warm winds and warm ocean currents coming from the north and encountered and reported by practically all arctic explorers; the presence of the limbs and branches of trees with green foliage upon them floating southward from the far north, far above the latitude where any such trees are found upon the outer crust; then there is the phenomenon of the northern lights, which in the light of David Innes' theory may easily be explained as rays of light from the central sun of the inner world, breaking occasionally through the fog and cloud banks above the polar opening. Again there is the pollen, which often thickly covers the snow and ice in portions of the polar regions. This pollen could not come from elsewhere than the inner world. And in addition to all this is the insistence of the far northern tribes of Eskimos that their forefathers came from a country to the north."

"Did not Amundson and Ellsworth in the Norge expedition definitely disprove the theory of a north polar opening in the earth's crust, and have not airplane flights been made over a considerable portion of the hitherto unexplored regions near the pole?" demanded the ape-man.

"The answer to that is that the polar opening is so large that a ship, a dirigible or an airplane could dip down over the edge into it a short distance and return without ever being aware of the fact, but the most tenable theory is that in most instances explorers have merely followed around the outer rim of the orifice, which would largely explain the peculiar and mystifying action of compasses and other scientific instruments at points near the so-called north pole—matters which have greatly puzzled all arctic explorers."

"You are convinced then that there is not only an inner world but that there is an entrance to it at the north pole?" asked Tarzan.

"I am convinced that there is an inner world, but I am not convinced of the existence of a polar opening," replied Gridley. "I can only say that I believe there is sufficient evidence to warrant the organization of an expedition such as I have suggested."

"Assuming that a polar opening into an inner world exists, by just what means do you purpose accomplishing the discovery and exploration of it?"

"The most practical means of transportation that exists today for carrying out my plan would be a specially constructed rigid airship, built along the lines of the modern Zeppelin. Such a ship, using helium gas, would show a higher factor of safety than any other means of transportation at our disposal. I have given the matter considerable thought and I feel sure that if there is such a polar opening, the obstacles that would confront us in an attempt to enter the inner world would be far less than those encountered by the Norge in its famous trip across the pole to Alaska, for there is no question in my mind but that it made a wide detour in following the rim of the polar orifice and covered a far greater distance than we shall have to cover to reach a reasonably safe anchorage below the cold, polar sea that David Innes discovered north of the land of the Korsars before he was finally taken prisoner by them.

"The greatest risk that we would have to face would be a possible inability to return to the outer crust, owing to the depletion of our helium gas that might be made necessary by the maneuvering of the ship. But that is only the same chance of life or death that every explorer and scientific investigator must be willing to assume in the prosecution of his labors. If it were but possible to build a hull sufficiently light, and at the same time sufficiently strong, to withstand atmospheric pressure, we could dispense with both the dangerous hydrogen gas and the rare and expensive helium gas and have the assurance of the utmost safety and maximum of buoyancy in a ship supported entirely by vacuum tanks."

"Perhaps even that is possible," said Tarzan, who was now evincing increasing interest in Gridley's proposition.

The American shook his head. "It may be possible some day," he said, "but not at present with any known material. Any receptacle having sufficient strength to withstand the atmospheric pressure upon a vacuum would have a weight far too great for the vacuum to lift."

"Perhaps," said Tarzan, "and, again, perhaps not."

"What do you mean?" inquired Gridley.

"What you have just said," replied Tarzan, "reminds me of something that a young friend of mine recently told me. Erich von Harben is something of a scientist and explorer himself, and the last time that I saw him he had just returned from a second expedition into the Wiramwazi Mountains, where he told me that he had discovered a lake-dwelling tribe using canoes made of a metal that was apparently as light as cork and stronger than steel. He brought some samples of the metal back with him, and at the time I last saw him he was conducting some experiments in a little laboratory he has rigged up at his father's mission."

"Where is this man?" demanded Gridley.

"Dr. von Harben's mission is in the Urambi country," replied the ape-man, "about four marches west of where we now are."

Far into the night the two men discussed plans for the project, for Tarzan was now thoroughly interested, and the next day they turned back toward the Urambi country and von Harben's mission, where they arrived on the fourth day and were greeted by Dr. von Harben and his son, Erich, as well as by the latter's wife, the beautiful Favonia of Castrum Mare.

It is not my intention to weary you with a recital of the details of the organization and equipment of the Pellucidarian expedition, although that portion of it which relates to the search for and discovery of the native mine containing the remarkable metal now known as Harbenite, filled as it was with adventure and excitement, is well worth a volume by itself.

While Tarzan and Erich von Harben were locating the

mine and transporting the metal to the seacoast, Jason Gridley was in Friedrichshafen in consultation with the engineers of the company he had chosen to construct the specially designed airship in which the attempt was to be made to reach the inner world.

Exhaustive tests were made of the samples of Harbenite brought to Friedrichshafen by Jason Gridley. Plans were drawn, and by the time the shipment of the ore arrived everything was in readiness to commence immediate construction, which was carried on secretly. And six months later, when the O-220, as it was officially known, was ready to take the air, it was generally considered to be nothing more than a new design of the ordinary type of rigid airship, destined to be used as a common carrier upon one of the already numerous commercial airways of Europe.

The great cigar-shaped hull of the O-220 was 997 feet in length and 150 feet in diameter. The interior of the hull was divided into six large, air-tight compartments, three of which, running the full length of the ship, were above the medial line and three below. Inside the hull and running along each side of the ship, between the upper and lower vaccum tanks, were long corridors in which were located the engines, motors and pumps, in addition to supplies of gasoline and oil.

The internal location of the engine room was made possible by the elimination of fire risk, which is an ever-present source of danger in airships which depend for their lifting power upon hydrogen gas, as well as to the absolutely fireproof construction of the O-220; every part of which, with the exception of a few cabin fittings and furniture, was of Harbenite, this metal being used throughout except for certain bushings and bearings in motors, generators and propellers.

Connecting the port and starboard engine and fuel corridors were two transverse corridors, one forward and one aft, while bisecting these transverse corridors were two climbing shafts extending from the bottom of the ship to the top.

The upper end of the forward climbing shaft terminated in a small gun and observation cabin at the top of the ship, along which was a narrow walking-way extending from the forward cabin to a small turret near the tail of the ship, where provision had been made for fixing a machine gun.

The main cabin, running along the keel of the ship, was an integral part of the hull, and because of this entirely rigid construction, which eliminated the necessity for cabins suspended below the hull, the O-220 was equipped with landing gear in the form of six, large, heavily tired wheels projecting below the bottom of the main cabin. In the extreme stern of the keel cabin a small scout monoplane was carried in such a way that it could be lowered through the bottom of the ship and launched while the O-220 was in flight.

Eight air-cooled motors drove as many propellers, which were arranged in pairs upon either side of the ship and staggered in such a manner that the air from the forward propellers would not interfere with those behind.

The engines, developing 5600 horsepower, were capable of driving the ship at a speed of 105 miles per hour.

In the O-220 the ordinary axial wire, which passes the whole length of the ship through the center, consisted of a tubular shaft of Harbenite from which smaller tubular braces radiated, like the spokes of a wheel, to the tubular girders, to which the Harbenite plates of the outer envelope were welded.

Owing to the extreme lightness of Harbenite, the total weight of the ship was 75 tons, while the total lift of its vacuum tanks was 225 tons.

For purposes of maneuvering the ship and to facilitate landing, each of the vacuum tanks was equipped with a bank of eight air valves operated from the control cabin at the forward end of the keel; while six pumps, three in the starboard and three in the port engine corridors, were designed to expel the air from the tanks when it became necessary to renew the vacuum. Special rudders and elevators were also operated from the forward control cabin as well as from an auxiliary position aft in the port engine corridor, in the event that the control cabin steering gear should break down.

In the main keel cabin were located the quarters for the officers and crew, gun and ammunition room, provision room, galley, additional gasoline and oil storage tanks, and water tanks, the latter so constructed that the contents of any of them might be emptied instantaneously in case of an emergency, while a proportion of the gasoline and oil tanks were slip tanks that might be slipped through the bottom of the ship in cases of extreme emergency when it was necessary instantaneously to reduce the weight of the load.

This, then, briefly, was the great, rigid airship in which Jason Gridley and Tarzan of the Apes hoped to discover the north polar entrance to the inner world and rescue David Innes, Emperor of Pellucidar, from the dungeons of the Korsars.

II

PELLUCIDAR

JUST BEFORE daybreak of a clear June morning, the O-220 moved slowly from its hangar under its own power. Fully loaded and equipped, it was to make its test flight under load conditions identical with those which would obtain when it set forth upon its long journey. The three lower tanks were still filled with air and she carried an excess of water ballast sufficient to overcome her equilibrium, so that while she moved lightly over the ground she moved with entire safety and could be maneuvered almost as handily as an automobile.

As she came into the open her pumps commenced to expel the air from the three lower tanks, and at the same time a portion of her excess water ballast was slowly discharged, and almost immediately the huge ship rose slowly and gracefully from the ground.

The entire personnel of the ship's company during the test flight was the same that had been selected for the expedition. Zuppner, who had been chosen as captain, had been in charge of the construction of the ship and had a considerable part in its designing. There were two mates, Von Horst and Dorf, who had been officers in the Imperial air forces, as also had the navigator, Lieutenant Hines. In addition to these there were twelve engineers and eight mechanics, a negro cook and two Filipino cabin-boys.

Tarzan was commander of the expedition, with Jason Gridley as his lieutenant, while the fighting men of the ship consisted of Muviro and nine of his Waziri warriors.

As the ship rose gracefully above the city, Zuppner, who was at the controls, could scarce restrain his enthusiasm.

"The sweetest thing I ever saw!" he exclaimed. "She responds to the lightest touch."

"I am not surprised at that," said Hines; "I knew she'd do it. Why we've got twice the crew we need to handle her."

"There you go again, Lieutenant," said Tarzan, laughing; "but do not think that my insistence upon a large crew was based upon any lack of confidence in the ship. We are going into a strange world. We may be gone a long time. If we reach our destination we shall have fighting, as each of you men who volunteered has been informed many times, so that while we may have twice as many men as we need for the trip in, we may yet find ourselves short handed on the return journey, for not all of us will return."

"I suppose you are right," said Hines; "but with the feel of this ship permeating me and the quiet peacefulness of the scene below, danger and death seem remote."

"I hope they are," returned Tarzan, "and I hope that we shall return with every man that goes out with us, but I believe in being prepared and to that end Gridley and I have been studying navigation and we want you to give us a chance at some practical experience before we reach our destination."

Zuppner laughed. "They have you marked already, Hines," he said.

The Lieutenant grinned. "I'll teach them all I know," he said; "but I'll bet the best dinner that can be served in Berlin that if this ship returns I'll still be her navigator."

"That is a case of heads-I-win, tails-you-lose," said Gridley.

"And to return to the subject of preparedness," said Tarzan, "I am going to ask you to let my Waziri help the mechanics and engineers. They are highly intelligent men, quick to learn, and if some calamity should overtake us we cannot have too many men familiar with the engines, and other machinery of the ship."

"You are right," said Zuppner, "and I shall see that it is done."

The great, shining ship sailed majestically north; Ravensburg fell astern and half an hour later the somber gray ribbon of the Danube lay below them.

The longer they were in the air the more enthusiastic Zuppner became. "I had every confidence in the successful outcome of the trial flight," he said; "but I can assure you that I did not look for such perfection as I find in this ship. It marks a new era in aeronautics, and I am convinced that long before we cover the four hundred miles to Hamburg that we shall have established the entire air worthiness of the O-220 to the entire satisfaction of each of us."

"To Hamburg and return to Friedrichshafen was to have been the route of the trial trip," said Tarzan, "but why turn back at Hamburg?"

The others turned questioning eyes upon him as the purport of his query sank home.

"Yes, why?" demanded Gridley.

Zuppner shrugged his shoulders. "We are fully equipped and provisioned," he said.

"Then why waste eight hundred miles in returning to Friedrichshafen?" demanded Hines.

"If you are all agreeable we shall continue toward the north," said Tarzan. And so it was that the trial trip of the O-220 became an actual start upon its long journey toward the interior of the earth, and the secrecy that was desired for the expedition was insured.

The plan had been to follow the Tenth Meridian east of Greenwich north to the pole. But to avoid attracting unnecessary notice a slight deviation from this course was found desirable, and the ship passed to the west of Hamburg and out across the waters of the North Sea, and thus due north, passing to the west of Spitzbergen and out across the frozen polar wastes.

Maintaining an average cruising speed of about 75 miles per hour, the O-220 reached the vicinity of the north pole about midnight of the second day, and excitement ran high when Hines announced that in accordance with his calculation they should be directly over the pole. At Tarzan's suggestion the ship circled slowly at an altitude of a few hundred feet above the rough, snow-covered ice.

"We ought to be able to recognize it by the Italian flags," said Zuppner, with a smile. But if any reminders of the passage of the Norge remained below them, they were effectually hidden by the mantle of many snows.

The ship made a single circle above the desolate ice pack before she took up her southerly course along the 170th East Meridian.

From the moment that the ship struck south from the pole Jason Gridley remained constantly with Hines and Zuppner eagerly and anxiously watching the instruments, or gazing down upon the bleak landscape ahead. It was Gridley's belief that the north polar opening lay in the vicinity of 85 north latitude and 170 east longitude. Before him were compass, aneroids, bubble statoscope, air speed indicator, inclinometers, rise and fall indicator, bearing plate, clock and thermometers; but the instrument that commanded his closest attention was the compass, for Jason Gridley held a theory and upon the correctness of it depended their success in finding the north polar opening.

For five hours the ship flew steadily toward the south, when she developed an apparent tendency to fall off toward the west.

"Hold her steady, Captain," cautioned Gridley, "for if I am correct we are now going over the lip of the polar opening, and the deviation is in the compass only and not in our course. The further we go along this course the more erratic the compass will become and if we were presently to move upward, or in other words, straight out across the polar opening toward its center, the needle would spin erratically in a circle. But we could not reach the center of the polar opening because of the tremendous altitude which this would require. I believe that we are now on the eastern verge of the opening and if whatever deviation from the present course you make is to the starboard we shall slowly spiral downward into Pellucidar, but your compass will be useless for the next four to six hundred miles."

Zuppner shook his head, dubiously. "If this weather holds, we may be able to do it," he said, "but if it commences to blow I doubt my ability to keep any sort of a course if I am not to follow the compass."

"Do the best you can," said Gridley, "and when in doubt put her to starboard."

So great was the nervous strain upon all of them that for hours at a time scarcely a word was exchanged.

"Look!" exclaimed Hines suddenly. "There is open water just ahead of us."

"That, of course, we might expect," said Zuppner, "even if there is no polar opening, and you know that I have been skeptical about that ever since Gridley first explained his theory to me."

"I think," said Gridley, with a smile, "that really I am the only one in the party who has had any faith at all in the theory, but please do not call it my theory for it is not, and even I should not have been surprised had the theory proven to be a false one. But if any of you has been watching the sun for the last few hours, I think that you will have to agree with me that even though there may be no polar opening into an inner world, there must be a great depression at this point in the earth's crust and that we had gone down into it for a considerable distance, for you will notice that the midnight sun is much lower than it should be and that the further we continue upon this course the lower it drops—eventually it will set completely, and if I am not much mistaken we shall soon see the light of the eternal noonday sun of Pellucidar."

Suddenly the telephone rang and Hines put the receiver to his ear. "Very good, sir," he said, after a moment, and hung up. "It was Von Horst, Captain, reporting from the observation cabin. He has sighted land dead ahead."

"Land!" exclaimed Zuppner. "The only land our chart shows in this direction is Siberia."

"Siberia lies over a thousand miles south of 85, and we cannot be over three hundred miles south of 85," said Gridley.

"Then we have either discovered a new arctic land, or we are approaching the northern frontiers of Pellucidar," said Lieutenant Hines.

"And that is just what we are doing," said Gridley. "Look at your thermometer."

"The devil!" exclaimed Zuppner. "It is only twenty degrees above zero Fahrenheit."

"You can see the land plainly now," said Tarzan. "It looks desolate enough, but there are only little patches of snow here and there."

"This corresponds with the land Innes described north of Korsar," said Gridley.

Word was quickly passed around the ship to the other officers and the crew that there was reason to believe that the land below them was Pellucidar. Excitement ran high, and every man who could spare a moment from his duties was aloft on the walkingway, or peering through portholes for a glimpse of the inner world.

Steadily the O-220 forged southward and just as the rim of the midnight sun disappeared from view below the horizon astern, the glow of Pellucidar's central sun was plainly visible ahead.

The nature of the landscape below was changing rapidly. The barren land had fallen astern, the ship had crossed a range of wooded hills and now before it lay a great forest that stretched on and on seemingly curving upward to be lost eventually in the haze of the distance. This was indeed Pellucidar—the Pellucidar of which Jason Gridley had dreamed.

Beyond the forest lay a rolling plain dotted with clumps of trees, a well-watered plain through which wound numerous streams, which emptied into a large river at its opposite side.

Great herds of game were grazing in the open pasture land and nowhere was there sight of man.

"This looks like heaven to me," said Tarzan of the Apes. "Let us land, Captain.

Slowly the great ship came to earth as air was taken into the lower vacuum tanks.

Short ladders were run out, for the bottom of the cabin was only six feet above the ground, and presently the entire ship's company, with the exception of a watch of an officer and two men, were knee deep in the lush grasses of Pellucidar.

"I thought we might get some fresh meat," said Tarzan, "but the ship has frightened all the game away."

"From the quantity of it I saw, we shall not have to go far to bag some," said Dorf.

"What we need most right now, however, is rest," said Tarzan. "For weeks every man has been working at high pitch in completing the preparation for the expedition and I doubt if one of us has had over two hours sleep in the last three days. I suggest that we remain here until we are all thoroughly rested and then take up a systematic search for the city of Korsar."

The plan met with general approval and preparations were made for a stay of several days.

"I believe," said Gridley to Captain Zuppner, "that it would be well to issue strict orders that no one is to leave the ship, or rather its close vicinity, without permission from you and that no one be allowed to venture far afield except in parties commanded by an officer, for we have every assurance that we shall meet with savage men and far more savage beasts everywhere within Pellucidar."

"I hope that you will except me from that order," said Tarzan, smiling.

"I believe that you can take care of yourself in any country," said Zuppner.

"And I can certainly hunt to better effect alone than I can with a party," said the ape-man.

"In any event," continued Zuppner, "the order comes from you as commander, and no one will complain if you exempt yourself from its provisions since I am sure that none of the rest of us is particularly anxious to wander about Pellucidar alone."

Officers and men, with the exception of the watch, which changed every four hours, slept the clock around.

Tarzan of the Apes was the first to complete his sleep and leave the ship. He had discarded the clothing that had encumbered and annoyed him since he had left his own African jungle to join in the preparation of the O-220, and it was no faultlessly attired Englishman that came from the cabin and dropped to the ground below, but instead an almost naked and primitive warrior, armed with hunting knife, spear, a bow and arrows, and the long rope which Tarzan always carried, for in the hunt he preferred the weapons of his youth to the firearms of civilization.

Lieutenant Dorf, the only officer on duty at the time, saw him depart and watched with unfeigned admiration as the black-haired jungle lord moved across the open plain and disappeared in the forest.

There were trees that were familiar to the eyes of the ape-man, and trees such as he had never seen before, but it was a forest and that was enough to lure Tarzan of the Apes and permit him to forget the last few weeks that had been spent amidst the distasteful surroundings of civilization. He was happy to be free from the ship, too, and, while he liked all his companions, he was yet glad to be alone.

In the first flight of his new-found freedom Tarzan was like a boy released from school. Unhampered by the hated vestments of civilization, out of sight of anything that might even remotely remind him of the atrocities with which man scars the face of nature, he filled his lungs with the free air of Pellucidar, leaped into a nearby tree and swung away through the forest, his only concern for the moment the joyousness of exultant vitality and life. On he sped through the primeval forest of Pellucidar. Strange birds, startled by his swift and silent passage, flew screaming from his path, and strange beasts slunk to cover beneath him. But Tarzan did not care; he was not hunting; he was not even searching for the new in this new world. For the moment he was only living.

24

While this mood dominated him Tarzan gave no thought to the passage of time any more than he had given thought to the timelessness of Pellucidar, whose noonday sun, hanging perpetually at zenith, gives a lie to us of the outer crust who rush frantically through life in mad and futile effort to beat the earth in her revolutions. Nor did Tarzan reckon upon distance or direction, for such matters were seldom the subjects of conscious consideration upon the part of the ape-man, whose remarkable ability to meet every and any emergency he unconsciously attributed to powers that lay within himself, not stopping to consider that in his own jungle he relied upon the friendly sun and moon and stars as guides by day and night, and to the myriad familiar things that spoke to him in a friendly, voiceless language that only the jungle people can interpret.

As his mood changed Tarzan reduced his speed, and presently he dropped to the ground in a well-marked game trail. Now he let his eyes take in the new wonders all about him. He noticed the evidences of great age as betokened by the enormous size of the trees and the hoary stems of the great vines that clung to many of them—suggestions of age that made his own jungle seem modern—and he marvelled at the gorgeous flowers that bloomed in riotous profusion upon every hand, and then of a sudden something gripped him about the body and snapped him high into the air.

Tarzan of the Apes had nodded. His mind occupied with the wonders of this new world had permitted a momentary relaxation of that habitual wariness that distinguishes creatures of the wild.

Almost in the instant of its occurrence the ape-man realized what had befallen him. Although he could easily imagine its disastrous sequel, the suggestion of a smile touched his lips—a rueful smile—and one that was perhaps tinged with disgust for himself, for Tarzan of the Apes had been caught in as primitive a snare as was ever laid for unwary beasts.

A rawhide noose, attached to the downbent limb of an overhanging tree, had been buried in the trail along which he had been passing and he had struck the trigger—that was the whole story. But its sequel might have had less unfortunate possibilities had the noose not pinioned his arms to his sides as it closed about him.

He hung about six feet above the trail, caught securely about the hips, the noose imprisoning his arms between elbows and wrists and pinioning them securely to his sides. And to add to his discomfort and helplessness, he swung head downward, spinning dizzily like a human plumb-bob.

He tried to draw an arm from the encircling noose so that he might reach his hunting knife and free himself, but the weight of his body constantly drew the noose more tightly about him and every effort upon his part seemed but to strengthen the relentless grip of the rawhide that was pressing deep into his flesh.

He knew that the snare meant the presence of men and that doubtless they would soon come to inspect their noose, for his own knowledge of primitive hunting taught him that they would not leave their snares long untended, since in the event of a catch, if they would have it at all, they must claim it soon lest it fall prey to carnivorous beasts or birds. He wondered what sort of people they were and if he might not make friends with them, but whatever they were he hoped that they would come before the beasts of prey came. And while such thoughts were running through his mind, his keen ears caught the sound of approaching footsteps, but they were not the steps of men. Whatever was approaching was approaching across the wind and he could detect no scent spoor; nor, upon the other hand, he realized, could the beast scent him. It was coming leisurely and as it neared him, but before it came in sight along the trail, he knew that it was a hoofed animal and, therefore, that he had little reason to fear its approach unless, indeed, it might prove to be some strange Pellucidarian creature with characteristics entirely unlike any that he knew upon the outer crust.

But even as he permitted these thoughts partially to reassure him, there came strongly to his nostrils a scent that always caused the short hairs upon his head to rise, not in fear but in natural reaction to the presence of an hereditary enemy. It was not an odor that he had ever smelled before.

It was not the scent spoor of Numa the lion, nor Sheeta the leopard, but it was the scent spoor of some sort of great cat. And now he could hear its almost silent approach through the underbrush and he knew that it was coming down toward the trail, lured either by knowledge of his presence or by that of the beast whose approach Tarzan had been awaiting.

It was the latter who came first into view—a great ox-like animal with wide-spread horns and shaggy coat—a huge bull that advanced several yards along the trail after Tarzan discovered it before it saw the ape-man dangling in front of it. It was the thag of Pellucidar, the Bos Primigenus of the paleontologist of the outer crust, a long extinct progenitor of the bovine races of our own world.

For a moment it stood eyeing the man dangling in its path.

Tarzan remained very quiet. He did not wish to frighten it away for he realized that one of them must be the prey of the carnivore sneaking upon them, but if he expected the thag to be frightened he soon realized his error in judgment for, uttering low grumblings, the great bull pawed the earth with a front foot, and then, lowering his massive horns, gored it angrily, and the ape-man knew that he was working his short temper up to charging pitch; nor did it seem that this was to take long for already he was advancing menacingly to the accompaniment of thunderous bellowing. His tail was up and his head down as he broke into the trot that preluded the charge.

The ape-man realized that if he was ever struck by those massive horns or that heavy head, his skull would be crushed like an eggshell.

The dizzy spinning that had been caused by the first stretching of the rawhide to his weight had lessened to a gentle turning motion, so that sometimes he faced the thag and sometimes in the opposite direction. The utter helplessness of his position galled the ape-man and gave him more concern than any consideration of impending death. From childhood he had walked hand in hand with the Grim Reaper and he had looked upon death in so many forms that it held no terror for him. He knew that it was the final experience of all created things, that it must as inevitably come to him as to others and while he loved life and did not wish to die, its mere approach induced within him no futile hysteria. But to die without a chance to fight for life was not such an end as Tarzan of the Apes would have chosen. And now, as his body slowly revolved and his eyes were turned away from the charging thag, his heart sank at the thought that he was not even to be vouchsafed the meager satisfaction of meeting death face to face.

In the brief instant that he waited for the impact, the air was rent by as horrid a scream as had ever broken upon the ears of the ape-man and the bellowing of the bull rose suddenly to a higher pitch and mingled with that other awesome sound.

Once more the dangling body of the ape-man revolved and his eyes fell upon such a scene as had not been vouchsafed to men of the outer world for countless ages.

Upon the massive shoulders and neck of the great thag clung a tiger of such huge proportions that Tarzan could scarce credit the testimony of his own eyes. Great saber-like tusks, projecting from the upper jaw, were buried deep in the neck of the bull, which, instead of trying to escape, had stopped in its tracks and was endeavoring to dislodge the great beast of prey, swinging its huge horns backward in an attempt to rake the living death from its shoulders, or again shaking its whole body violently for the same purpose and all the while bellowing in pain and rage.

Gradually the saber-tooth changed its position until it had attained a hold suited to its purpose. Then with lightning-like swiftness it swung back a great forearm and delivered a single, terrific blow on the side of the thag's head—a titanic blow that crushed that mighty skull and dropped the huge bull dead in its tracks. And then the carnivore settled down to feast upon its kill.

During the battle the saber-tooth had not noticed the ape-man; nor was it until after he had commenced to feed upon the thag that his eye was attracted by the revolving body swinging above the trail a few yards away. Instantly

28

the beast stopped feeding; his head lowered and flattened, his upper lip turned back in a hideous snarl. He watched the ape-man. Low, menacing growls rumbled from his cavernous throat; his long, sinuous tail lashed angrily as slowly he arose from the body of his kill and advanced toward Tarzan of the Apes.

III

THE GREAT CATS

THE EBBING TIDE of the great war had left human flotsam stranded upon many an unfamiliar beach. In its full flow it had lifted Robert Jones, high private in the ranks of a labor battalion, from uncongenial surroundings and landed him in a prison camp behind the enemy line. Here his good nature won him friends and favors, but neither one nor the other served to obtain his freedom. Robert Jones seemed to have been lost in the shuffle. And finally, when the evacuation of the prison had been completed, Robert Jones still remained, but he was not downhearted. He had learned the language of his captors and had made many friends among them. They found him a job and Robert Jones of Alabama was content to remain where he was. He had been graduated from body servant to cook of an officers' mess and it was in this capacity that he had come under the observation of Captain Zuppner, who had drafted him for the O-220 expedition.

Robert Jones yawned, stretched, turned over in his narrow berth aboard the O-220, opened his eyes and sat up with an exclamation of surprise. He jumped to the floor and stuck his head out of an open port.

"Lawd, niggah!" he exclaimed; "you all suah done overslep' yo'sef."

For a moment he gazed up at the noonday sun shining down upon him and then, hastily dressing, hurried into his galley.

" 'S funny," he soliloquized; "dey ain't no one stirrin'—mus' all of overslep' demsef." He looked at the clock on the galley wall. The hour hand pointed to six. He cocked his ear and listened. "She ain't stopped," he muttered. Then he went to the door that opened from the galley through the ship's side and pushed it back. Leaning far out he looked up again at the sun. Then he shook his head. "Dey's sumpin wrong," he said. "Ah dunno whether to cook breakfas', dinner or supper."

Jason Gridley, emerging from his cabin, sauntered down the narrow corridor toward the galley. "Good morning, Bob!" he said, stopping in the open doorway. "What's the chance for a bite of breakfast?"

"Did you all say breakfas', suh?" inquired Robert.

"Yes," replied Gridley; "just toast and coffee and a couple of eggs—anything you have handy."

"Ah knew it!" exclaimed the black. "Ah knew dat ol' clock couldn't be wrong, but Mistah Sun he suah gone hay wire."

Gridley grinned. "I'll drop down and have a little walk," he said. "I'll be back in fifteen minutes. Have you seen anything of Lord Greystoke?"

"No suh, Ah ain't seen nothin' o' Massa Ta'zan sence yesterday."

"I wondered," said Gridley; "he is not in his cabin."

For fifteen minutes Gridley walked briskly about in the vicinity of the ship. When he returned to the mess room he found Zuppner and Dorf awaiting breakfast and greeted them with a pleasant "good morning."

"I don't know whether it's good morning or good evening," said Zuppner.

"We have been here twelve hours," said Dorf, "and it is just the same time that it was when we arrived. I have been on watch for the last four hours and if it hadn't been for the chronometer I could not swear that I had been on fifteen minutes or that I had not been on a week."

"It certainly induces a feeling of unreality that is hard to explain," said Gridley.

"Where is Greystoke?" asked Zuppner. "He is usually an early riser."

"I was just asking Bob," said Gridley, "but he has not seen him."

"He left the ship shortly after I came on watch," said Dorf. "I should say about three hours ago, possibly longer. I saw him cross the open country and enter the forest."

"I wish he had not gone out alone," said Gridley.

"He strikes me as a man who can take care of himself," said Zuppner.

"I have seen some things during the last four hours," said Dorf, "that make me doubt whether any man can take care of himself alone in this world, especially one armed only with the primitive weapons that Greystoke carried with him."

"You mean that he carried no firearms?" demanded Zuppner.

"He was armed with a bow and arrows, a spear and a rope," said Dorf, "and I think he carried a hunting knife as well. But he might as well have had nothing but a pea-shooter if he met some of the things I have seen since I went on watch."

"What do you mean?" demanded Zuppner. "What have you seen?"

Dorf grinned sheepishly. "Honestly, Captain, I hate to tell you," he said, "for I'm damned if I believe it myself."

"Well, out with it," exclaimed Zuppner. "We will make allowances for your youth and for the effect that the sun and horizon of Pellucidar may have had upon your eyesight or your veracity."

"Well," said Dorf, "about an hour ago a bear passed within a hundred yards of the ship."

"There is nothing remarkable about that," said Zuppner.

"There was a great deal that was remarkable about the bear, however," said Dorf.

"In what way?" asked Gridley.

"It was fully as large as an ox," said Dorf, "and if I were going out after bear in this country I should want to take along field artillery."

"Was that all you saw—just a bear?" asked Zuppner.

"No," said Dorf, "I saw tigers, not one but fully a dozen, and they were as much larger than our Bengal tigers as the bear was larger than any bear of the outer crust that I have ever seen. They were perfectly enormous and they were armed with the most amazing fangs you ever saw—great curved fangs that extended from their upper jaws to lengths of from eight inches to a foot. They came down to this stream here to drink and then wandered away, some of them toward the forest and some down toward that big river yonder."

"Greystoke couldn't do much against such creatures as those even if he had carried a rifle," said Zuppner.

"If he was in the forest, he could escape them," said Gridley.

Zuppner shook his head. "I don't like the looks of it," he said. "I wish that he had not gone out alone."

"The bear and the tigers were bad enough," continued Dorf, "but I saw another creature that to me seemed infinitely worse."

Robert, who was more or less a privileged character, had entered from the galley and was listening with wide-eyed interest to Dorf's account of the creatures he had seen, while Victor, one of the Filipino cabin-boys, served the officers.

"Yes," continued Dorf, "I saw a mighty strange creature. It flew directly over the ship and I had an excellent view of it. At first I thought that it was a bird, but when it approached more closely I saw that it was a winged reptile. It had a long, narrow head and it flew so close that I could see its great jaws, armed with an infinite number of long, sharp teeth. Its head was elongated above the eyes and came to a sharp point. It was perfectly immense and must have had a wing spread of at least twenty feet. While I was watching it, it dropped suddenly to earth only a short distance beyond the ship, and when it arose again it was carrying in its talons some animal that must have been fully as large as a good sized sheep, with which it flew away without apparent effort. That the creature is carnivorous is evident as is also the fact that it has sufficient strength to carry away a man."

Robert Jones covered his large mouth with a pink palm and with hunched and shaking shoulders turned and tip-toed from the room. Once in the galley with the door closed, he gave himself over to unrestrained mirth.

"What is the matter with you?" asked Victor.

"Lawd-a-massy!" exclaimed Robert. "Ah allus thought some o' dem gem'n in dat dere Adventurous Club in Bummingham could lie some, but, shucks, dey ain't in it with this Lieutenant Dorf. Did you all heah him tell about dat flyin' snake what carries off sheep?"

But back in the mess room the white men took Dorf's statement more seriously.

"That would be a pterodactyl," said Zuppner.

"Yes," replied Dorf. "I classified it as a Pteranodon."

"Don't you think we ought to send out a search party?" asked Gridley.

"I am afraid Greystoke would not like it," replied Zuppner.

"It could go out under the guise of a hunting party," suggested Dorf.

"If he has not returned within an hour," said Zuppner, "we shall have to do something of the sort."

Hines and Von Horst now entered the mess room, and when they learned of Tarzan's absence from the ship and had heard from Dorf a description of some of the animals that he might have encountered, they were equally as apprehensive as the others of his safety.

"We might cruise around a bit, sir," suggested Von Horst to Zuppner.

"But suppose he returns to this spot during our absence?" asked Gridley.

"Could you return the ship to this anchorage again?" inquired Zuppner.

"I doubt it," replied the Lieutenant. "Our instruments are almost worthless under the conditions existing in Pellucidar."

"Then we had better remain where we are," said Gridley, "until he returns."

"But if we send a searching party after him on foot, what assurance have we that it will be able to find its way back to the ship?" demanded Zuppner.

"That will not be so difficult," said Gridley. "We can always blaze our trail as we go and thus easily retrace our steps."

"Yes, that is so," agreed Zuppner.

"Suppose," said Gridley, "that Von Horst and I go out with Muviro and his Waziri. They are experienced trackers, prime fighting men and they certainly know the jungle."

"Not this jungle," said Dorf.

"But at least they know any jungle better than the rest of us," insisted Gridley.

"I think your plan is a good one," said Zuppner, "and anyway as you are in command now, the rest of us gladly place ourselves under your orders."

"The conditions that confront us here are new to all of us," said Gridley. "Nothing that anyone of us can suggest or command can be based upon any personal experience or knowledge that the rest do not possess, and in matters of this kind I think that we had better reach our decision after full discussion rather than to depend blindly upon official priority of authority."

"That has been Greystoke's policy," said Zuppner, "and it has made it very easy and pleasant for all of us. I quite agree with you, but I can think of no more feasible plan than that which you have suggested."

"Very good," said Gridley. "Will you accompany me, Lieutenant?" he asked, turning to Von Horst.

The officer grinned. "Will I?" he exclaimed. "I should never have forgiven you if you had left me out of it."

"Fine," said Gridley. "And now, I think, we might as well make our preparations at once and get as early a start as possible. See that the Waziri have eaten, Lieutenant, and tell Muviro that I want them armed with rifles. These fellows can use them all right, but they rather look with scorn upon anything more modern than their war spears and arrows."

"Yes, I discovered that," said Hines. "Muviro told me a few days ago that his people consider firearms as something of an admission of cowardice. He told me that they use them for target practice, but when they go out after lions or rhino they leave their rifles behind and take their spears and arrows."

"After they have seen what I saw," said Dorf, "they will have more respect for an express rifle."

"See that they take plenty of ammunition, Von Horst," said Gridley, "for from what I have seen in this country we shall not have to carry any provisions."

"A man who could not live off this country would starve to death in a meat market," said Zuppner.

Von Horst left to carry out Gridley's orders while the latter returned to his cabin to prepare for the expedition.

The officers and crew remaining with the O-220 were all on hand to bid farewell to the expedition starting out in search of Tarzan of the Apes, and as the ten stalwart Waziri warriors marched away behind Gridley and Von Horst, Robert Jones, watching from the galley door, swelled with pride. "Dem niggahs is sho nuf hot babies," he exclaimed. "All dem flyin' snakes bettah clear out de country now." With the others Robert watched the little party as it crossed the plain and until it had disappeared within the dark precincts of the forest upon the opposite side. Then he glanced up at the noonday sun, shook his head, elevated his palms in resignation and turned back into his galley.

Almost immediately after the party had left the ship, Gridley directed Muviro to take the lead and watch for Tarzan's trail since, of the entire party, he was the most experienced tracker; nor did the Waziri chieftain have any difficulty in following the spoor of the ape-man across the plain and into the forest, but here, beneath a great tree, it disappeared.

"The Big Bwana took to the trees here," said Muviro, "and no man lives who can follow his spoor through the lower, the middle or the upper terraces."

"What do you suggest, then, Muviro?" asked Gridley.

"If this were his own jungle," replied the warrior, "I should feel sure that when he took to the trees he would move in a straight line toward the place he wished to go; unless he happened to be hunting, in which case his direction would be influenced by the sign and scent of game."

"Doubtless he was hunting here," said Von Horst.

"If he was hunting," said Muviro, "he would have moved in a straight line until he caught the scent spoor of game or came to a well-beaten game trail."

"And then what would he do?" asked Gridley.

"He might wait above the trail," replied Muviro, "or he might follow it. In a new country like this, I think he would follow it, for he has always been interested in exploring every new country he entered."

"Then let us push straight into the forest in this same direction until we strike a game trail," said Gridley.

Muviro and three of his warriors went ahead, cutting brush were it was necessary and blazing the trees at frequent intervals that they might more easily retrace their steps to the ship. With the aid of a small pocket compass Gridley directed the line of advance, which otherwise it would have been difficult to hold accurately beneath that eternal noonday sun, whose warm rays filtered down through the foliage of the forest.

"God! What a forest!" exclaimed Von Horst. "To search for a man here is like the proverbial search for the needle in a haystack."

"Except," said Gridley, "that one might stand a slight chance of finding the needle."

"Perhaps we had better fire a shot occasionally," suggested Von Horst.

"Excellent," said Gridley. "The rifles carry a much heavier charge and make a louder report than our revolvers."

After warning the others of his intention, he directed one of the blacks to fire three shots at intervals of a few seconds, for neither Gridley nor Von Horst was armed with rifles, each of the officers carrying two .45 caliber Colts. Thereafter, at intervals of about half an hour, a single shot was fired, but as the searching party forced its way on into the forest each of its members became gloomily impressed with the futility of their search.

Presently the nature of the forest changed. The trees were set less closely together and the underbrush, while still forming an almost impenetrable screen, was less dense than it had been heretofore and here they came upon a wide game trail, worn by countless hoofs and padded feet to a depth of two feet or more below the surface of the surrounding ground, and here Jason Gridley blundered.

"We won't bother about blazing the trees as long as we follow this trail," he said to Muviro, "except at such places as it may fork or be crossed by other trails."

It was, after all, a quite natural mistake since a few blazed trees along the trail would not serve any purpose in following it back when they wished to return.

The going here was easier and as the Waziri warriors swung along at a brisk pace, the miles dropped quickly behind them and already had the noonday sun so cast its spell upon them that the element of time seemed not to enter into their calculations, while the teeming life about them absorbed the attention of blacks and whites alike.

Strange monkeys, some of them startlingly man-like in appearance and of large size, watched them pass. Birds of both gay and somber plumage scattered protestingly before their advance, and again dim bulks loomed through the undergrowth and the sound of padded feet was everywhere.

At times they would pass through a stretch of forest as silent as the tomb, and then again they seemed to be surrounded by a bedlam of hideous growls and roars and screams.

"I'd like to see some of those fellows," said Von Horst, after a particularly savage outburst of sound.

"I am surprised that we haven't," replied Gridley; "but I imagine that they are a little bit leery of us right now, not alone on account of our numbers but because of the, to them strange and unfamiliar, odors which must surround us. These would naturally increase the suspicion which must have been aroused by the sound of our shots."

"Have you noticed," said Von Horst, "that most of the noise seems to come from behind us; I mean the more savage, growling sounds. I have heard squeals and noises that sounded like the trumpeting of elephants to the right and to the left and ahead, but only an occasional growl or

37

roar seems to come from these directions and then always at a considerable distance."

"How do you account for it?" asked Gridley.

"I can't account for it," replied Von Horst. "It is as though we were moving along in the center of a procession with all the savage carnivores behind us."

"This perpetual noonday sun has its compensations," remarked Gridley with a laugh, "for at least it insures that we shall not have to spend the night here."

At that instant the attention of the two men was attracted by an exclamation from one of the Waziri behind them. "Look, Bwana! Look!" cried the man, pointing back along the trail. Following the direction of the Waziri's extended finger, Gridley and Von Horst saw a huge beast slinking slowly along the trail in their rear.

"God!" exclaimed Von Horst, "and I thought Dorf was exaggerating."

"It doesn't seem possible," exclaimed Gridley, "that five hundred miles below our feet automobiles are dashing through crowded streets lined by enormous buildings; that there the telegraph, the telephone and the radio are so commonplace as to excite no comment; that countless thousands live out their entire lives without ever having to use a weapon in self-defense, and yet at the same instant we stand here facing a saber-tooth tiger in surroundings that may not have existed upon the outer crust for a million years."

"Look at them!" exclaimed Von Horst. "If there is one there are a dozen of them."

"Shall we fire, Bwana?" asked one of the Waziri.

"Not yet," said Gridley. "Close up and be ready. They seem to be only following us."

Slowly the party fell back, a line of Waziri in the rear facing the tigers and backing slowly away from them. Muviro dropped back to Gridley's side.

"For a long time, Bwana," he said, "there has been the spoor of many elephants in the trail, or spoor that looked like the spoor of elephants, though it was different. And just now I sighted some of the beasts ahead. I could not make them out distinctly, but if they are not elephants they are very much like them."

"We seem to be between the devil and the deep sea," said Von Horst.

"And there are either elephants or tigers on each side of us," said Muviro. "I can hear them moving through the brush."

Perhaps the same thought was in the minds of all these men, that they might take to the trees, but for some reason no one expressed it. And so they continued to move slowly along the trail until suddenly it broke into a large, open area in the forest, where the ground was scantily covered with brush and there were few trees. Perhaps a hundred acres were included in the clearing and then the forest commenced again upon all sides.

And into the clearing, along numerous trails that seemed to center at this spot, came as strange a procession as the eyes of these men had ever rested upon. There were great ox-like creatures with shaggy coats and wide-spreading horns. There were red deer and sloths of gigantic size. There were mastodon and mammoth, and a huge, elephantine creature that resembled an elephant and yet did not seem to be an elephant at all. Its great head was four feet long and three feet wide. It had a short, powerful trunk and from its lower jaw mighty tusks curved downward, their points bending inward toward the body. At the shoulder it stood at least ten feet above the ground, and in length it must have been fully twenty feet. But what resemblance it bore to an elephant was lessened by its small, pig-like ears.

The two white men, momentarily forgetting the tigers behind them in their amazement at the sight ahead, halted and looked with wonder upon the huge gathering of creatures within the clearing.

"Did you ever see anything like it?" exclaimed Gridley.

"No, nor anyone else," replied Von Horst.

"I could catalog a great many of them," said Gridley, "although practically all are extinct upon the outer crust. But that fellow there gets me," and he pointed to the elphantine creature with the downward pointing tusks.

"A Dinotherium of the Miocene," said Von Horst.

Muviro had stopped beside the two whites and was gazing in wide-eyed astonishment at the scene before him.

"Well," asked Gridley, "what do you make of it, Muviro?"

"I think I understand now, Bwana," replied the black, "and if we are ever going to escape our one chance is to cross that clearing as quickly as possible. The great cats are herding these creatures here and presently there will be such a killing as the eyes of man have never before seen. If we are not killed by the cats, we shall be trampled to death by these beasts in their efforts to escape or to fight the tigers."

"I believe you are right, Muviro," said Gridley.

"There is an opening just ahead of us," said Von Horst.

Gridley called the men around him and pointed out across the clearing to the forest upon the opposite side. "Apparently our only chance now," he said, "is to cross before the cats close in on these beasts. We have already come into the clearing too far to try to take refuge in the trees on this side for the saber-tooths are too close. Stick close together and fire at nothing unless we are charged."

"Look!" exclaimed Von Horst. "The tigers are entering the clearing from all sides. They have surrounded their quarry."

"There is still the one opening ahead of us, Bwana," said Muviro.

Already the little party was moving slowly across the clearing, which was covered with nervous beasts moving irritably to and fro, their whole demeanor marked by nervous apprehension. Prior to the advent of the tigers the animals had been moving quietly about, some of them grazing on the short grass of the clearing or upon the leaves and twigs of the scattered trees growing in it; but with the appearance of the first of the carnivores their attitude changed. A huge, bull mastodon raised his trunk and trumpeted shrilly, and instantly every herbivore was on the alert. And as eyes or nostrils detected the presence of the great cats, or the beasts became excited by the excitement of their fellows, each added his voice to the pandemonium that now reigned. To the squealing, trumpeting and bellowing of the quarry were added the hideous growls and roars of the carnivores.

"Look at those cats!" cried Von Horst. "There must be hundreds of them." Nor was his estimate an exaggeration for from all sides of the clearing, with the exception of a single point opposite them, the cats were emerging from the forest and starting to circle the herd. That they did not rush it immediately evidenced their respect for the huge beasts they had corraled, the majority of which they would not have dared to attack except in superior numbers.

Now a mammoth, a giant bull with tail raised and ears up-cocked, curled his trunk above his head and charged. But a score of the great cats, growling hideously, sprang to meet him, and the bull, losing his nerve, wheeled in a wide circle and returned to the herd. Had he gone through that menacing line of fangs and talons, as with his great size and weight and strength he might have done, he would have opened a hole through which a stampede of the other animals would have carried the bulk of them to safety.

The frightened herbivores, their attention centered upon the menacing tigers, paid little attention to the insignificant man-things passing among them. But there were some exceptions. A thag, bellowing and pawing the earth directly in their line of march, terrified by the odor of the carnivores and aroused and angered by the excited trumpeting and squealing of the creatures about him, seeking to vent his displeasure upon something, lowered his head and charged them. A Waziri warrior raised his rifle to his shoulder and fired, and a prehistoric Bos Primigenus crashed to the impact of a modern bullet.

As the report of the rifle sounded above the other noises of the clearing, the latter were momentarily stilled, and the full attention of hunters and hunted was focused upon the little band of men, so puny and insignificant in the presence of the mighty beasts of another day. A dinotherium, his little ears up-cocked, his tail stiffly erect, walked slowly toward them. Almost immediately others followed his example until it seemed that the whole aggregation was converging upon them. The forest was yet a hundred yards away as Jason Gridley realized the seriousness of the emergency that now confronted them.

"We shall have to run for it," he said. "Give them a volley, and then beat it for the trees. If they charge, it will have to be every man for himself."

The Waziri wheeled and faced the slowly advancing herd and then, at Gridley's command, they fired. The thunderous volley had its effect upon the advancing beasts. They hesitated and then turned and retreated; but behind them were the carnivores. And once again they swung back in the direction of the men, who were now moving rapidly toward the forest.

"Here they come!" cried Von Horst. And a backward glance revealed the fact that the entire herd, goaded to terror by the tigers behind them, had broken into a mad stampede. Whether or not it was a direct charge upon the little party of men is open to question, but the fact that they lay in its path was sufficient to seal their doom if they were unable to reach the safety of the forest ahead of the charging quadrupeds.

"Give them another volley!" cried Gridley. And again the Waziri turned and fired. A dinotherium, a thag and two mammoths stumbled and fell to the ground, but the remainder of the herd did not pause. Leaping over the carcasses of their fallen comrades they thundered down upon the fleeing men.

It was now, in truth, every man for himself, and so close pressed were they that even the brave Waziri threw away their rifles as useless encumbrances to flight.

Several of the red deer, swifter in flight than the other members of the herd, had taken the lead, and, stampeding through the party, scattered them to left and right.

Gridley and Von Horst were attempting to cover the retreat of the Waziri and check the charge of the stampeding animals with their revolvers. They succeeded in turning a few of the leaders, but presently a great, red stag passed between them, forcing them to jump quickly apart to escape his heavy antlers, and behind him swept a nightmare of terrified beasts forcing them still further apart.

Not far from Gridley grew a single, giant tree, a short distance from the edge of the clearing, and finding himself alone and cut off from further retreat, the American turned and ran for it, while Von Horst was forced to bolt for the jungle which was now almost within reach.

Bowled over by a huge sloth, Gridley scrambled to his feet, and, passing in front of a fleeing mastodon, reached the tree just as the main body of the stampeding herd closed about it. Its great bole gave him momentary protection and an instant later he had scrambled among its branches.

Instantly his first thought was for his fellows, but where they had been a moment before was now only a solid mass of leaping, plunging, terrified beasts. No sign of a human being was anywhere to be seen and Gridley knew that no living thing could have survived the trampling of those incalculable tons of terrified flesh.

Some of them, he knew, must have reached the forest, but he doubted that all had come through in safety and he feared particularly for Von Horst, who had been some little distance in rear of the Waziri.

The eyes of the American swept back over the clearing to observe such a scene as probably in all the history of the world had never before been vouchsafed to the eyes of man. Literally thousands of creatures, large and small, were following their leaders in a break for life and liberty, while upon their flanks and at their rear hundreds of savage sabertooth tigers leaped upon them, dragging down the weaker, battling with the stronger, leaving the maimed and crippled behind that they might charge into the herd again and drag down others.

The mad rush of the leaders across the clearing had been checked as they entered the forest, and now those in the rear were forced to move more slowly, but in their terror they sought to clamber over the backs of those ahead. Red deer leaped upon the backs of mastodons and fled across the heaving bodies beneath them, as a mountain goat might leap from rock to rock. Mammoths raised their huge bulks upon lesser animals and crushed them to the ground. Tusks and horns were red with gore as the maddened beasts battled for their lives. The scene was sickening in its horror,

43

and yet fascinating in its primitive strength and savagery—and everywhere were the great, savage cats.

Slowly they were cutting into the herd from both sides in an effort to encircle a portion of it and at last they were successful, though within the circle there remained but a few scattered beasts that were still unmaimed or uncrippled. And then the great tigers turned upon these, closing in and drawing tighter their hideous band of savage fury.

In twos and threes and scores they leaped upon the remaining beasts and dragged them down until the sole creature remaining alive within their circle was a gigantic bull mammoth. His shaggy coat was splashed with blood and his tusks were red with gore. Trumpeting, he stood at bay, a magnificent picture of primordial power, of sagacity, of courage.

The heart of the American went out to that lone warrior trumpeting his challenge to overwhelming odds in the face of certain doom.

By hundreds the carnivores were closing in upon the great bull; yet it was evident that even though they outnumbered him so overwhelmingly, they still held him in vast respect. Growling and snarling, a few of them slunk in stealthy circles about him, and as he wheeled about with them, three of them charged him from the rear. With a swiftness that matched their own, the pachyderm wheeled to meet them. Two of them he caught upon his tusks and tossed them high into the air, and at the same instant a score of others rushed him from each side and from the rear and fastened themselves to his back and flanks. Down he went as though struck by lightning, squatting quickly upon his haunches and rolling over backward, crushing a dozen tigers before they could escape.

Gridley could scarce repress a cheer as the great fellow staggered to his feet and threw himself again upon the opposite side to the accompaniment of hideous screams of pain and anger from the tigers he pinioned beneath him. But now he was gushing blood from a hundred wounds, and other scores of the savage carnivores were charging him. Though he put up a magnificent battle the end was inevitable and at last they dragged him down, tearing him to pieces while he yet struggled to rise again and battle with them.

And then commenced the aftermath as the savage beasts fought among themselves for possession of their prey. For even though there was flesh to more than surfeit them all, in their greed, jealousy and ferocity, they must still battle one with another.

That they had paid heavily for their meat was evident by the carcasses of the tigers strewn about the clearing and as the survivors slowly settled down to feed, there came the jackals, the hyaenodons and the wild dogs to feast upon their leavings.

IV

THE SAGOTHS

As THE great cat slunk toward him, Tarzan of the Apes realized that at last he faced inevitable death, yet even in that last moment of life the emotion which dominated him was one of admiration for the magnificent beast drawing angrily toward him.

Tarzan of the Apes would have preferred to die fighting, if he must die; yet he felt a certain thrill as he contemplated the magnificence of the great beast that Fate had chosen to terminate his earthly career. He felt no fear, but a certain sense of anticipation of what would follow after death. The Lord of the Jungle subscribed to no creed. Tarzan of the Apes was not a church man; yet like the majority of those who have always lived close to nature he was, in a sense, intensely religious. His intimate knowledge of the stupendous forces of nature, of her wonders and her miracles had impressed him with the fact that their ultimate origin lay far beyond the conception of the finite mind of man, and thus incalculably remote from the farthest bounds of science. When he thought of God he liked to think of Him primitively, as a personal God. And while he realized that he knew nothing of such matters, he liked to believe that after death he would live again.

Many thoughts passed quickly through his mind as the saber-tooth advanced upon him. He was watching the long, glistening fangs that so soon were to be buried in his flesh when his attention was attracted by a sound among the trees about him. That the great cat had heard too was evident, for it stopped in its tracks and gazed up into the foliage of the trees above. And then Tarzan heard a rustling in the branches directly overhead, and looking up he saw what appeared to be a gorilla glaring down upon him.

Two more savage faces showed through the foliage above him and then in other trees about he caught glimpses of similar shaggy forms and fierce faces. He saw that they were like gorillas, and yet unlike them; that in some respects they were more man than gorilla, and in others more gorilla than man. He caught glimpses of great clubs wielded by hairy hands, and when his eyes returned to the saber-tooth he saw that the great beast had hesitated in its advance and was snarling and growling angrily as its eyes roved upward and around at the savage creatures glaring down upon it.

It was only for a moment that the cat paused in its advance upon the ape-man. Snarling angrily, it moved forward again and as it did so, one of the creatures in the tree above Tarzan reached down, and seizing the rope that held him dangling in mid-air, drew him swiftly upward. Then several things occurred simultaneously—the saber-tooth leaped to retrieve its prey and a dozen heavy cudgels hurtled through the air from the surrounding trees, striking the great cat heavily upon head and body with the result that the talons that must otherwise have inevitably been imbedded in the flesh of the ape-man grazed harmlessly by him, and an instant later he was drawn well up among the branches of the tree, where he was seized by three hairy brutes whose attitude suggested that he might have been as well off had he been left to the tender mercies of the saber-tooth.

Two of them, one on either side, seized an arm and the third grasped him by the throat with one hand while he held his cudgel poised above his head in the other. And then from the lips of the creature facing him came a sound that fell as startlingly upon the ears of the ape-man as had the first unexpected roar of the saber-tooth, but with far different effect.

"Ka-goda!" said the creature facing Tarzan.

In the language of the apes of his own jungle Ka-goda may be roughly interpreted according to its inflection as a command to surrender, or as an interrogation, "do you surrender?" or as a declaration of surrender.

This word, coming from the lips of a hairy gorilla man of the inner world, suggested possibilities of the most startling nature. For years Tarzan had considered the language of the great apes as the primitive root language of created things. The great apes, the lesser apes, the gorillas, the baboons and the monkeys utilized this with various degrees of refinement and many of its words were understood by jungle animals of other species and by many of the birds; but, perhaps, after the fashion that our domestic animals have learned many of the words in our vocabulary, with this difference that the language of the great apes has doubtless persisted unchanged for countless ages.

That these gorilla men of the inner world used even one word of this language suggested one of two possibilities—either they held an origin in common with the creatures of the outer crust, or else that the laws of evolution and progress were so constant that this was the only form of primitive language that could have been possible to any creatures emerging from the lower orders toward the estate of man. But the suggestion that impressed Tarzan most vividly was that this single word, uttered by the creature grasping him by the throat, postulated familiarity on the part of his fierce captors with the entire ape language that he had used since boyhood.

"Ka-goda?" inquired the bull.

"Ka-goda," said Tarzan of the Apes.

The brute, facing Tarzan, half lowered his cudgel as

47

though he were surprised to hear the prisoner answer in his own tongue. "Who are you?" he demanded in the language of the great apes.

"I am Tarzan—mighty hunter, mighty fighter," replied the ape-man.

"What are you doing in M'wa-lot's country?" demanded the gorilla man.

"I come as a friend," replied Tarzan. "I have no quarrel with your people."

The fellow had lowered his club now, and from other trees had come a score more of the shaggy creatures until the surrounding limbs sagged beneath their weight.

"How did you learn the language of the Sagoths?" demanded the bull. "We have captured gilaks in the past, but you are the first one who ever spoke or understood our language."

"It is the language of my people," replied Tarzan. "As a little balu, I learned it from Kala and other apes of the tribe of Kerchak."

"We never heard of the tribe of Kerchak," said the bull.

"Perhaps he is not telling the truth," said another. "Let us kill him; he is only a gilak."

"No," said a third. "Take him back to M'wa-lot that the whole tribe of M'wa-lot may join in the killing."

"That is good," said another. "Take him back to the tribe, and while we are killing him we shall dance."

The language of the great apes is not like our language. It sounds to man like growling and barking and grunting, punctuated at times by shrill screams, and it is practically untranslatable to any tongue known to man; yet it carried to Tarzan and the Sagoths the sense that we have given it. It is a means of communicating thought and there its similarity to the languages of men ceases.

Having decided upon the disposition of their prisoner, the Sagoths now turned their attention to the saber-tooth, who had returned to his kill, across the body of which he was lying. He was not feeding, but was gazing angrily up into the trees at his tormentors.

While three of the gorilla men secured Tarzan's wrists

48

behind his back with a length of buckskin thong, the others renewed their attention to the tiger. Three or four of them would cast well-aimed cudgels at his face at intervals so nicely timed that the great beast could do nothing but fend off the missiles as they sped toward him. And while he was thus occupied, the other Sagoths, who had already cast their clubs, sprang to the ground and retrieved them with an agility and celerity that would have done credit to the tiniest monkey of the jungle. The risk that they took bespoke great self-confidence and high courage since often they were compelled to snatch their cudgels from almost beneath the claws of the saber-tooth.

Battered and bruised, the great cat gave back inch by inch until, unable to stand the fusillade longer, it suddenly turned tail and bounded into the underbrush, where for some time the sound of its crashing retreat could be distinctly heard. And with the departure of the carnivore, the gorilla men leaped to the ground and fell upon the carcass of the thag. With heavy fangs they tore its flesh, oftentimes fighting among themselves like wild beasts for some particularly choice morsel; but unlike many of the lower orders of man upon similar occasions they did not gorge themselves, and having satisfied their hunger they left what remained to the jackals and wild dogs that had already gathered.

Tarzan of the Apes, silent spectator of this savage scene, had an opportunity during the feast to examine his captors more closely. He saw that they were rather lighter in build than the gorillas he had seen in his own native jungle, but even though they were not as heavy as Bolgani, they were yet mighty creatures. Their arms and legs were of more human conformation and proportion than those of a gorilla, but the shaggy brown hair covering their entire body increased their beast-like appearance, while their faces were even more brutal than that of Bolgani himself, except that the development of the skull denoted a brain capacity seemingly as great as that of man.

They were entirely naked, nor was there among them any suggestion of ornamentation, while their only weapons were clubs. These, however, showed indications of having been shaped by some sharp instrument as though an effort had been made to insure a firm grip and a well-balanced weapon.

Their feeding completed, the Sagoths turned back along the game trail in the same direction that Tarzan had been going when he had sprung the trigger of the snare. But before departing several of them reset the noose, covered it carefully with earth and leaves and set the trigger that it might be sprung by the first passing animal.

So sure were all their movements and so deft their fingers, Tarzan realized that though these creatures looked like beasts they had long since entered the estate of man. Perhaps they were still low in the scale of evolution, but unquestionably they were men with the brains of men and the faces and skins of gorillas.

As the Sagoths moved along the jungle trail they walked erect as men walk, but in other ways they reminded Tarzan of the great apes who were his own people, for they were given neither to laughter nor song and their taciturnity suggested the speechlessness of the alali. That certain of their sense faculties were more highly developed than in man was evidenced by the greater dependence they placed upon their ears and noses than upon their eyes in their unremitting vigil against surprise by an enemy.

While by human standards they might have been judged ugly and even hideous, they did not so impress Tarzan of the Apes, who recognized in them a certain primitive majesty of bearing and mien such as might well have been expected of pioneers upon the frontiers of humanity.

It is sometimes the custom of theorists to picture our primordial progenitors as timid, fearful creatures, fleeing from the womb to the grave in constant terror of the countless, savage creatures that beset their entire existence. But as it does not seem reasonable that a creature so poorly equipped for offense and defense could have survived without courage, it seems far more consistent to assume that with the dawning of reason came a certain superiority complex—a vast and at first stupid egotism—that knew caution, perhaps, but not fear; nor is any other theory tenable unless we are to suppose that from the loin of a rabbit-hearted creature sprang men who hunted the bison, the mammoth and the cave bear with crude spears tipped with stone.

The Sagoths of Pellucidar may have been analogous in the scale of evolution to the Neanderthal men of the outer crust, or they may, indeed, have been even a step lower; yet in their bearing there was nothing to suggest to Tarzan that they had reached this stage in evolution through the expedience of flight. Their bearing as they trod the jungle trail bespoke assurance and even truculence, as though they were indeed the lords of creation, fearing nothing. Perhaps Tarzan understood their attitude better than another might have since it had been his own always in the jungle—unquestioning fearlessness—with which a certain intelligent caution was not inconsistent.

They had come but a short distance from the scene of Tarzan's capture when the Sagoths stopped beside a hollow log, the skeleton of a great tree that had fallen beside the trail. One of the creatures tapped upon the log with his club—one, two; one, two; one, two, three. And then, after a moment's pause, he repeated the same tapping. Three times the signal boomed through the jungle and then the signaler paused, listening, while others stopped and put their ears against the ground.

Faintly through the air, more plainly through the ground, came an answering signal—one, two; one, two; one, two, three.

The creatures seemed satisfied and climbing into the surrounding trees, disposed themselves comfortably as though settling down to a wait. Two of them carried Tarzan easily aloft with them, as with his hands bound behind his back he could not climb unassisted.

Since they had started on the march Tarzan had not spoken, but now he turned to one of the Sagoths near him. "Remove the bonds from my wrists," he said. "I am not an enemy."

"Tar-gash," said he whom Tarzan had addressed, "the gilak wants his bonds removed."

Tar-gash, a large bull with noticeably long, white canine fangs, turned his savage eyes upon the ape-man. For a long

51

time he glared unblinkingly at the prisoner and it seemed to Tarzan that the mind of the half-brute was struggling with a new idea. Presently he turned to the Sagoth who had repeated Tarzan's request. "Take them off," he said.

"Why?" demanded another of the bulls. The tone was challenging.

"Because I, Tar-gash, say 'take them off,' " growled the other.

"You are not M'wa-lot. He is king. If M'wa-lot says take them off, we will take them off."

"I am not M'wa-lot, To-yad; I am Tar-gash, and Tar-gash says 'take them off.' "

To-yad swung to Tarzan's side. "M'wa-lot will come soon," he said. "If M'wa-lot says take them off, we shall take them off. We do not take orders from Tar-gash."

Like a panther, quickly, silently Tar-gash sprang straight for the throat of To-yad. There was no warning, not even an instant of hesitation. In this Tarzan saw that Tar-gash differed from the great apes with whom the Lord of the Jungle had been familiar upon the outer crust, for among them two bulls ordinarily must need have gone through a long preliminary of stiff-legged strutting and grumbled invective before either one launched himself upon the other in deadly combat. But the mind of Tar-gash had functioned with like celerity, so much so that decision and action had appeared to be almost simultaneous.

The impact of the heavy body of Tar-gash toppled To-yad from the branch upon which he had been standing, but so naturally arboreal were the two great creatures that even as they fell they reached out and seized the same branch and still fighting, each with his free hand and his heavy fangs, they hung there a second breaking their fall, and then dropped to the ground. They fought almost silently except for low growls, Tar-gash seeking the jugular of To-yad with those sharp, white fangs that had given him his name. To-yad, his every faculty concentrated upon defense, kept the grinning jaws from his flesh and suddenly twisting quickly around, tore loose from the powerful fingers of his opponent and sought safety in flight. But like a football player, Tar-gash launched himself through the air; his long hairy arms encircled the legs of the fleeing To-yad, bringing him heavily to the ground, and an instant later the powerful aggressor was on the back of his opponent and To-yad's jugular was at the mercy of his foe, but the great jaws of Tar-gash did not close.

"Ka-goda?" he inquired.

"Ka-goda," growled To-yad, and instantly Tar-gash arose from the body of the other bull.

With the agility of a monkey the victor leaped back into the branches of the tree. "Remove the bonds from the wrists of the gilak," he said, and at the same time he glared ferociously about him to see if there was another so mutinously minded as To-yad; but none spoke and none objected as one of the Sagoths who had dragged Tarzan up into the tree untied the bonds that secured his wrists.

"If he tries to run away from us," said Tar-gash, "kill him."

When his bonds were removed Tarzan expected that the Sagoths would take his knife away from him. He had lost his spear and bow and most of his arrows at the instant that the snare had snapped him from the ground, but though they had lain in plain view in the trail beneath the snare the Sagoths had paid no attention to them; nor did they now pay any attention to his knife. He was sure they must have seen it and he could not understand their lack of concern regarding it, unless they were ignorant of its purpose or held him in such contempt that they did not consider it worth the effort to disarm him.

Presently To-yad sneaked back into the tree, but he huddled sullenly by himself, apart from the others.

Faintly, from a distance, Tarzan heard something approaching. He heard it just a moment before the Sagoths heard it.

"They come!" announced Tar-gash.

"M'wa-lot comes," said another, glancing at To-yad. Now Tarzan knew why the primitive drum had been sounded, but he wondered why they were gathering.

At last they arrived, nor was it difficult for Tarzan to recognize M'wa-lot, the king among the others. A great bull walked in front—a bull with so much gray among the hairs

53

on his face that the latter had a slightly bluish complexion, and instantly the ape-man saw how the king had come by his name.

As soon as the Sagoths with Tarzan were convinced of the identity of the approaching party, they descended from the trees to the ground and when M'wa-lot had approached within twenty paces of them, he halted. "I am M'wa-lot," he announced. "With me are the people of my tribe."

"I am Tar-gash," replied the bull who seemed to be in charge of the other party. "With me are other bulls of the tribe of M'wa-lot."

This precautionary preliminary over, M'wa-lot advanced, followed by the bulls, the shes and the balus of his tribe.

"What is that?" demanded M'wa-lot, as his fierce eyes espied Tarzan.

"It is a gilak that we found caught in our snare," replied Tar-gash.

"That is the feast that you called us to?" demanded M'wa-lot, angrily. "You should have brought it to the tribe. It can walk."

"This is not the food of which the drum spoke," replied Tar-gash. "Nearby is the body of a thag that was killed by a tarag close by the snare in which this gilak was caught."

"Ugh!" grunted M'wa-lot. "We can eat the gilak later."

"We can have a dance," suggested one of Tarzan's captors. "We have eaten and slept many times since we have danced, M'wa-lot."

As the Sagoths, guided by Tar-gash, proceeded along the trail towards the body of the thag, the shes with balus growled savagely when one of the little ones chanced to come near to Tarzan. The bulls eyed him suspiciously and all seemed uneasy because of his presence. In these and in other ways the Sagoths were reminiscent of the apes of the tribe of Kerchak and to such an extent was this true that Tarzan, although a prisoner among them, felt strangely at home in this new environment.

A short distance ahead of the ape-man walked M'wa-lot, king of the tribe, and at M'wa-lot's elbow was To-yad. The two spoke in low tones and from the frequent glances they cast at Tar-gash, who walked ahead of them, it was evident that he was the subject of their conversation, the effect of which upon M'wa-lot seemed to be highly disturbing.

Tarzan could see that the shaggy chieftain was working himself into a frenzy of rage, the inciting cause of which was evidently the information that To-yad was imparting to him. The latter seemed to be attempting to goad him to greater fury, a fact which seemed to be now apparent to every member of the tribe with the exception of Tar-gash, who was walking in the lead, ahead of M'wa-lot and To-yad, for practically every other eye was turned upon the king, whose evident excitement had imparted a certain fierce restlessness to the other members of his party. But it was not until they had come within sight of the body of the thag that the storm broke and then, without warning, M'wa-lot swung his heavy club and leaped forward toward Tar-gash with the very evident intention of braining him from behind.

If the life of the ape-man in his constant battle for survival had taught him to act quickly, it also had taught him to think quickly. He knew that in all his savage company he had no friends, but he also knew that Tar-gash, from very stubbornness and to spite To-yad, might alone be expected to befriend him and now it appeared that Tar-gash himself might need a friend, for it was evident that no hand was to be raised in defense of him nor any voice in warning. And so Tarzan of the Apes, prompted both by considerations of self-interest and fair play, took matters into his own hands with such suddenness that he had already acted before any hand could be raised to stop him.

"Kreeg-ah, Tar-gash!" he cried, and at the same instant he sprang quickly forward, brushing To-yad aside with a single sweep of a giant arm that sent the Sagoth headlong into the underbrush bordering the trail.

At the warning cry of "Kreeg-ah," which in the language of the great apes is synonymous to beware, Tar-gash wheeled about to see the infuriated M'wa-lot with upraised club almost upon him and then he saw something else which made his savage eyes widen in surprise. The strange gilak, whom he had taken prisoner, had leaped close to M'wa-lot from behind. A smooth, bronzed arm slipped quickly about the king's neck and tightened. The gilak turned and stooped and surging forward with the king across his hip threw the great, hairy bull completely over his head and sent him sprawling at the feet of his astonished warriors. Then the gilak leaped to Tar-gash's side and, wheeling, faced the tribe with Tar-gash.

Instantly a score of clubs were raised against the two.

"Shall we remain and fight, Tar-gash?" demanded the ape-man.

"They will kill us," said Tar-gash. "If you were not a gilak, we might escape through the trees, but as you cannot escape we shall have to remain and fight."

"Lead the way," said Tarzan. "There is no Sagoth trail that Tarzan cannot follow."

"Come then," said Tar-gash, and as he spoke he hurled his club into the faces of the oncoming warriors and, turning, fled along the trail. A dozen mighty bounds he took and then leaped to the branch of an overhanging tree, and close behind him came the hairless gilak.

M'wa-lot's hairy warrior bulls pursued the two for a short distance and then gave up the chase as Tarzan was confident that they would, since among his own people it had usually been considered sufficient to run a recalcitrant bull out of the tribe and, unless he insisted upon returning, no particular effort was made to molest him.

As soon as it became evident that pursuit had been abandoned the Sagoth halted among the branches of a huge tree. "I am Tar-gash," he said, as Tarzan stopped near him.

"I am Tarzan," replied the ape-man.

"Why did you warn me?" asked Tar-gash.

"I told you that I did not come among you as an enemy," replied Tarzan, "and when I saw that To-yad had succeeded in urging M'wa-lot to kill you, I warned you because it was you that kept the bulls from killing me when I was captured."

"What were you doing in the country of the Sagoths?" asked Tar-gash.

"I was hunting," replied Tarzan.

"Where do you want to go now?" asked the Sagoth.

"I shall return to my people," replied Tarzan.

"Where are they?"

Tarzan of the Apes hesitated. He looked upward toward the sun, whose rays were filtering down through the foliage of the forest. He looked about him—everywhere was foliage. There was nothing in the foliage nor upon the boles or branches of the trees to indicate direction. Tarzan of the Apes was lost!

V
BROUGHT DOWN

JASON GRIDLEY, looking down from the branches of the tree in which he had found sanctuary, was held by a certain horrible fascination as he watched the feast of the great cats.

The scene that he had just witnessed—this stupendous spectacle of savagery—suggested to him something of what life upon the outer crust must have been at the dawn of humanity.

The suggestion was borne in upon him that perhaps this scene which he had witnessed might illustrate an important cause of the extinction of all of these animals upon the outer crust.

The action of the great saber-tooth tigers of Pellucidar in rounding up the other beasts of the forest and driving them to this clearing for slaughter evidenced a development of intelligence far beyond that attained by the carnivores of the outer world of the present day, such concerted action by any great number for the common good being unknown.

Gridley saw the vast number of animals that had been slaughtered and most of them uselessly, since there was more flesh there than the surviving tigers could consume before it reached a stage of putrefaction that would render it un-palatable even to one of the great cats. And this fact suggested the conviction that the cunning of the tigers had reached a plane where it might reasonably be expected to react upon themselves and eventually cause their extinction, for in their savage fury and lust for flesh they had slaughtered indiscriminately males and females, young and old. If this slaughter went on unchecked for ages, the natural prey of the tigers must become extinct and then, goaded by starvation, they would fall upon one another.

The last stage of the ascendancy of the great cats upon the outer crust must have been short and terrible and so eventually it would prove here in Pellucidar.

And just as the great cats may have reached a point where their mental development had spelled their own doom, so in the preceding era the gigantic, carnivorous dinosaurs of the Jurassic may similarly have caused the extinction of their own contemporaries and then of themselves. Nor did Jason Gridley find it difficult to apply the same line of reasoning to the evolution of man upon the outer crust and to his own possible extinction in the not far remote future. In fact, he recalled quite definitely that statisticians had shown that within two hundred years or less the human race would have so greatly increased and the natural resources of the outer world would have been so depleted that the last generation must either starve to death or turn to cannibalism to prolong its hateful existence for another short period.

Perhaps, thought Gridley, in nature's laboratory each type that had at some era dominated all others represented an experiment in the eternal search for perfection. The invertebrate had given way to fishes, the fishes to the reptiles, the reptiles to the birds and mammals, and these, in turn, had been forced to bow to the greater intelligence of man.

What would be next? Gridley was sure that there would be something after man, who is unquestionably the Creator's greatest blunder, combining as he does all the vices of preceding types from invertebrates to mammals, while possessing few of their virtues.

As such thoughts were forced upon his mind by the scene below him they were accompanied by others of more immediate importance, first of which was concern for his fellows.

Nowhere about the clearing did he see any sign of a human being alive or dead. He called aloud several times but received no reply, though he realized that it was possible that above the roaring and the growling of the feeding beasts his voice might not carry to any great distance. He began to have hopes that his companions had all escaped, but he was still greatly worried over the fate of Von Horst.

The subject of second consideration was that of his own escape and return to the O-220. He had it in his mind that at nightfall the beasts might retire and unconsciously he glanced upward at the sun to note the time, when the realization came to him that there would never be any night, that forever throughout all eternity it would be noon here. And then he began to wonder how long he had been gone from the ship, but when he glanced at his watch he realized that that meant nothing. The hour hand might have made an entire circle since he had last looked at it, for in the excitement of all that had transpired since they had left the O-220 how might the mind of man, unaided, compute time?

But he knew that eventually the beasts must get their fill and leave. After them, however, there would be the hyaenodons and the jackals with their fierce cousins, the wild dogs. As he watched these, sitting at a respectful distance from the tigers or slinking hungrily in the background, he realized that they might easily prove as much of a bar to his escape as the saber-tooth tigers themselves.

The hyaenodons especially were most discouraging to contemplate. Their bodies were as large as that of a full grown mastiff. They walked upon short, powerful legs and their broad jaws were massive and strong. Dark, shaggy hair covered their backs and sides, turning to white upon their breasts and bellies.

Gnawing hunger assailed Jason Gridley and also an overpowering desire to sleep, convincing him that he must have been many hours away from the O-220, and yet the beasts beneath him continued to feed.

A dead thag lay at the foot of the tree in which the American kept his lonely vigil. So far it had not been fed upon and the nearest tiger was fifty yards away. Gridley was hungry, so hungry that he eyed the thag covetously. He glanced about him, measuring the distance from the tree to the nearest tiger and trying to compute the length of time that it would take him to clamber back to safety should he descend to the ground. He had seen the tigers in action and he knew how swiftly they could cover ground and that one of them could leap almost as high as the branch upon which he sat.

Altogether the chance of success seemed slight for the plan he had in mind in the event that the nearest tiger took exception to it. But great though the danger was, hunger won. Gridley drew his hunting knife and lowered himself gently to the ground, keeping an alert eye upon the nearest tiger. Quickly he sliced several long strips of flesh from the thag's hind quarter.

The tarag feeding fifty yards away looked up. Jason sliced another strip, returned his knife to its sheath and climbed quickly back to safety. The tarag lowered its head upon its kill and closed its eyes.

The American gathered dead twigs and small branches that still clung to the living tree and with them he built a small fire in a great crotch.

Here he cooked some of the meat of the thag; the edges were charred, the inside was raw, but Jason Gridley could have sworn that never before in his life had he tasted such delicious food.

How long his culinary activities employed him, he did not know, but when he glanced down again at the clearing he saw that most of the tigers had quitted their kills and were moving leisurely toward the forest, their distended bellies proclaiming how well they had surfeited themselves. And as the tigers retired, the hyaenodons, the wild dogs and the jackals closed in to the feast.

The hyaenodons kept the others away and Gridley saw another long wait ahead of him; nor was he mistaken. And when the hyaenodons had had their fill and gone, the wild dogs came and kept the jackals away.

In the meantime Gridley had fashioned a rude platform among the branches of the tree, and here he had slept, awakening refreshed but assailed by a thirst that was almost overpowering.

The wild dogs were leaving now and Gridley determined to wait no longer. Already the odor of decaying flesh was warning him of worse to come and there was the fear too that the tigers might return to their kills.

Descending from the tree he skirted the clearing, keeping close to the forest and searching for the trail by which his party had entered the clearing. The wild dogs, slinking away, turned to growl at him, baring menacing fangs. But knowing how well their bellies were filled, he entertained little fear of them; while for the jackals he harbored that contempt which is common among all creatures.

Gridley was dismayed to note that many trails entered the clearing; nor could he recognize any distinguishing mark that might suggest the one by which he had come. Whatever footprints his party had left had been entirely obliterated by the pads of the carnivores.

He tried to reconstruct his passage across the clearing to the tree in which he had found safety and by this means he hit upon a trail to follow, although he had no assurance that it was the right trail. The baffling noonday sun shining down upon him seemed to taunt him with his helplessness.

As he proceeded alone down the lonely trail, realizing that at any instant he might come face to face with some terrible beast of a long dead past, Jason Gridley wondered how the ape-like progenitors of man had survived to transmit any of their characteristics however unpleasant to a posterity. That he could live to reach the O-220 he much doubted. The idea that he might live to take a mate and raise a family was preposterous.

While the general aspect of the forest through which he was passing seemed familiar, he realized that this might be true no matter what trail he was upon and now he reproached himself for not having had the trees along the trail blazed. What a stupid ass he had been, he thought; but his regrets were not so much for himself as for the others, whose safety had been in his hands.

Never in his life had Jason Gridley felt more futile or helpless. To trudge ceaselessly along that endless trail, having not the slightest idea whether it led toward the O-220 or in the opposite direction was depressing, even maddening; yet there was naught else to do. And always that damned noon-day sun staring unblinkingly down upon him—the cruel sun that could see his ship, but would not lead him to it.

His thirst was annoying, but not yet overpowering, when he came to a small stream that was crossed by the trail. Here he drank and rested for a while, built a small fire, cooked some more of his thag meat, drank again and took up his weary march—but much refreshed.

Aboard the O-220, as the hours passed and hope waned, the spirit of the remaining officers and members of the crew became increasingly depressed as apprehension for the safety of their absent comrades increased gradually until it became eventually an almost absolute conviction of disaster.

"They have been gone nearly seventy-two hours now," said Zuppner, who, with Dorf and Hines, spent most of his time in the upper observation cabin or pacing the narrow walkingway along the ship's back. "I never felt helpless before in my life," he continued ruefully, "but I am free to admit that I don't know what in the devil to do."

"It just goes to show," said Hines, "how much we depend upon habit and custom and precedence in determining all our action even in the face of what we are pleased to call emergency. Here there is no custom, habit or precedence to guide us."

"We have only our own resources to fall back upon," said Dorf, "and it is humiliating to realize that we have no resources."

"Not under the conditions that surround us," said Zuppner. "On the outer crust there would be no question but that we should cruise around in search of the missing members of our party. We could make rapid excursions, returning to our base often; but here in Pellucidar if we should lose sight of our base there is not one of us who believes he could return the ship to this same anchorage. And that is a chance we cannot take for the only hope those men have is that the ship shall be here when they return."

One hundred and fifty feet below them Robert Jones leaned far out of the galley doorway in an effort to see the noonday sun shining down upon the ship. His simple, good-natured face wore a puzzled expression not untinged with awe, and as he drew back into the galley he extracted a rabbit's foot from his trousers pocket. Gently he touched each eye with it and then rubbed it vigorously upon the top of his head at the same time muttering incoherently below his breath.

From the vantage point of the walkingway far above, Lieutenant Hines scanned the landscape in all directions through powerful glasses as he had done for so long that it seemed he knew every shrub and tree and blade of grass within sight. The wild life of savage Pellucidar that crossed and re-crossed the clearing had long since become an old story to these three men. Again and again as one animal or another had emerged from the distant forest the glasses had been leveled upon it until it could be identified as other than man; but now Hines voiced a sudden, nervous exclamation.

"What is it?" demanded Zuppner. "What do you see?"

"It's a man!" exclaimed Hines. "I'm sure of it."

"Where?" asked Dorf, as he and Zuppner raised their glasses to their eyes.

"About two points to port."

"I see it," said Dorf. "It's either Gridley or Von Horst, and whoever it is he is alone."

"Take ten of the crew at once, Lieutenant," said Zuppner, turning to Dorf. "See that they are well armed and go out and meet him. Lose no time," he shouted after the Lieutenant, who had already started down the climbing shaft.

The two officers upon the top of the O-220 watched Dorf and his party as it set out to meet the man they could see trudging steadily toward the ship. They watched them as they approached one another, though, owing to the contour of the land, which was rolling, neither Dorf nor the man he had gone to meet caught sight of one another until they were less than a hundred yards apart. It was then that the Lieutenant recognized the other as Jason Gridley.

As they hastened forward and clasped hands it was typical

of the man that Gridley's first words were an inquiry relative to the missing members of the party.

Dorf shook his head. "You are the only one that has returned," he said.

The eager light died out of Gridley's eyes and he suddenly looked very tired and much older as he greeted the engineers and mechanics who made up the party that had come to escort him back to the ship.

"I have been within sight of the ship for a long time," he said. "How long, I do not know. I broke my watch back in the forest a way trying to beat a tiger up a tree. Then another one treed me just on the edge of the clearing in plain view of the ship. It seems as though I have been there a week. How long have I been gone, Dorf?"

"About seventy-two hours."

Gridley's face brightened. "Then there is no reason to give up hope yet for the others," he said. "I honestly thought I had been gone a week. I have slept several times, I never could tell how long; and then I have gone for what seemed long periods without sleep because I became very tired and excessively hungry and thirsty."

During the return march to the ship Jason insisted upon hearing a detailed account of everything that had happened since his departure, but it was not until they had joined Zuppner and Hines that he narrated the adventures that had befallen him and his companions during their ill-fated expedition.

"The first thing I want," he told them after he had been greeted by Zuppner and Hines, "is a bath, and then if you will have Bob cook a couple of cows I'll give you the details of the expedition while I am eating them. A couple of handfuls of Bos Primigenus and some wild fruit have only whetted my appetite."

A half hour later, refreshed by a bath, a shave and fresh clothing, he joined them in the mess room.

As the three men seated themselves, Robert Jones entered from the galley, his black face wreathed in smiles.

"Ah'm suttinly glad to see you all, Mas' Jason," said Robert.

"Ah knew sumpin was a-goin' to happen though—Ah knew we was a-goin' to have good luck."

"Well, I'm glad to be back, Bob," said Gridley, "and I don't know of anyone that I am any happier to see than you, for I sure have missed your cooking. But what made you think that we're going to have good luck?"

"Ah jes had a brief conversation with mah rabbit's foot. Dat ole boy he never fails me. We suah be out o' luck if Ah lose him."

"Oh, I've seen lots of rabbits around, Bob," said Zuppner. "We can get you a bushel of them in no time."

"Yes suh, Cap'n, but you can't get 'em in de dahk of de moon where dey ain't no dahk an' dey ain't no moon, an' othe'wise dey lacks efficiency."

"It's a good thing, then, that we brought you along," said Jason, "and a mighty good thing for Pellucidar, for she never has had a really effective rabbit's foot before in all her existence. But I can see where you're going to need that rabbit's foot pretty badly yourself in about a minute, Bob."

"How's dat, suh?" demanded Robert.

"The spirits tell me that something is going to happen to you if you don't get food onto this table in a hurry," laughed Gridley.

"Yes suh, comin' right up," exclaimed the black as he hastened into the galley.

As Gridley ate, he went over the adventures of the last seventy-two hours in careful detail and the three men sought to arrive at some definite conjecture as to the distance he had covered from the ship and the direction.

"Do you think that you could lead another party to the clearing where you became separated from Von Horst and the Waziri?" asked Zuppner.

"Yes, of course I could," replied Gridley, "because from the point that we entered the forest we blazed the trees up to the time we reached the trail, which we followed to the left. In fact I would not be needed at all and if we decide to send out such a party, I shall not accompany it."

The other officers looked at him in surprise and for a moment there was an embarrassed silence.

"I have what I consider a better plan," continued Gridley. "There are twenty-seven of us left. In the event of absolute necessity, twelve men can operate the ship. That will leave fifteen to form a new searching party. Leaving me out, you would have fourteen, and after you have heard my plan, if you decide upon sending out such a party, I suggest that Lieutenant Dorf command it, leaving you, Captain Zuppner, and Hines to navigate the ship in the event that none of us returns, or that you finally decide to set out in search of us."

"But I thought that you were not going," said Zuppner.

"I am not going with the searching party. I am going alone in the scout plane, and my advice would be that you send out no searching party for at least twenty-four hours after I depart, for in that time I shall either have located those who are missing or have failed entirely."

Zuppner shook his head, dubiously. "Hines, Dorf and I have discussed the feasibility of using the scout plane," he said. "Hines was very anxious to make the attempt, although he realizes better than any of us that once a pilot is out of sight of the O-220 he may never be able to locate it again, for you must remember that we know nothing concerning any of the landmarks of the country in the direction that our search must be prosecuted."

"I have taken all that into consideration," replied Gridley, "and I realize that it is at best but a forlorn hope."

"Let me undertake it," said Hines. "I have had more flying experience than any of you with the possible exception of Captain Zuppner, and it is out of the question that we should risk losing him."

"Any one of you three is probably better fitted to undertake such a flight than I," replied Gridley; "but that does not relieve me of the responsibility. I am more responsible than any other member of this party for our being where we are and, therefore, my responsibility for the safety of the missing members of the expedition is greater than that of any of the rest of you. Under the circumstances, then, I could not permit anyone else to undertake this flight. I think that you will all understand and appreciate how I feel and that you will do me the favor to interpose no more objection."

It was several minutes thereafter before anyone spoke, the four seeming to be immersed in the business of sipping their coffee and smoking their cigarettes. It was Zuppner who broke the silence.

"Before you undertake this thing," he said, "you should have a long sleep, and in the meantime we will get the plane out and have it gone over thoroughly. You must have every chance for success that we can give you."

"Thank you!" said Gridley. "I suppose you are right about the sleep. I hate to waste the time, but if you will call me the moment that the ship is ready I shall go to my cabin at once and get such sleep as I can in the meantime."

While Gridley slept, the scout plane, carried aft in the keel cabin, was lowered to the ground, where it underwent a careful inspection and test by the engineers and officers of the O-220.

Even before the plane was ready Gridley appeared at the cabin door of the O-220 and descended to the ground.

"You did not sleep long," said Zuppner.

"I do not know how long," said Gridley, "but I feel rested and anyway I could not have slept longer, knowing that those fellows are out there somewhere waiting and hoping for succor."

"What route do you expect to follow," asked Zuppner, "and how are you planning to insure a reasonable likelihood of your being able to return?"

"I shall fly directly over the forest as far as I think it at all likely that they could have marched in the time that they have been absent, assuming that they became absolutely confused and have traveled steadily away from the ship. As soon as I have gained sufficient altitude to make any observation I shall try and spot some natural landmark, like a mountain or a body of water, near the ship and from time to time, as I proceed, I shall make a note of similar landmarks. I believe that in this way I can easily find my way back, since at the furthest I cannot proceed over two hundred and fifty miles from the O-220 and return to it with the fuel that I can carry.

"After I have reached the furthest possible limits that I think the party could have strayed, I shall commence circling, depending upon the noise of the motor to attract their attention and, of course, assuming that they will find some means of signaling their presence to me, which they can do even in wooded country by building smudges."

"You expect to land?" inquired Zuppner, nodding at the heavy rifle which Gridley carried.

"If I find them in open country, I shall land; but even if I do not find them it may be necessary for me to come down and my recent experiences have taught me not to venture far in Pellucidar without a rifle."

After a careful inspection, Gridley shook hands with the three remaining officers and bid farewell to the ship's company, all of whom were anxious observers of his preparation for departure.

"Good-bye, old man," said Zuppner, "and may God and luck go with you."

Gridley pressed the hand of the man he had come to look upon as a staunch and loyal friend, and then took his seat in the open cockpit of the scout plane. Two mechanics spun the propeller, the motor roared and a moment later the block was kicked away and the plane rolled out across the grassy meadowland towards the forest at the far side. The watchers saw it rise swiftly and make a great circle and they knew that Gridley was looking for a landmark. Twice it circled above the open plain and then darted away across the forest.

It had not been until he had made that first circle that Jason Gridley had realized the handicap that this horizonless landscape of Pellucidar had placed upon his chances of return. He had thought of a mountain standing boldly out against the sky, for such a landmark would have been almost constantly within the range of his vision during the entire flight.

There were mountains in the distance, but they stood out against no background of blue sky nor upon any horizon. They simply merged with the landscape beyond them, curving upward in the distance. Twice he circled, his keen eyes searching for any outstanding point in the topography of the country beneath him, but there was nothing that was more apparent than the grassy plain upon which the O-220 rested.

He felt that he could not waste time and fuel by searching longer for a landmark that did not exist, and while he realized that the plain would be visible for but a comparatively short distance he was forced to accept it as his sole guide in lieu of a better one.

Roaring above the leafy roof of the primeval forest, all that transpired upon the ground below was hidden from him and it was tantalizing to realize that he might have passed directly over the heads of the comrads he sought, yet there was no other way. Returning, he would either circle or hold an exaggerated zig-zag course, watching carefully for sign of a signal.

For almost two hours Jason Gridley held a straight course, passing over forest, plain and rolling, hilly country, but nowhere did he see any sign of those he sought. Already he had reached the limit of the distance he had planned upon coming when there loomed ahead of him in the distance a range of lofty mountains. These alone would have determined him to turn back, since his judgment told him that the lost members of the party, should they have chanced to come this far, would be now have realized that they were traveling in the wrong direction.

As he banked to turn he caught a glimpse out of the corner of an eye of something in the air above him and looking quickly back, Jason Gridley caught his breath in astonishment.

Hovering now, almost above him, was a gigantic creature, the enormous spread of whose wings almost equalled that of the plane he was piloting. The man had a single glimpse of tremendous jaws, armed with mighty teeth, in the very instant that he realized that this mighty anachronism was bent upon attacking him.

Gridley was flying at an altitude of about three thousand feet when the huge pteranodon launched itself straight at the ship. Jason sought to elude it by diving. There was a terrific crash, a roar, a splintering of wood and a grinding of metal as the pteranodon swooped down upon its prey and full into the propeller.

What happened then, happened so quickly that Jason Gridley could not have reconstructed the scene five seconds later.

The plane turned completely over and at the same instant Gridley jumped. He jerked the rip cord of his parachute. Something struck him on the head and he lost consciousness.

VI

A PHORORHACOS OF THE MIOCENE

"Where are your people?" Tar-gash asked again.

Tarzan shook his head. "I do not know," he said.

"Where is your country?" asked Tar-gash.

"It is a long way off," replied the ape-man. "It is not in Pellucidar;" but that the Sagoth could not understand any more than he could understand that a creature might be lost at all, for inherent in him was that same homing instinct that marked all the creatures of Pellucidar and which constitutes a wise provision of nature in a world without guiding celestial bodies.

Had it been possible to transport Tar-gash instantly to any point within that mighty inner world, elsewhere than upon the surface of an ocean, he could have unerringly found his way to the very spot where he was born, and because that power was instinctive he could not understand why Tarzan did not possess it.

"I know where there is a tribe of men," he said, presently. "Perhaps they are your people. I shall lead you to them."

As Tarzan had no idea as to the direction in which the ship lay and as it was remotely possible that Tar-gash was referring to the members of the O-220 expedition, he felt that he was as well off following where Tar-gash led as elsewhere, and so he signified his readiness to accompany the Sagoth.

"How long since you saw this tribe of men," he asked after a while, "and how long have they lived where you saw them?"

Upon the Sagoth's reply to these questions, the ape-man felt that he might determine the possibility of the men to whom Tar-gash referred being the members of his own party, for if they were newcomers in the district then the chances were excellent that they were the people he sought; but his questions elicited no satisfactory reply for the excellent reason that time meant nothing to Tar-gash. And so the two set out upon a leisurely search for the tribe of men that Tar-gash knew of. It was leisurely because for Tar-gash time did not exist; nor had it ever been a very important factor in the existence of the ape-man, except in occasional moments of emergency.

They were a strangely assorted pair—one a creature just standing upon the threshold of humanity, the other an English Lord in his own right, who was, at the same time, in many respects as primitive as the savage, shaggy bull into whose companionship chance had thrown him.

At first Tar-gash had been inclined to look with contempt upon this creature of another race, which he considered far inferior to his own in strength, agility, courage and wood-craft, but he soon came to hold the ape-man in vast respect. And because he could respect his prowess he became attached to him in bonds of loyalty that were as closely akin to friendship as the savage nature of his primitive mind permitted.

They hunted together and fought together. They swung through the trees when the great cats hunted upon the ground, or they followed game trails ages old beneath the hoary trees of Pellucidar or out across her rolling, grassy, flower-spangled meadowland.

They lived well upon the fat of the land for both were mighty hunters.

Tarzan fashioned a new bow and arrows and a stout spear, and these, at first, the Sagoth refused even to notice, but presently when he saw how easily and quickly they brought game to their larder he evinced a keen interest and Tarzan taught him how to use the weapons and later how to fashion them.

The country through which they traveled was well watered and was alive with game. It was partly wooded with great stretches of open land, where tremendous herds of herbivores grazed beneath the eternal noonday sun, and because of these great herds the beasts of prey were numerous—and such beasts!

Tarzan had thought that there was no world like his own world and no jungle like his own jungle, but the more deeply he dipped into the wonders of Pellucidar the more enamored he became of this savage, primitive world, teeming with the wild life he loved best. That there were few men was Pellucidar's chiefest recommendation. Had there been none the ape-man might have considered this the land of ultimate perfection, for who is there more conversant with the cruelty and inconsideration of man than the savage beasts of the jungle?

The friendship that had developed between Tarzan and the Sagoth—and that was primarily based upon the respect which each felt for the prowess of the other—increased as each seemed to realize other admirable, personal qualities and characteristics in his companion, not the least of which being a common taciturnity. They spoke only when conversation seemed necessary, and that, in reality, was seldom.

If man spoke only when he had something worth while to say and said that as quickly as possible, ninety-eight per cent of the human race might as well be dumb, thereby establishing a heavenly harmony from pate to tonsil.

And so the companionship of Tar-gash, coupled with the romance of strange sights and sounds and odors in this new world, acted upon the ape-man as might a strong drug, filling him with exhilaration and dulling his sense of responsibility, so that the necessity of finding his people dwindled to a matter of minor importance. Had he known that some of them were in trouble his attitude would have changed immediately, but this he did not know. On the contrary he was only aware that they had every facility for insuring their safety and their ultimate return to the outer world and that his absence would not handicap them in any particular. However, when he did give the matter thought he knew that he must return to them, that he must find them, and that sooner or later he must go back with them to the world from which they had come.

But all such considerations were quite remote from his thoughts as he and Tar-gash were crossing a rolling, tree-dotted plain in their search for the tribe of men to which the Sagoth was guiding him. By comparison with other plains they had crossed, this one seemed strangely deserted, but the reason for this was evident in the close-cropped grass which suggested that great herds had grazed it off before moving on to new pastures. The absence of life and movement was slightly depressing and Tarzan found himself regretting the absence of even the dangers of the teeming land through which they had just come.

They were well out toward the center of the plain and could see the solid green of a great forest curving upward into the hazy distance when the attention of both was attracted by a strange, droning noise that brought them to a sudden halt. Simultaneously both turned and looked backward and up into the sky from which the sound seemed to come.

Far above and just emerging from the haze of the distance was a tiny speck. "Quick!" exclaimed Tar-gash. "It is a thipdar," and motioning Tarzan to follow him he ran swiftly to concealment beneath a large tree.

"What is a thipdar?" asked Tarzan, as the two halted beneath the friendly shade.

"A thipdar," said the Sagoth, "is a thipdar;" nor could he describe it more fully other than to add that the thipdars were sometimes used by the Mahars either to protect them or to hunt their food.

"Is the thipdar a living thing?" demanded Tarzan.

"Yes," replied Tar-gash. "It lives and is very strong and very fierce."

"Then that is not a thipdar," said Tarzan.

"What is it then?" demanded the Sagoth.

"It is an aeroplane," replied Tarzan.

"What is that?" inquired the Sagoth.

"It would be hard to explain it to you," replied the ape-man. "It is something that the men of my world build and in which they fly through the air," and as he spoke he stepped out into the opening, where he might signal the pilot of the plane, which he was positive was the one carried by the O-220 and which, he assumed, was prosecuting a search for him.

"Come back," exclaimed Tar-gash. "You cannot fight a thipdar. It will swoop down and carry you off if you are out in the open."

"It will not harm me," said Tarzan. "One of my friends is in it."

"And you will be in it, too, if you do not come back under the tree," replied Tar-gash.

As the plane approached, Tarzan ran around in a small circle to attract the pilot's attention, stopping occasionally to wave his arms, but the plane sped on above him and it was evident that its pilot had not seen him.

Until it faded from sight in the distance, Tarzan of the Apes stood upon the lonely plain, watching the ship that was bearing his comrade away from him.

The sight of the ship awakened Tarzan to a sense of his responsibility. He realized now that someone was risking his life to save him and with this thought came a determination to exert every possible effort to locate the O-220.

The passage of the plane opened many possibilities for conjecture. If it was circling, which was possible, the direction of its flight as it passed over him would have no bearing upon the direction of the O-220, and if it were not circling, then how was he to know whether it was traveling away from the ship in the beginning of its quest, or was returning to it having concluded its flight.

"That was not a thipdar," said Tar-gash, coming from beneath the tree and standing at Tarzan's side. "It is a creature that I have never seen before. It is larger and must be even more terrible than a thipdar. It must have been very angry, for it growled terribly all the time."

"It is not alive," said Tarzan. "It is something that the men of my country build that they may fly through the air. Riding in it is one of my friends. He is looking for me."

The Sagoth shook his head. "I am glad he did not come down," he said. "He was either very angry or very hungry, otherwise he would not have growled so loudly."

It was apparent to Tarzan that Tar-gash was entirely incapable of comprehending his explanation of the aeroplane and that he would always believe it was a huge, flying reptile; but that was of no importance—the thing that troubled Tarzan being the question of the direction in which he should now prosecute his search for the O-220, and eventually he determined to follow in the direction taken by the airship, for as this coincided with the direction in which Tar-gash assured him he would find the tribe of human beings for which they were searching, it seemed after all the wisest course to pursue.

The drone of the motor had died away in the distance when Tarzan and Tar-gash took up their interrupted journey across the plain and into broken country of low, rocky hills.

The trail, which was well marked and which Tar-gash said led through the hills, followed the windings of a shallow canyon, which was rimmed on one side by low cliffs, in the face of which there were occasional caves and crevices. The bottom of the canyon was strewn with fragments of rock of various sizes. The vegetation was sparse and there was every indication of an aridity such as Tarzan had not previously encountered since he left the O-220, and as it seemed likely that both game and water would be scarce here, the two pushed on at a brisk, swinging walk.

It was very quiet and Tarzan's ears were constantly upon the alert to catch the first sound of the hum of the motor of the returning aeroplane, when suddenly the silence was shattered by the sound of hoarse screeching which seemed to be coming from a point further up the canyon.

Tar-gash halted. "Dyal," he said.

Tarzan looked at the Sagoth questioningly.

"It is a Dyal," repeated Tar-gash, "and it is angry."

"What is a Dyal?" asked Tarzan.

"It is a terrible bird," replied the Sagoth; "but its meat is good, and Tar-gash is hungry."

That was enough. No matter how terrible the Dyal might be, it was meat and Tar-gash was hungry, and so the two beasts of prey crept warily forward, stalking their quarry. A vagrant breeze, wafting gently down the canyon, brought to the nostrils of the ape-man a strange, new scent. It was a bird scent, slightly suggestive of the scent of an ostrich, and from its volume Tarzan guessed that it might come from a very large bird, a suggestion that was borne out by the loud screeching of the creature, intermingled with which was a scratching and a scraping sound.

Tar-gash, who was in the lead and who was taking advantage of all the natural shelter afforded by the fragments of rock with which the canyon bed was strewn, came to a halt upon the lower side of a great boulder, behind which he quickly withdrew, and as Tarzan joined him he signalled the ape-man to look around the corner of the boulder.

Following the suggestion of his companion, Tazan saw the author of the commotion that had attracted their attention. Being a savage jungle beast, he exhibited no outward sign of the astonishment he felt as he gazed upon the mighty creature that was clawing frantically at a crevice in the cliffside.

To Tarzan it was a nameless creature of another world. To Tar-gash it was simply a Dyal. Neither knew that he was looking upon a Phororhacos of the Miocene. They saw a huge creature whose crested head, larger than that of a horse, towered eight feet above the ground. Its powerful, curved beak gaped wide as it screeched in anger. It beat its short, useless wing in a frenzy of rage as it struck with its mighty three-toed talons at something just within the fissure before it. And then it was that Tarzan saw that the thing at which it struck was a spear, held by human hands—a pitifully inadequate weapon with which to attempt to ward off the attack of the mighty Dyal.

As Tarzan surveyed the creature he wondered how Tar-gash, armed only with his puny club, might hope to pit himself in successful combat against it. He saw the Sagoth creep stealthily out from behind their rocky shelter and move slowly to another closer to the Dyal and behind it, and so absorbed was the bird in its attack upon the man within the fissure that it did not notice the approach of the enemy in its rear.

The moment that Tar-gash was safely concealed behind the new shelter, Tarzan followed him and now they were within fifty feet of the great bird.

The Sagoth, grasping his club firmly by the small end, arose and ran swiftly from his concealment, straight toward the giant Dyal, and Tarzan followed, fitting an arrow to his bow.

Tar-gash had covered but half the distance when the sound of his approach attracted the attention of the bird. Wheeling about, it discovered the two rash creatures who dared to interfere with its attack upon its quarry, and with a loud screech and wide distended beak it charged them.

The instant that the Dyal had turned and discovered them, Tar-gash had commenced whirling his club about his head and as the bird charged he launched it at one of those mighty legs, and on the instant Tarzan understood the purpose of the Sagoth's method of attack. The heavy club, launched by the mighty muscles of the beast man, would snap the leg bone that it struck, and then the enormous fowl would be at the mercy of the Sagoth. But if it did not strike the leg, what then? Almost certain death for Tar-gash.

Tarzan had long since had reason to appreciate his companion's savage disregard of life in the pursuit of flesh, but this seemed the highest pinnacle to which rashness might ascend and still remain within the realm of sanity.

And, indeed, there happened that which Tarzan had feared—the club missed its mark. Tarzan's bow sang and an arrow sank deep into the breast of the Dyal. Tar-gash leaped swiftly to one side, eluding the charge, and another arrow pierced the bird's feathers and hide. And then the ape-man sprang quickly to his right as the avalanche of destruction bore down upon him, its speed undiminished by the force of the two arrows buried so deeply within it.

Before the Dyal could turn to pursue either of them, Tar-gash hurled a rock, many of which were scattered upon the ground about them. It struck the Dyal upon the side of the head, momentarily dazing him, and Tarzan drove home two more arrows. As he did so, the Dyal wheeled drunkenly toward him and as he faced about a great spear drove past Tarzan's shoulder and plunged deep into the breast of the maddened creature, and to the impact of this last missile it went down, falling almost at the feet of the ape-man.

Ignorant though he was of the strength and the methods of attack and defense of this strange bird, Tarzan neverthe-less hesitated not an instant and as the Dyal fell he was upon it with drawn hunting knife.

So quickly was he in and out that he had severed its windpipe and was away again before he could become en-tangled in its death struggle, and then it was that for the first time he saw the man who had cast the spear.

Standing erect, a puzzled expression upon his face, was a tall, stalwart warrior, his slightly bronzed skin gleaming in the sunlight, his shaggy head of hair bound back by a deer-skin band.

For weapons, in addition to his spear, he carried a stone knife, thrust into the girdle that supported his G-string. His eyes were well set and intelligent. His features were regular and well cut. Altogether he was as splendid a specimen of manhood as Tarzan had ever beheld.

Tar-gash, who had recovered his club, was advancing toward the stranger. "I am Tar-gash," he said. "I kill."

The stranger drew his stone knife and waited, looking first at Tar-gash and then at Tarzan.

The ape-man stepped in front of Tar-gash. "Wait," he commanded. "Why do you kill?"

"He is a gilak," replied the Sagoth.

"He saved you from the Dyal," Tarzan reminded Tar-gash. "My arrows would not stop the bird. Had it not been for his spear, one or both of us must have died."

The Sagoth appeared puzzled. He scratched his head in

perplexity. "But if I do not kill him, he will kill me," he said finally.

Tarzan turned toward the stranger. "I am Tarzan," he said. "This is Tar-gash," and he pointed at the Sagoth and waited.

"I am Thoar," said the stranger.

"Let us be friends," said Tarzan. "We have no quarrel with you."

Again the stranger looked puzzled.

"Do you understand the language of the Sagoths?" asked Tarzan, thinking that possibly the man might not have understood him.

Thoar nodded. "A little," he said; "but why should we be friends?"

"Why should we be enemies?" countered the ape-man.

Thoar shook his head. "I do not know," he said. "It is always thus."

"Together we have slain the Dyal," said Tarzan. "Had we not come it would have killed you. Had you not cast your spear it would have killed us. Therefore, we should be friends, not enemies. Where are you going?"

"Back to my own country," replied Thoar, nodding in the direction that Tarzan and Tar-gash had been travelling.

"We, too, are going in that direction," said Tarzan. "Let us go together. Six hands are better than four."

Thoar glanced at the Sagoth.

"Shall we all go together as friends, Tar-gash?" demanded Tarzan.

"It is not done," said the Sagoth, precisely as though he had behind him thousands of years of civilization and culture.

Tarzan smiled one of his rare smiles. "We shall do it, then," he said. "Come!"

As though taking it for granted that the others would obey his command, the ape man turned to the body of the Dyal and, drawing his hunting knife, fell to work cutting off portions of the meat. For a moment Thoar and Tar-gash hesitated, eyeing each other suspiciously, and then the bronzed warrior walked over to assist Tarzan and presently Tar-gash joined them.

Thoar exhibited keen interest in Tarzan's steel knife,

which slid so easily through the flesh while he hacked and hewed laboriously with his stone implement; while Tar-gash seemed not particularly to notice either of the implements as he sunk his strong fangs into the breast of the Dyal and tore away a large hunk of the meat, which he devoured raw. Tarzan was about to do the same, having been raised exclusively upon a diet of raw meat, when he saw Thoar preparing to make fire, which he accomplished by the primitive expedient of friction. The three ate in silence, the Sagoth carrying his meat to a little distance from the others, perhaps because in him the instinct of the wild beast was stronger.

When they had finished they followed the trail upward toward the pass through which it led across the hills, and as they went Tarzan sought to question Thoar concerning his country and its people, but so limited is the primitive vocabulary of the Sagoths and so meager Thoar's knowledge of this language that they found communication difficult and Tarzan determined to master Thoar's tongue.

Considerable experience in learning new dialects and languages rendered the task far from difficult and as the ape-man never for a moment relinquished a purpose he intended to achieve, nor ever abandoned a task that he had set himself until it had been successfully concluded, he made rapid progress which was greatly facilitated by the interest which Thoar took in instructing him.

As they reached the summit of the low hills, they saw, hazily in the far distance, what appeared to be a range of lofty mountains.

"There," said Thoar, pointing, "lies Zoram."

"What is Zoram?" asked Tarzan.

"It is my country," replied the warrior. "It lies in the Mountains of the Thipdars."

This was the second time that Tarzan had heard a reference to thipdars. Tar-gash had said the aeroplane was a thipdar and now Thoar spoke of the Mountains of the Thipdars. "What is a thipdar?" he asked.

Thoar looked at him in astonishment. "From what country

do you come," he demanded, "that you do not know what a thipdar is and do not speak the language of the gilaks?"

"I am not of Pellucidar," said Tarzan.

"I could believe that," said Thoar, "if there were any other place from which you could be, but there is not, except Molop Az, the flaming sea upon which Pellucidar floats. But the only inhabitants of the Molop Az are the little demons, who carry the dead who are buried in the ground, piece by piece, down to Molop Az, and while I have never seen one of these little demons I am sure that they are not like you."

"No," said Tarzan, "I am not from Molop Az, yet sometimes I have thought that the world from which I come is inhabited by demons, both large and small."

As they hunted and ate and slept and marched together, these three creatures found their confidence in one another increasing so that even Tar-gash looked no longer with suspicion upon Thoar, and though they represented three distinct periods in the ascent of man, each separated from the other by countless thousands of years, yet they had so much in common that the advance which man had made from Tar-gash to Tarzan seemed scarcely a fair recompense for the time and effort which Nature must have expended.

Tarzan could not even conjecture the length of time he had been absent from the O-220, but he was confident that he must be upon the wrong trail, yet it seemed futile to turn back since he could not possibly have any idea as to what direction he should take. His one hope was that either he might be sighted by the pilot of the plane, which he was certain was hunting for him, or that the O-220, in cruising about, would eventually pass within signaling distance of him. In the meantime he might as well be with Tar-gash and Thoar as elsewhere.

The three had eaten and slept again and were resuming their journey when Tarzan's keen eyes espied from the summit of a low hill something lying upon an open plain at a considerable distance ahead of them. He did not know what it was, but he was sure that whatever it was, it was not a part of the natural landscape, there being about it that indefinable suggestion of discord, or, more properly, lack of harmony with its surroundings that every man whose perception has not been dulled by city dwelling will understand. And as it was almost instinctive with Tarzan to investigate anything that he did not understand, he turned his footsteps in the direction of the thing that he had seen.

The object that had aroused his curiosity was hidden from him almost immediately after he started the descent of the hill upon which he had stood when he discovered it; nor did it come again within the range of his vision until he was close upon it, when to his astonishment and dismay he saw that it was the wreck of an aeroplane.

VII

THE RED FLOWER OF ZORAM

Jana, The Red Flower of Zoram, paused and looked back across the rocky crags behind and below her. She was very hungry and it had been long since she had slept, for behind her, dogging her trail, were the four terrible men from Pheli, which lies at the foot of the Mountains of the Thipdars, beyond the land of Zoram.

For just an instant she stood erect and then she threw herself prone upon the rough rock, behind a jutting fragment that partially concealed her, and here she looked back along the way she had come, across a pathless waste of tumbled granite. Mountain-bred, she had lived her life among the lofty peaks of the Mountains of the Thipdars, considering contemptuously the people of the lowland to which those who pursued her belonged. Perchance, if they followed her here she might be forced to concede them some measure of courage and possibly to look upon them with a slightly lessened contempt, yet even so she would never abate her effort to escape them.

Bred in the bone of The Red Flower was loathing of the

men of Pheli, who ventured occasionally into the fastnesses of the Mountains of the Thipdars to steal women, for the pride and the fame of the mountain people lay in the beauty of their girls, and so far had this fame spread that men came from far countries, out of the vast river basin below their lofty range, and risked a hundred deaths in efforts to steal such a mate as Jana, The Red Flower of Zoram.

The girl's sister, Lana, had been thus stolen, and within her memory two other girls of Zoram, by the men from the lowland, and so the fear, as well as the danger, was ever present. Such a fate seemed to The Red Flower worse than death, since not only would it take her forever from her beloved mountains, but make her a low-country woman and her children low-country children than which, in the eyes of the mountain people, there could be no deeper disgrace, for the mountain men mated only with mountain women, the men of Zoram, and Clovi, and Daroz taking mates from their own tribes or stealing them from their neighbors.

Jana was beloved by many of the young warriors of Zoram, and though, as yet, there had been none who had fired her own heart to love she knew that some day she would mate with one of them, unless in the meantime she was stolen by a warrior from another tribe.

Were she to fall into the hands of one from either Clovi or Daroz she would not be disgraced and she might even be happy, but she was determined to die rather than to be taken by the men from Pheli.

Long ago, it seemed to her now, who had no means for measuring time, she had been searching for thipdar eggs among the lofty crags above the caverns that were the home of her people when a great hairy man leaped from behind a rock and endeavored to seize her. Active as a chamois, she eluded him with ease, but he stood between her and the village and when she sought to circle back she discovered that he had three companions who effectually barred her way, and then had commenced the flight and the pursuit that had taken her far from Zoram among lofty peaks where she had never been before.

EDGAR RICE BURROUGHS

Not far below her, four squat, hairy men had stopped to rest. "Let us turn back," growled one. "You can never catch her, Skruk, in country like this, which is fit only for thipdars and no place for men."

Skruk shook his bullet head. "I have seen her," he said, "and I shall have her if I have to chase her to the shores of Molop Az."

"Our hands are torn by the sharp rock," said another. "Our sandals are almost gone and our feet bleed. We cannot go on. We shall die."

"You may die," said Skruk, "but until then you shall go on. I am Skruk, the chief, and I have spoken."

The others growled resentfully, but when Skruk took up the pursuit again they followed him. Being from a low country they found strenuous exertion in these high altitudes exhausting, it is true, but the actual basis for their disinclination to continue the pursuit was the terror which the dizzy heights inspired in them and the perilous route along which The Red Flower of Zoram was leading them.

From above Jana saw them ascending, and knowing that they were again upon the right trail she stood erect in plain view of them. Her single, soft garment made from the pelt of tarag cubs, whipped about her naked legs, half revealing, half concealing the rounded charms of her girlish figure. The noonday sun shone down upon her light, bronzed skin, glistening from the naked contours of a perfect shoulder and imparting golden glints to her hair that was sometimes a lustrous brown and again a copper bronze. It was piled loosely upon her head and held in place by slender, hollow bones of the dimorphodon, a little long-tailed cousin of the thipdar. The upper ends of these bone pins were ornamented with carving and some of them were colored. A fillet of soft skin ornamented in colors encircled her brow and she wore bracelets and anklets made of the vertebræ of small animals, strung upon leather thongs. These, too, were carved and colored. Upon her feet were stout, little sandals, soled with the hide of the mastodon and from the center of her headband rose a single feather. At her hip was a stone knife and in her right hand a light spear.

84

She stooped and picking up a small fragment of rock hurled it down at Skruk and his companions. "Go back to your swamps, jaloks of the low country," she cried. "The Red Flower of Zoram is not for you," and then she turned and sped away across the pathless granite.

To her left lay Zoram, but there was a mighty chasm between her and the city. Along its rim she made her way, sometimes upon its very verge, but unshaken by the frightful abyss below her. Constantly she sought for a means of descent, since she knew that if she could cross it she might circle back toward Zoram, but the walls rose sheer for two thousand feet offering scarce a handhold in a hundred feet.

As she rounded the shoulder of the peak she saw a vast country stretching away below her—a country that she had never seen before—and she knew that she had crossed the mighty range and was looking on the land that lay beyond. The fissure that she had been following she could see widening below her into a great canyon that led out through foothills to a mighty plain. The slopes of the lower hills were wooded and beyond the plain were forests.

This was a new world to Jana of Zoram, but it held no lure for her; it did not beckon to her for she knew that savage beasts and savage men of the low countries roamed its plains and forests.

To her right rose the mountains she had rounded; to her left was the deep chasm, and behind her were Skruk and his three companions.

For a moment she feared that she was trapped, but after advancing a few yards she saw that the sheer wall of the abyss had given way to a tumbled mass of broken ledges. But whether there were any means of descent, even here, she did not know—she could only hope.

From pausing often to search for a way down into the gorge, Jana had lost precious time and now she became suddenly award that her pursuers were close behind her. Again she sprang forward, leaping from rock to rock, while they redoubled their speed and stumbled after her in pursuit, positive now that they were about to capture her.

Jana glanced below, and a hundred feet beneath her she

saw a tumbled mass of granite that had fallen from above and formed a wide ledge. Just ahead the mountain jutted out forming an overhanging cliff.

She glanced back. Skruk was already in sight. He was stumbling awkwardly along in a clumsy run and breathing heavily, but he was very near and she must choose quickly.

There was but one way—over the edge of the cliff lay temporary escape or certain death. A leather thong, attached a foot below the point of her spear, she fastened around her neck, letting the spear hang down her back, threw herself upon the ground and slid over the edge of the cliff. Perhaps there were handholds; perhaps not. She glanced down. The face of the cliff was rough and not perpendicular, leaning in a little toward the mountain. She felt about with her toes and finally she located a protuberance that would hold her weight. Then she relinquished her hold upon the top of the cliff with one hand and searched about for a crevice in which to insert her fingers, or a projection to which she could cling.

She must work quickly for already the footsteps of the Phelians were sounding above her. She found a hold to which she might cling with scarcely more than the tips of her fingers, but it was something and the horror of the lowland was just above her and only death below.

She relinquished her hold upon the cliff edge with her other hand and lowered herself very slowly down the face of the cliff, searching with her free foot for another support. One foot, two, three she descended, and then attracted by a noise above her she glanced up and saw the hairy face of Skruk just above her.

"Hold my legs," he shouted to his companions, at the same time throwing himself prone at the edge of the cliff, and as they obeyed his command he reached down a long, hairy arm to seize Jana, and the girl was ready to let go all holds and drop to the jagged rocks beneath when Skruk's hand should touch her. Still looking upward she saw the fist of the Pehlian but a few inches from her face.

The outstretched fingers of the man brushed the hair of the girl. One of her groping feet found a tiny ledge and she

86

lowered herself from immediate danger of capture. Skruk was furious, but that one glance into the upturned face of the girl so close beneath him only served to add to his determination to possess her. No lengths were too far now to go to achieve his heart's desire, but as he glanced down that frightful escarpment his savage heart was filled with fear for the safety of his prize. It seemed incredible that she had descended as far as she had without falling and she had only commenced the descent. He knew that he and his companions could not follow the trail that she was blazing and he realized, too, that if they menaced her from above she might be urged to a greater haste that would spell her doom.

With these thoughts in his mind Skruk arose to his feet and turned to his companions. "We shall seek an easier way down," he said in a low voice, and then leaning over the cliff edge, he called down to Jana. "You have beaten me, mountain girl," he said. "I go back now to Pheli in the lowland. But I shall return and then I shall take you with me as my mate."

"May the thipdars catch you and tear out your heart before ever you reach Pheli again," cried Jana. But Skruk made no reply and she saw that they were going back the way that they had come, but she did not know that they were merely looking for an easier way into the bottom of the gorge toward which she was descending, or that Skruk's words had been but a ruse to throw her off her guard.

The Red Flower of Zoram, relieved of immediate necessity for haste, picked her way cautiously down the face of the cliff to the first ledge of tumbled granite. Here, by good fortune, she found the egg of a thipdar, which furnished her with both food and drink.

It was a long, slow descent to the bottom of the gorge, but finally the girl accomplished it, and in the meantime Skruk and his companions had found an easier way and had descended into the gorge several miles above her.

For a moment after she reached the bottom Jana was undecided as to what course to pursue. Instinct urged her to turn upward along the gorge in the general direction of Zoram, but her judgment prompted her to descend and skirt the base of the mountain to the left in search of an easier route back across them. And so she came leisurely down toward the valley, while behind her followed the four men from Pheli.

The canyon wall at her left, while constantly lessening in height as she descended, still presented a formidable obstacle, which it seemed wiser to circumvent than to attempt to surmount, and so she continued on downward toward the mouth of the canyon, where it debauched upon a lovely valley.

Never before in all her life had Jana approached the lowland so closely. Never before had she dreamed how lovely the lowland country might be, for she had always been taught that it was a horrid place and no fit abode for the stalwart tribes of the mountains.

The lure of the beauties and the new scenes unfolding before her, coupled with a spirit of exploration which was being born within her, led her downward into the valley much farther than necessity demanded.

Suddenly her attention was attracted by a strange sound coming suddenly from on high—a strange, new note in the diapason of her savage world, and glancing upward she finally descried the creature that must be the author of it.

A great thipdar, it appeared to be, moaning dismally far above her head—but what a thipdar! Never in her life had she seen one as large as this.

As she watched she saw another thipdar, much smaller, soaring above it. Suddenly the lesser one swooped upon its intended prey. Faintly she heard sounds of shattering and tearing and then the two combatants plunged earthward. As they did so she saw something separate itself from the mass and as the two creatures, partially supported by the wings of the larger, fell in a great, gliding spiral a most remarkable thing happened to the piece that had broken loose. Something shot out of it and unfolded above it in the air— something that resembled a huge toadstool, and as it did so the swift flight of the falling body was arrested and it floated slowly earthward, swinging back and forth as she had seen a heavy stone do when tied at the end of a buckskin thong.

As the strange thing descended nearer, Jana's eyes went wide in surprise and terror as she recognized the dangling body as that of a man.

Her people had few superstitions, not having advanced sufficiently in the direction of civilization to have developed a priesthood, but here was something that could be explained according to no natural logic. She had seen two great, flying reptiles meet in battle, high in air and out of one of them had come a man. It was incredible, but more than all it was terrifying. And so The Red Flower of Zoram, reacting in the most natural way, turned and fled.

Back toward the canyon she raced, but she had gone only a short distance when, directly in front of her, she saw Skruk and his three companions.

They, too, had seen the battle in mid-air and they had seen the thing floating downward toward the ground, and while they had not recognized it for what it was they had been terrified and were themselves upon the point of fleeing when Skruk descried Jana running toward them. Instantly every other consideration was submerged in his desire to have her and growling commands to his terrified henchmen he led them toward the girl.

When Jana discovered them she turned to the right and tried to circle about them, but Skruk sent one to intercept her and when she turned in the opposite direction, the four spread out across her line of retreat so as to effectually bar her escape in that direction.

Choosing any fate rather than that which must follow her capture by Skruk, Jana turned again and fled down the valley and in pursuit leaped the four squat, hairy men of Pheli.

At the instant that Jason Gridley had pulled the rip cord of his parachute a fragment of the broken propeller of his plane had struck him a glancing blow upon the head, and when he regained consciousness he found himself lying upon a bed of soft grasses at the head of a valley, where a canyon, winding out of lofty mountains, opened onto leveller land.

Disgusted by the disastrous end of his futile search for his companions, Gridley arose and removed the parachute harness. He was relieved to discover that he had suffered no more serious injury than a slight abrasion of the skin upon one temple.

His first concern was for his ship and though he knew that it must be a total wreck he hoped against hope that he might at least salvage his rifle and ammunition from it. But even as the thought entered his mind it was forced into the background by a chorus of savage yelps and growls that caused him to turn his eyes quickly to the right. At the summit of a little rise of ground a short distance away he saw four of the ferocious wolf dogs of Pellucidar. As hyaenodons they were known to the paleontologists of the outer crust, and as jaloks to the men of the inner world. As large as full grown mastiffs they stood there upon their short, powerful legs, their broad, strong jaws parted in angry growls, their snarling lips drawn back to reveal their powerful fangs.

As he discovered them Jason became aware that their attention was not directed upon him—that they seemed not as yet to have discovered him—and as he looked in the direction that they were looking he was astounded to see a girl running swiftly toward them, and at a short distance behind the girl four men, who were apparently pursuing her.

As the vicious growls of the jaloks broke angrily upon the comparative silence of the scene, the girl paused and it was evident that she had not before been aware of the presence of this new menace. She glanced at them and then back at her pursuers.

The hyaenodons advanced toward her at an easy trot. In piteous bewilderment she glanced about her. There was but one way open for escape and then as she turned to flee in that direction her eyes fell upon Jason Gridley, straight ahead in her path of flight and again she hesitated.

To the man came an intuitive understanding of her quandary. Menaced from the rear and upon two sides by known enemies, she was suddenly faced by what might indeed by another, cutting off all hope of retreat.

Acting impulsively and in accordance with the code that dominates his kind, Gridley ran toward the girl, shouting words of encouragement and motioning her to come to him.

Shruk and his companions were closing in upon her from behind and from her right, while upon her left came the jaloks. For just an instant longer, she hesitated and then seemingly determined to place her fate in the hands of an unknown, rather than surrender it to the inevitable doom which awaited her either at the hands of the Phelians or the fangs of the jaloks, she turned and sped toward Gridley, and behind her came the four beasts and the four men.

As Gridley ran forward to mee the girl he drew one of his revolvers, a heavy .45 caliber Colt.

The hyaenodons were charging now and the leader was close behind her, and at that instant Jana tripped and fell, and simultaneously Jason reached her side, but so close was the savage beast that when Jason fired the hyaenodon's body fell across the body of the girl.

The shot, a startling sound to which none of them was accustomed, brought the other hyaenodons to a sudden stop, as well as the four men, who were racing rapidly forward under Skruk's command in an effort to save the girl from the beasts.

Quickly rolling the body of the jalok from its intended victim, Jason lifted the girl to her feet and as he did so she snatched her stone knife from its scabbard. Jason Gridley did not know how near he was to death at that instant. To Jana, every man except the men of Zoram was a natural enemy. The first law of nature prompted her to kill lest she be killed, but in the instant before she struck the blade home she saw something in the eyes of this man, something in the expression upon his face that she had never seen in the eyes or face of any man before. As plainly as though it had been spoken in words she understood that this stranger was prompted by solicitousness for her safety; that he was prompted by a desire to befriend rather than to harm her, and though in common with the jaloks and the Phelians she had been terrified by the loud noise and the smoke that had burst from the strange stick in his hand she knew that this had been the means that he had taken to protect her from the jaloks.

Her knife hand dropped to her side, and, as a slow smile lighted the face of the stranger, The Red Flower of Zoram smiled back in response.

They stood as they had when he had lifted her from the ground, his left arm about her shoulders supporting her and he maintained this unconscious gesture of protection as he turned to face the girl's enemies, who, after their first fright, seemed on the point of returning to the attack.

Two of the hyaenodons, however, had transferred their attention to Skruk and his companions, while the third was slinking bare fanged, toward Jason and Jana.

The men of Pheli stood ready to receive the charge of the hyaenodons, having taken positions in line, facing their attackers, and at sufficient intervals to permit them properly to wield their clubs. As the beasts charged two of the men hurled their weapons, each singling out one of the fierce carnivores. Skruk hurled his weapon with the greater accuracy, breaking one of the forelegs of the beast attacking him, and as it went down the Phelian standing next to Skruk leaped forward and rained heavy blows upon its skull.

The cudgel aimed at the other beast struck it a glancing blow upon the shoulder, but did not stop it and an instant later it was upon the Phelian whose only defense now was his crude stone knife. But his companion, who had reserved his club for such an emergency, leaped in and swung lustily at the savage brute, while Skruk and the other, having disposed of their adversary, came to the assistance of their fellows.

The savage battle between men and beast went unnoticed by Jason, whose whole attention was occupied by the fourth wolfdog as it moved forward to attack him and his companion.

Jana, fully aware that the attention of each of the men was fully centered upon the attacking beasts, realized that now was the opportune moment to make a break for freedom. She felt the arm of the stranger about her shoulders, but it rested there lightly—so lightly that she might easily disengage herself by a single, quick motion. But there was something in the feel of that arm about her that imparted to her a sense of greater safety than she had felt since she had left the caverns of her people—perhaps the protective instinct which dominated the man subconsciously exerted its natural reaction upon the girl to the end that instead of fleeing she was content to remain, sensing greater safety where she was than elsewhere.

And then the fourth hyaenodon charged, growling, to be met by the roaring bark of the Colt. The creature stumbled and went down, stopped by the force of the heavy charge—but only for an instant—again it was up, maddened by pain, desperate in the face of death. Bloody foam crimsoned its jowls as it leaped for Jason's throat.

Again the Colt spoke, and then the man went down beneath the heavy body of the wolf dog, and at the same instant the Phelians dispatched the second of the beasts which had attacked them.

Jason Gridley was conscious of a great weight upon him as he was borne to the ground and he sought to send those horrid jaws from his throat by interposing his left forearm, but the jaws never closed and when Gridley struggled from beneath the body of the beast and scrambled to his feet he saw the girl tugging upon the shaft of her crude, stone-tipped spear in an effort to drag it from the body of the jalok.

Whether his last bullet or the spear had dispatched the beast the man did not know, and he was only conscious of gratitude and admiration for the brave act of the slender girl, who had stood her ground at his side, facing the terrible beast without loss of poise or resourcefulness.

The four jaloks lay dead, but Jason Gridley's troubles were by no means over, for scarcely had he arisen after the killing of the second beast when the girl seized him by the arm and pointed toward something behind him.

"They are coming," she said. "They will kill you and take me. Oh, do not let them take me!"

Jason did not understand a word that she had said, but it was evident from her tone of voice and from the expression upon her beautiful face that she was more afraid of the four men approaching them than she had been of the hyaenodons, and as he turned to face them he could not wonder, for the men of Pheli looked quite as brutal as the hyaenodons and there was nothing impressive or magnificent in their appearance as there had been in the mien of the savage carnivores—a fact which is almost universally noticeable when a comparison is made between the human race and the so-called lower orders.

Gridley raised his revolver and levelled it at the leading Phelian, who happened to be another than Skruk. "Beat it!" he said. "Your faces frighten the young lady."

"I am Gluf," said the Phelian. "I kill."

"If I could understand you I might agree with you," replied Jason, "but your exuberant whiskers and your diminutive forehead suggest that you are all wet."

He did not want to kill the man, but he realized that he could not let him approach too closely. But if he had any compunction in the matter of manslaughter, it was evident that the girl did not for she was talking volubly, evidently urging him to some action, and when she realized that he could not understand her she touched his pistol with a brown forefinger and then pointed meaningly at Gluf.

The fellow was now within fifteen paces of them and Jason could see that his companions were starting to circle them. He knew that something must be done immediately and prompted by humanitarian motives he fired his Colt, aiming above the head of the approaching Phelian. The sharp report stopped all four of them, but when they realized that none of them was injured they broke into a torrent of taunts and threats, and Gluf, inspired only by a desire to capture the girl so that they might return to Pheli, resumed his advance, at the same time commencing to swing his club menacingly. Then it was that Jason Gridley regretfully shot, and shot to kill. Gluf stopped in his tracks, stiffened, whirled about and sprawled forward upon his face.

Wheeling upon the others, Gridley fired again, for he

realized that those menacing clubs were almost as effective at short range as was his Colt. Another Phelian dropped in his tracks, and then Skruk and his remaining companion turned and fled.

"Well," said Gridley, looking about him at the bodies of the four hyaenodons and the corpses of the two men, "this is a great little country, but I'll be gosh-darned if I see how anyone grows up to enjoy it."

The Red Flower of Zoram stood looking at him admiringly. Everything about this stranger aroused her interest, piqued her curiosity and stimulated her imagination. In no particular was he like any other man she had ever seen. Not one item of his strange apparel corresponded to anything that any other human being of her acquaintance wore. The remarkable weapon, which spat smoke and fire to the accompaniment of a loud roar, left her dazed with awe and admiration; but perhaps the outstanding cause for astonishment, when she gave it thought, was the fact that she was not afraid of this man. Not only was the fear of strangers inherent in her, but from earliest childhood she had been taught to expect only the worst from men who were not of her own tribe and to flee from them upon any and all occasions. Perhaps it was his smile that had disarmed her, or possibly there was something in his friendly, honest eyes that had won her immediate trust and confidence. Whatever the cause, however, the fact remained that The Red Flower of Zoram made no effort to escape from Jason Gridley, who now found himself completely lost in a strange world, which in itself was quite sad enough without having added to it responsibilities for the protection of a strange, young woman, who could understand nothing that he said to her and whom, in turn, he could not understand.

VIII

JANA AND JASON

TAR-GASH and Thoar looked with wonder upon the wreckage of the plane and Tarzan hastily searched it for the body of the pilot. The ape-man experienced at least temporary relief when he discovered that there was no body there, and a moment later he found footprints in the turf upon the opposite side of the plane—the prints of a booted foot which he recognized immediately as having been made by Jason Gridley—and this evidence assured him that the American had not been killed and apparently not even badly injured by the fall. And then he discovered something else which puzzled him exceedingly. Mingling with the footprints of Gridley and evidently made at the same time were those of a small sandaled foot.

A further brief examination revealed the fact that two persons, one of them Gridley and the other apparently a female or a youth of some Pellucidarian tribe, who had accompanied him, had approached the plane after it had crashed, remained in its vicinity for a short time and then returned in the direction from which they had come. With the spoor plain before him there was nothing for Tarzan to do other than to follow it.

The evidence so far suggested that Gridley had been forced to abandon the plane in air and that he had safely made a parachute descent, but where and under what circumstances he had picked up his companion, Tarzan could not even hazard a guess.

He found it difficult to get Thoar away from the aeroplane, the strange thing having so fired his curiosity and imagination that he must need remain near it and ask a hundred questions concerning it.

With Tar-Gash, however, the reaction was entirely different. He had glanced at it with only a faint show of curiosity or interest, and then he had asked one question, "What is it?"

".This is the thing that passed over us and which you said was a flying reptile," replied Tarzan. "I told you at that time that one of my friends was in it. Something happened and the thing fell, but my friend escaped without injury."

"It has no eyes," said Tar-gash. "How could it see to fly?"

"It was not alive," replied Tarzan.

"I heard it growl," said the Sagoth; nor was he ever convinced that the thing was not some strange form of living creature.

They had covered but a short distance along the trail made by Gridley and Jana, after they had left the aeroplane, when they came upon the carcass of a huge pteranodon. Its head was crushed and battered and almost severed from its body and a splinter of smooth wood projected from its skull—a splinter that Tarzan recognized as a fragment of an aeroplane propeller—and instantly he knew the cause of Gridley's crash.

Half a mile further on the three discovered further evidence, some of it quite startling. An opened parachute lay stretched upon the ground where it had fallen and at short distances from it lay the bodies of four hyaenodons and two hairy men.

An examination of the bodies revealed the fact that both of the men and two of the hyaenodons had died from bullet wounds. Everywhere upon the trampled turf appeared the imprints of the small sandals of Jason's companion. It was evident to the keen eyes of Tarzan that two other men, both natives, had taken part in the battle which had been waged here. That they were of the same tribe as the two that had fallen was evidenced by the imprints of their sandals, which were of identical make, while those of Tarzan's companion differed materially from all the others.

As he circled about, searching for further evidence, he saw that the two men who had escaped had run rapidly for some distance toward the mouth of a large canyon, and that, apparently following their retreat, Jason and his companion had set out in search of the plane. Later they had returned to the scene of the battle, and when they had departed they also had gone toward the mountains, but along a line considerably to the right of the trail made by the fleeing natives.

Thoar, too, was much interested in the various tracks that the participants in the battle by the parachute had left, but he said nothing until after Tarzan had completed his investigation.

"There were four men and either a woman or a youth here with my friend," said Tarzan.

"Four of them were low countrymen from Pheli," said Thoar, "and the other was a woman of Zoram."

"How do you know?" asked Tarzan, who was always anxious to add to his store of woodcraft.

"The low country sandals are never shaped to the foot as closely as are those of the mountain tribes," replied Thoar, "and the soles are much thinner, being made usually of the hides of the thag, which is tough enough for people who do not walk often upon anything but soft grasses or in soggy marshland. The sandals of the mountain tribes are soled with the thick hide of Maj, the cousin of Tandor. If you will look at the spoor you will see that they are not worn at all, while there are holes in the sandals of these dead men of Pheli."

"Are we near Zoram?" asked Tarzan.

"No," replied Thoar. "It lies across the highest range ahead of us."

"When we first met, Thoar, you told me that you were from Zoram."

"Yes, that is my country," replied Thoar.

"Then, perhaps, this woman is someone whom you know?"

"She is my sister," replied Thoar.

Tarzan of the Apes looked at him in surprise. "How do you know?" he demanded.

"I found an imprint where there was no turf, only soft earth, and there the spoor was so distinct that I could recognize the sandals as hers. So familiar with her work am I that I could recognize the stitching alone, where the sole is joined to the upper part of the sandal, and in addition there are the notches, which indicate the tribe. The people of Zoram have three notches in the underside of the sole at the toe of the left sandal."

"What was your sister doing so far from her own country and how is it that she is with my friend?"

"It is quite plain," replied Thoar. "These men of Pheli sought to capture her. One of them wanted her for his mate, but she eluded them and they pursued her across the Mountains of the Thipdars and down into this valley, where she was set upon by jaloks. The man from your country came and killed the jaloks and two of the Phelians and drove the other two away. It is evident that my sister could not escape him, and he captured her."

Tarzan of the Apes smiled. "The spoor does not indicate that she ever made any effort to escape him," he said.

Thoar scratched his head. "That is true," he replied, "and I cannot understand it, for the women of my tribe do not care to mate with the men of other tribes and I know that Jana, my sister, would rather die than mate outside the Mountains of the Thipdars. Many times has she said so and Jana is not given to idle talk."

"My friend would not take her by force," said Tarzan. "If she has gone with him, she has gone with him willingly. And I think that when we find them you will discover that he is simply accompanying her back to Zoram, for he is the sort of man who would not permit a woman to go alone and unprotected."

"We shall see," said Thoar, "but if he has taken Jana against her wishes, he must die."

As Tarzan, Tar-gash and Thoar followed the spoor of Jason and Jana a disheartened company of men rounded the end of the great Mountains of the Thipdars, fifty miles to the east of them, and entered the Gyor Cors, or great Plains of the Gyors.

The party consisted of ten black warriors and a white man, and, doubtless, never in the history of mankind had eleven men been more completely and hopelessly lost than these.

Muviro and his warriors, than whom no better trackers

ever lived, were totally bewildered by their inability even to back-track successfully.

The stampeding of the maddened beasts, from which they had barely escaped with their lives and then only by what appeared nothing short of a miracle, had so obliterated all signs of the party's former spoor that though they were all confident that they had gone but a short distance from the clearing, into which the beasts had been herded by the tarags, they had never again been able to locate the clearing, and now they were wandering hopelessly and, in accordance with Von Horst's plans, keeping as much in the open as possible in the hope that the cruising O-220 might thus discover them, for Von Horst was positive that eventually his companions would undertake a search for them.

Aboard the O-220 the grave fear that had been entertained for the safety of the thirteen missing members of the ship's company had developed into a conviction of disaster when Gridley failed to return within the limit of the time that he might reasonably be able to keep the scout plane in the air.

Then it was that Zuppner had sent Dorf out with another searching party, but at the end of seventy hours they had returned to report absolute failure. They had followed the trail to a clearing where jackals fed upon rotting carrion, but beyond this there was no sign of spoor to suggest in what direction their fellows had wandered.

Going and coming they had been beset by savage beasts and so ruthless and determined had been the attacks of the giant tarags that Dorf reported to Zuppner that he was confident that all of the missing members of the party must by this time have been destroyed by these great cats.

"Until we have proof of that, we must not give up hope," replied Zuppner, "nor may we relinquish our efforts to find them, whether dead or alive, and that we cannot do by remaining here."

There was nothing now to delay the start. While the motors were warming up, the anchor was drawn in and the air expelled from the lower vacuum tanks. As the giant ship rose from the ground Robert Jones jotted down a brief note in a greasy memorandum book: "We sailed from here at noon."

When Skruk and his companion had left the field to the victorious Jason, the latter had returned his six-gun to its holster and faced the girl. "Well," he inquired, "what now?"

She shook her head. "I cannot understand you," she said. "You do not speak the language of gilaks."

Jason scratched his head. "That being the case," he said, "and as it is evident that we are never going to get anywhere on conversation which neither one of us understands, I am going to have a look around for my ship, in the meantime, praying to all the gods that my thirty-thirty and ammunition are safe. It's a cinch that she did not burn for she must have fallen close by and I could have seen the smoke."

Jana listened attentively and shook her head.

"Come on," said Jason, and started off in the direction that he thought the ship might lie.

"No, not that way," exclaimed Jana, and running forward she seized his arm and tried to stop him, pointing back to the tall peaks of the Mountains of the Thipdars, where Zoram lay.

Jason essayed the difficult feat of explaining in a weird sign language of his own invention that he was looking for an aeroplane that had crashed somewhere in the vicinity, but the conviction soon claimed him that that would be a very difficult thing to accomplish even if the person to whom he was trying to convey the idea knew what an aeroplane was, and so he ended up by grinning good naturedly, and, seizing the girl by the hand, gently leading her in the direction he wished to go.

Again that charming smile disarmed The Red Flower of Zoram and though she knew that this stranger was leading her away from the caverns of her people, yet she followed docilely, though her brow was puckered in perplexity as she tried to understand why she was not afraid, or why she was willing to go with this stranger, who evidently was not even a gilak, since he could not speak the language of men.

A half hour's search was rewarded by the discovery of the

wreck of the plane, which had suffered far less damage than Jason had expected.

It was evident that in its plunge to earth it must have straightened out and glided to a landing. Of course, it was wrecked beyond repair, even if there had been any facilities for repairs, but it had not burned and Jason recovered his thirty-thirty and all his ammunition.

Jana was intensely interested in the plane and examined every portion of it minutely. Never in her life had she wished so much to ask questions, for never in her life had she seen anything that had so aroused her wonder. And here was the one person in all the world who could answer her questions, but she could not make him understand one of them. For a moment she almost hated him, and then he smiled at her and pressed her hand, and she forgave him and smiled back.

"And now," said Jason, "where do we go from here? As far as I am concerned one place is as good as another."

Being perfectly well aware that he was hopelessly lost, Jason Gridley felt that the only chance he had of being reunited with his companions lay in the possibility that the O-220 might chance to cruise over the very locality where he happened to be, and no matter whither he might wander, whether north or south or east or west, that chance was as slender in one direction as another, and, conversely, equally good. In an hour the O-220 would cover a distance fully as great as he could travel in several days of outer earthly time. And so even if he chanced to be moving in a direction that led away from the ship's first anchorage, he could never go so far that it might not easily and quickly overtake him, if its search should chance to lead in his direction. Therefore he turned questioningly to the girl, pointing first in one direction, and then in another, while he looked inquiringly at her, attempting thus to convey to her the idea that he was ready and willing to go in any direction she chose, and Jana, sensing his meaning, pointed toward the lofty Mountains of the Thipdars.

"There," she said, "lies Zoram, the land of my people."

"Your logic is unassailable," said Jason, "and I only wish

I could understand what you are saying, for I am sure that anyone with such beautiful teeth could never be uninteresting."

Jana did not wait to discuss the matter, but started forthwith for Zoram and beside her walked Jason Gridley of California.

Jana's active mind had been working rapidly and she had come to the conclusion that she could not for long endure the constantly increasing pressure of unsatisfied curiosity. She must find some means of communicating with this interesting stranger and to the accomplishment of this end she could conceive of no better plan than teaching the man her language. But how to commence! Never in her experience or that of her people had the necessity arisen for teaching a language. Previously she had not dreamed of the existence of such a means. If you can feature such a state, which is doubtful, you must concede to this primitive girl of the stone age a high degree of intelligence. This was no accidental blowing off of the lid of the teapot upon which might be built a theory. It required, as a matter of fact, a greater reasoning ability. Give a steam engine to a man who had never heard of steam and ask him to make it go—Jana's problem was almost as difficult. But the magnitude of the reward spurred her on, for what will one not do to have one's curiosity satisfied, especially if one happens to be a young and beautiful girl and the object of one's curiosity an exceptionally handsome young man. Skirts may change, but human nature never.

And so The Red Flower of Zoram pointed at herself with a slim, brown forefinger and said, "Jana." She repeated this several times and then she pointed at Jason, raising her eyebrows in interrogation.

"Jason," he said, for there was no misunderstanding her meaning. And so the slow, laborious task began as the two trudged upward toward the foothills of the Mountains of the Thipdars.

There lay before them a long, hard climb to the higher altitudes, but there was water in abundance in the tumbling brooks, dropping down the hillside, and Jana knew the edible plants, and nuts, and fruits which grew in riotous profusion in many a dark, deep ravine, and there was game in plenty to be brought down, when they needed meat, by Jason's thirty-thirty.

As they proceeded in their quest for Zoram, Jason found greater opportunity to study his companion and he came to the conclusion that nature had attained the pinnacle of physical perfection with the production of this little savage. Every line and curve of that lithe, brown body sang of symmetry, for The Red Flower of Zoram was a living poem of beauty. If he had thought that her teeth were beautiful he was forced to admit that they held no advantage in that respect over her eyes, her nose or any other of her features. And when she fell to with her crude stone knife and helped him skin a kill and prepare the meat for cooking, when he saw the deftness and celerity with which she made fire with the simplest and most primitive of utensils, when he witnessed the almost uncanny certitude with which she located nests of eggs and edible fruit and vegetables, he was conscious that her perfections were not alone physical and he became more than ever anxious to acquire a sufficient understanding of her tongue to be able to communicate with her, though he realized that he might doubtless suffer a rude awakening and disillusionment when, through an understanding of her language, he might be able to judge the limitations of her mind.

When Jana was tired she went beneath a tree, and, making a bed of grasses, curled up and fell asleep immediately, and, while she slept, Gridley watched, for the dangers of this primitive land were numerous and constant. Fully as often as he shot for food he shot to protect them from some terrible beast, until the encounters became as prosaic and commonplace as does the constant eluding of death by pedestrians at congested traffic corners in cities of the outer crust.

When Jason felt the need of sleep, Jana watched and sometimes they merely rested without sleeping, usually beneath a tree for there they found the greatest protection from their greatest danger, the fierce and voracious thipdars from which the mountains took their name. These hideous, flying reptiles were a constant menace, but so thoroughly had nature developed a defense against them that the girl could hear their wings at a greater distance than either of them could see the creatures.

Jason had no means for determining how far they had travelled, or how long they had been upon their way, but he was sure that considerable outer earthly time must have elapsed since he had met the girl, when they came to a seemingly insurmountable obstacle, for already he had made considerable progress toward mastering her tongue and they were exchanging short sentences, much to Jana's delight, her merry laughter often marking one of Jason's more flagrant errors in pronunciation or construction.

And now they had come to a deep chasm with overhanging walls that not even Jana could negotiate. To Jason it resembled a stupendous fault that might have been caused by the subsidence of the mountain range for it paralleled the main axis of the range. And if this were true he knew that it might extend for hundreds of miles, effectually barring the way across the mountains by the route they were following.

For a long time Jana sought a means of descent into the crevice. She did not want to turn to the left as that route might lead her eventually back to the canyon that she had descended when pursued by Skruk and his fellows and she well knew how almost unscalable were the perpendicular sides of this terrific gorge. Another thing, perhaps, which decided her against the left hand route was the possibility that in that direction they might again come in contact with the Phelians, and so she led Jason toward the right and always she searched for a way to the bottom of the rift.

Jason realized that they were consuming a great deal of time in trying to cross, but he became also aware of the fact that time meant nothing in timeless Pellucidar. It was never a factor with which to reckon for the excellent reason that it did not exist, and when he gave the matter thought he was conscious of a mild surprise that he, who had been always a slave of time, so easily and naturally embraced the irresponsible existence of Pellucidar. It was not only the fact that time itself seemed not to matter but that the absence of this greatest of all task masters singularly affected one's outlook upon every other consideration of existence. Without time there appeared to be no accountability for one's acts since it is to the future that the slaves of time have learned to look for their reward or punishment. Where there is no time, there is no future. Jason Gridley found himself affected much as Tarzan had been in that the sense of his responsibility for the welfare of his fellows seemed deadened. What had happened to them had happened and no act of his could alter it. They were not there with him and so he could not be of assistance to them, and as it was difficult to visualize the future beneath an eternal noonday sun how might one plan ahead for others or for himself?

Jason Gridley gave up the riddle with a shake of his head and found solace in contemplation of the profile of The Red Flower of Zoram.

"Why do you look at me so much?" demanded the girl; for by now they could make themselves understood to one another.

Jason Gridley flushed slightly and looked quickly away. Her question had been very abrupt and surprising and for the first time he realized that he had been looking at her a great deal. He started to answer, hesitated and stopped. Why *had* he been looking at her so much? It seemed silly to say that it was because she was beautiful.

"Why do you not say it, Jason?" she inquired.

"Say what?" he demanded.

"Say the thing that is in your eyes when you look at me," she replied.

Gridley looked at her in astonishment. No one but an imbecile could have misunderstood her meaning, and Jason Gridley was no imbecile.

Could it be possible that he had been looking at her *that* way? Had he gone stark mad that he was even subconsciously entertaining such thoughts of this little barbarian who seized her meat in both hands and tore pieces from it with her flashing, white teeth, who went almost as naked as the beasts

106

of the field and with all their unconsciousness of modesty? Could it be that his eyes had told this untutored savage that he was harboring thoughts of love for her? The artificialities of a thousand years of civilization rose up in horror against such a thought.

Upon the screen of his memory there was flashed a picture of the haughty Cynthia Furnois of Hollywood, daughter of the famous director, Abelard Furnois, né Abe Fink. He recalled Cynthia's meticulous observance of the minutest details of social usages and the studied perfection of her deportment that had sometimes awed him. He saw, too, the aristocratic features of Barbara Green, daughter of old John Green, the Los Angeles realtor, from Texas. It is true that old John was no purist and that his total disregard of the social precedence of forks often shocked the finer sensibilities that Mrs. Green and Barbara had laboriously achieved in the universities of Montmarte and Cocoanut Grove, but Barbara had had two years at Marlborough and knew her suffixes and her hardware.

Of course Cynthia was a rotten little snob, not only on the surface but to the bottom of her shallow, selfish soul, while Barbara's snobbishness, he felt, was purely artificial, the result of mistaking for the genuine the silly artificialities and affectations of the almost celebrities and sudden rich that infest the public places of Hollywood.

But nevertheless these two did, after a fashion, reflect the social environment to which he was accustomed and as he tried to answer Jana's question he could not but picture her seated at dinner with a company made up of such as these. Of course, Jana was a bully companion upon an adventure such as that in which they were engaged, but modern man cannot go adventuring forever in the Stone Age. If his eyes had carried any other message to Jana than that of friendly comradeship he felt sorry, for he realized that in fairness to her, as well as to himself, there could never be anything more than this between them.

As Jason hesitated for a reply, the eyes of The Red Flower of Zoram searched his soul and slowly the half expectant smile faded from her lips. Perhaps she was a savage little barbarian of the Stone Age, but she was no fool and she was a woman.

Slowly she drew her slender figure erect as she turned away from him and started back along the rim of the rift toward the great gorge through which she had descended from the higher peaks when Skruk and his fellows had been pursuing her.

"Jana," he exclaimed, "don't be angry. Where are you going?"

She stopped and with her haughty little chin in air turned a withering look back upon him across a perfect shoulder. "Go your way, jalok," she said, "and Jana will go hers."

IX

TO THE THIPDAR'S NEST

HEAVY CLOUDS formed about the lofty peaks of the Mountains of the Thipdars—black, angry clouds that rolled down the northern slopes, spreading far to east and west.

"The waters have come again," said Thoar. "They are falling upon Zoram. Soon they will fall here too."

It looked very dark up there above them and presently the clouds swept out across the sky, blotting out the noonday sun.

It was a new landscape upon which Tarzan looked—a sullen, bleak and forbidding landscape. It was the first time that he had seen Pellucidar in shadow and he did not like it. The effect of the change was strikingly apparent in Thoar and Tar-gash. They seemed depressed, almost fearful. Nor was it man alone that was so strangely affected by the blotting out of the eternal sunlight, for presently from the upper reaches of the mountains the lower animals came, pursuing the sunlight. That they, too, were strangely affected and filled with terror was evidenced by the fact that the carnivores and their prey trotted side by side and that none of them paid any attention to the three men.

"Why do they not attack us, Thoar?" asked Tarzan.

"They know that the water is about to fall," he replied, "and they are afraid of the falling water. They forget their hunger and their quarrels as they seek to escape the common terror."

"Is the danger so great then?" asked the ape-man.

"Not if we remain upon high ground," replied Thoar. "Sometimes the gulleys and ravines fill with water in an instant, but the only danger upon the high land is from the burning spears that are hurled from the black clouds. But if we stay in the open, even these are not dangerous for, as a rule, they are aimed at trees. Do not go beneath a tree while the clouds are hurling their spears of fire."

As the clouds shut off the sunlight, the air became suddenly cold. A raw wind swept down from above and the three men shivered in their nakedness.

"Gather wood," said Tarzan. "We shall build a fire for warmth." And so the three gathered firewood and Tarzan made fire and they sat about it, warming their naked hides; while upon either side of them the brutes passed on their way down toward the sunlight.

The rain came. It did not fall in drops, but in great enveloping blankets that seemed to beat them down and smother them. Inches deep it rolled down the mountainside, filling the depressions and the gulleys, turning the canyons into raging torrents.

The wind lashed the falling water into a blinding maelstrom that the eye could not pierce a dozen feet. Terrified animals stampeded blindly, constituting themselves the greatest menace of the storm. The lightning flashed and the thunder roared, and the beasts progressed from panic to an insanity of fear.

Above the roar of the thunder and the howling of the wind rose the piercing shrieks and screams of the monsters of another day, and in the air above flapped shrieking reptiles fighting toward the sunlight against the pounding wrath of the elements. Giant pteranodons, beaten to the ground, staggered uncertainly upon legs unaccustomed to the task, and through it all the three beast-men huddled at the spot where their fire had been, though not even an ash remained.

It seemed to Tarzan that the storm lasted a great while, but like the others he was enured to the hardships and discomforts of primitive life. Where a civilized man might have railed against fate and cursed the elements, the three beast-men sat in stoic silence, their backs hunched against the storm, for each knew that it would not last forever and each knew that there was nothing he could say or do to lessen its duration or abate its fury.

Had it not been for the example set by Tarzan and Thoar, Tar-gash would have fled toward the sunlight with the other beasts, not that he was more fearful than they, but that he was influenced more by instinct than by reason. But where they stayed, he was content to stay, and so he squatted there with them, in dumb misery, waiting for the sun to come again.

The rain lessened; the howling wind died down; the clouds passed on and the sun burst forth upon a steaming world. The three beast-men arose and shook themselves.

"I am hungry," said Tarzan.

Thoar pointed about them to where lay the bodies of lesser beasts that had been crushed in the mad stampede for safety.

Now even Thoar was compelled to eat his meat raw, for there was no dry wood wherewith to start a fire, but to Tarzan and Tar-gash this was no hardship. As Tarzan ate, the suggestion of a smile smoldered in his eyes. He was recalling a fussy old nobleman with whom he had once dined at a London club and who had almost suffered a stroke of apoplexy because his bird had been slightly underdone.

When the three had filled their bellies, they arose to continue their search for Jana and Jason, only to discover that the torrential rain had effectually erased every vestige of the spoor that they had been following.

"We cannot pick up their trail again," said Thoar, "until we reach the point where they continued on again after the waters ceased to fall. To the left is a deep canyon, whose walls are difficult to scale. In front of us is a fissure, which extends along the base of the mountains for a considerable distance in both directions. But if we go to the right we shall find a place where we can descend into it and cross it. This is the way that they should have gone. Perhaps there we shall pick up their trail again." But though they continued on and crossed the fissure and clambered upward toward the higher peaks, they found no sign that Jana or Jason had come this way.

"Perhaps they reached your country by another route," suggested Tarzan.

"Perhaps," said Thoar. "Let us continue on to Zoram. There is nothing else that we can do. There we can gather the men of my tribe and search the mountains for them."

In the ascent toward the summit Thoar sometimes followed trails that for countless ages the rough pads of the carnivores had followed, or again he led them over trackless wastes of granite, taking such perilous chances along dizzy heights that Tarzan was astonished that any of them came through alive.

Upon a bleak summit they had robbed a thipdar's nest of its eggs and the three were eating when Thoar became suddenly alert and listening. To the ears of the ape-man came faintly a sound that resembled the dismal flapping of distant wings.

"A thipdar," said Thoar, "and there is no shelter for us."

"There are three of us," said Tarzan. "What have we to fear?"

"You do not know them," said Thoar. "They are hard to kill and they are never defeated until they are killed. Their brains are very small. Sometimes when we have cut them open it has been difficult to find the brain at all, and having no brain they have no fear of anything, not even death, for they cannot know what death is; nor do they seem to be affected much by pain, it merely angers them, making them more terrible. Perhaps we can kill it, but I wish that there were a tree."

"How do you know that it will attack us?" asked Tarzan.

111

"It is coming in this direction. It cannot help but see us, and whatever living thing they see they attack."

"Have you ever been attacked by one?" asked Tarzan.

"Yes," replied Thoar; "but only when there was no tree or cave. The men of Zoram are not ashamed to admit that they fear the mighty thipdars."

"But if you have killed them in the past, why may we not kill this one?" demanded the ape-man.

"We may," replied Thoar, "but I have never chanced to have an encounter with one, except when there were a number of my tribesmen with me. The lone hunter who goes forth and never returns is our reason for fearing the thipdar. Even when there are many of us to fight them, always there are some killed and many injured."

"It comes," said Tar-gash, pointing.

"It comes," said Thoar, grasping his spear more firmly.

Down to their ears came a sound resembling the escaping of steam through a petcock.

"It has seen us," said Thoar.

Tarzan laid his spear upon the ground at his feet, plucked a handful of arrows from his quiver and fitted one to his bow. Tar-gash swung his club slowly to and fro and growled.

On came the giant reptile, the dismal flapping of its wings punctuated occasionally by a loud and angry hiss. The three men waited, poised, ready, expectant.

There were no preliminaries. The mighty pteranodon drove straight toward them. Tarzan loosed a bolt which drove true to its mark, burying its head in the breast of the pterodactyl. The hiss became a scream of anger and then in rapid succession three more arrows buried themselves in the creature's flesh.

That this was a warmer reception than it had expected was evidenced by the fact that it rose suddenly upward, skimmed above their heads as though to abandon the attack, and then, quite suddenly and with a speed incomprehensible in a creature of its tremendous size, wheeled like a sparrow hawk and dove straight at Tarzan's back.

So quickly did the creature strike that there could be no

defense. The ape-man felt sharp talons half buried in his naked flesh and simultaneously he was lifted from the ground.

Thoar raised his spear and Tar-gash swung his cudgel, but neither dared strike for fear of wounding their comrade. And so they were forced to stand there futilely inactive and watch the monster bear Tarzan of the Apes away across the tops of the Mountains of the Thipdars.

In silence they stood watching until the creature passed out of sight beyond the summit of a distant peak, the body of the ape-man still dangling in its talons. Then Tar-gash turned and looked at Thoar.

"Tarzan is dead," said the Sagoth. Thoar of Zoram nodded sadly. Without another word Tar-gash turned and started down toward the valley from which they had ascended. The only bond that had united these two hereditary enemies had parted, and Tar-gash was going his way back to the stamping grounds of his tribe.

For a moment Thoar watched him, and then, with a shrug of his shoulders, he turned his face toward Zoram.

As the pteranodon bore him off across the granite peaks, Tarzan hung limply in its clutches, realizing that if Fate held in store for him any hope of escape it could not come in midair and if he were to struggle against his adversary, or seek to battle with it, death upon the jagged rocks below would be the barren reward of success. His one hope lay in retaining consciousness and the power to fight when the creature came to the ground with him. He knew that there were birds of prey that kill their victims by dropping them from great heights, but he hoped that the pteranodons of Pellucidar had never acquired this disconcerting habit.

As he watched the panorama of mountain peaks passing below him, he realized that he was being carried a considerable distance from the spot at which he had been seized; perhaps twenty miles.

The flight at last carried them across a frightful gorge and a short distance beyond the pteranodon circled a lofty granite peak, toward the summit of which it slowly dropped, and there, below him, Tarzan of the Apes saw a nest of small thipdars, eagerly awaiting with wide distended jaws the flesh that their savage parent was bringing to them.

The nest rested upon the summit of a lofty granite spire, the entire area of the summit encompassing but a few square yards, the walls dropping perpendicularly hundreds of feet to the rough granite of the lofty peak the spire surmounted. It was, indeed, a precarious place at which to stage a battle for life. Cautiously, Tarzan of the Apes drew his keen hunting knife from its sheath. Slowly his left hand crept upward against his body and passed over his left shoulder until his fingers touched the thipdar's leg. Cautiously, his fingers encircled the scaly, bird-like ankle just above the claws.

The reptile was descending slowly toward its nest. The hideous demons below were screeching and hissing in anticipation. Tarzan's feet were almost in their jaws when he struck suddenly upward with his blade at the breast of the thipdar.

It was no random thrust. What slender chance for life the ape-man had depended upon the accuracy and the strength of that single blow. The giant pteranodon emitted a shrill scream, stiffened convulsively in mid-air and, as it collapsed, relaxed its hold upon its prey, dropping the ape-man into the nest among the gaping jaws of its frightful brood.

Fortunately for Tarzan there were but three of them and they were still very young, though their teeth were sharp and their jaws strong.

Striking quickly to right and left with his blade he scrambled from the nest with only a few minor cuts and scratches upon his legs.

Lying partially over the edge of the spire was the body of the dead thipdar. Tarzan gave it a final shove and watched it as it fell three hundred feet to the rocks below. Then he turned his attention to a survey of his surroundings, but almost hopelessly since the view that he had obtained of the spire while the thipdar was circling it assured him that there was little or no likelihood that he could find any means of descent.

The young thipdars were screaming and hissing, but they had made no move to leave their nest as Tarzan started a close investigation of the granite spire upon the lofty summit of which it seemed likely that he would terminate his adventurous career.

Lying flat upon his belly he looked over the edge, and thus moving slowly around the periphery of the lofty aerie he examined the walls of the spire with minute attention to every detail.

Again and again he crept around the edge until he had catalogued within his memory every projection and crevice and possible handhold that he could see from above.

Several times he returned to one point and then he removed the coils of his grass rope from about his shoulders and holding the two ends in one hand, lowered the loop over the edge of the spire. Carefully he noted the distance that it descended from the summit and what a pitiful span it seemed—that paltry twenty-five feet against the three hundred that marked the distance from base to apex.

Releasing one end of the rope, he let that fall to its full length, and when he saw where the lower end touched the granite wall he was satisfied that he could descend at least that far, and below that another twenty-five feet. But it was difficult to measure distances below that point and from there on he must leave everything to chance.

Drawing the rope up again he looped the center of it about a projecting bit of granite, permitting the ends to fall over the edge of the cliff. Then he seized both strands of the rope tightly in one hand and lowered himself over the edge. Twenty feet below was a projection that gave him precarious foothold and a little crevice into which he could insert the fingers of his left hand. Almost directly before his face was the top of a buttress-like projection and below him he knew that there were many more similar to it. It was upon these that he had based his slender hope of success.

Gingerly he pulled upon one strand of the rope with his right hand. So slender was his footing upon the rocky escarpment that he did not dare draw the rope more than a few inches at a time lest the motion throw him off his balance. Little by little he drew it in until the upper end passed around the projection over which the rope had been looped at the summit and fell upon him. And as it descended he held his breath for fear that even this slight weight might topple him to the jagged rocks below.

And now came the slow process of drawing the rop unaided through one hand, fingering it slowly an inch at a time until the center was in his grasp. This he looped over the top of the projection in front of him, seating it as securely as he could, and then he grasped both strands once more in his right hand and was ready to descend another twenty-five feet.

This stage of the descent was the most appalling of all, since the rope was barely seated upon a shelving protuberance from which he was aware it might slip at any instant. And so it was with a sense of unspeakable relief that he again found foothold near the end of the frail strands that were supporting him.

At this point the surface of the spire became much rougher. It was broken by fissures and horizontal cracks that had not been visible from above, with the result that compared with the first fifty feet the descent from here to the base was a miracle of ease, and it was not long before Tarzan stood again squarely upon his two feet and level ground. And now for the first time he had an opportunity to take stock of his injuries.

His legs were scratched and cut by the teeth and talons of the young thipdars, but these wounds were as nothing to those left by the talons of the adult reptile upon his back and shoulders. He could feel the deep wounds, but he could not see them; nor the clotted blood that had dried upon his brown skin.

The wounds pained and his muscles were stiff and sore, but his only fear lay in the possibility of blood poisoning and that did not greatly worry the ape-man, who had been repeatedly torn and mauled by carnivores since childhood.

A brief survey of his position showed him that it would be practically impossible for him to recross the stupendous gorge that yawned between him and the point at which he had been so ruthlessly torn from his companions. And with that discovery came the realization that there was little or no likelihood that the people toward which Tar-gash had been attempting to guide him could be the members of the O-220 expedition. Therefore it seemed useless to attempt the seemingly impossible feat of finding Thoar and Tar-gash again among this maze of stupendous peaks, gorges and ravines. And so he determined merely to seek a way out of the mountains and back to the forests and plains that held a greater allure for him than did the rough and craggy contours of inhospitable hills. And to the accomplishment of this end he decided to follow the line of least resistance, seeking always the easiest avenues of descent.

Below him, in various directions, he could see the timber line and toward this he hastened to make his way.

As he descended the way became easier, though on several occasions he was again compelled to resort to his rope to lower himself from one level to another. Then the steep crags gave place to leveler land upon the shoulders of the mighty range and here, where earth could find lodgment, vegetation commenced. Grasses and shrubs, at first, then stunted trees and finally what was almost a forest, and here he came upon a trail.

It was a trail that offered infinite variety. For a while it wound through a forest and then climbed to a ledge of rock that projected from the face of a cliff and overhung a stupendous canyon.

He could not see the trail far ahead for it was continually rounding the shoulders of jutting crags.

As he moved along it, sure-footed, silent, alert, Tarzan of the Apes became aware that somewhere ahead of him other feet were treading probably the same trail.

What wind there was was eddying up from the canyon below and carrying the scent spoor of the creature ahead of him as well as his own up toward the mountain top, so that it was unlikely that either might apprehend the presence of the other by scent; but there was something in the sound of the footsteps that even at a distance assured Tarzan that they were not made by man, and it was evident too that

117

they were going in the same direction as he for they were not growing rapidly more distinct, but very gradually as though he was slowly overhauling the author of them.

The trail was narrow and only occasionally, where it crossed some ravine or shallow gulley, was there a place where one might either descend or ascend from it.

To meet a savage beast upon it, therefore, might prove, to say the least, embarrassing but Tarzan had elected to go this way and he was not in the habit of turning back whatever obstacles in the form of man or beast might bar his way. And, too, he had the advantage over the creature ahead of him whatever it might be, since he was coming upon it from behind and was quite sure that it had no knowledge of his presence, for Tarzan well knew that no creature could move with greater silence than he, when he elected to do so, and now he passed along that trail as noiselessly as the shadow of a shadow.

Curiosity caused him to increase his speed that he might learn the nature of the thing ahead, and as he did so and the sound of its footsteps increased in volume, he knew that he was stalking some heavy, four-footed beast with padded feet—that much he could tell, but beyond that he had no idea of the identity of the creature; nor did the winding trail at any time reveal it to his view. Thus the silent stalker pursued his way until he knew that he was but a short distance behind his quarry when there suddenly broke upon his ears the horrid snarling and growling of an enraged beast just ahead of him.

There was something in the tone of that awful voice that increased the ape-man's curiosity. He guessed from the volume of the sound that it must come from the throat of a tremendous beast, for the very hills seemed to shake to the thunder of its roars.

Guessing that it was attacking or was about to attack some other creature, and spurred, perhaps, entirely by curiosity, Tarzan hastened forward at a brisk trot, and as he rounded the shoulder of a buttressed crag his eyes took in a scene that galvanized him into instant action.

A hundred feet ahead the trail ended at the mouth of a

great cave, and in the entrance to the cave stood a boy—
a lithe, handsome youth of ten or twelve—while between
the boy and Tarzan a huge cave bear was advancing angrily
upon the former.

The boy saw Tarzan and at the first glance his eyes
lighted with hope, but an instant later, evidently recognizing
that the newcomer was not of his own tribe, the expression
of hopelessness that had been there before returned to his
face, but he stood his ground bravely, his spear and his
crude stone knife ready.

The scene before the ape-man told its own story. The bear,
returning to its cave, had unexpectedly discovered the youth
emerging from it, while the latter, doubtless equally surprised, found himself cornerd with no avenue of escape open
to him.

By the primitive jungle laws that had guided his youth,
Tarzan of the Apes was under no responsibility to assume
the dangerous rôle of savior, but there had always burned
within his breast the flame of chivalry, bequeathed him by
his English parents, that more often than not found him
jeopardizing his own life in the interests of others. This child
of a nameless tribe in an unknown world might hold no
claim upon the sympathy of a savage beast, or even of savage
men who were not of his tribe. And perhaps Tarzan of the
Apes would not have admitted that the youth had any claim
upon him, yet in reality he exercised a vast power over the
ape-man—a power that lay solely in the fact that he was a
child and that he was helpless.

One may analyze the deeds of a man of action and speculate upon them, whereas the man himself does not appear
to do so at all—he merely acts; and thus it was with Tarzan
of the Apes. He saw an emergency confronting him and
he was ready to meet it, for since the moment that he had
known that there was a beast upon the trail ahead of him
he had had his weapons in readiness, years of experience with
primitive men and savage beasts having taught him the value
of preparedness.

His grass rope was looped in the hollow of his left arm
and in the fingers of his left hand were grasped his spear,

his bow and three extra arrows, while a fourth arrow was ready in his right hand.

One glance at the beast ahead of him had convinced him that only by a combination of skill and rare luck could he hope to destroy this titanic monster with the relatively puny weapons with which he was armed, but he might at least divert its attention from the lad and by harassing it draw it away until the boy could find some means of escape. And so it was that within the very instant that his eyes took in the picture his bow twanged and a heavy arrow sank deeply into the back of the bear close to its spine, and at the same time Tarzan voiced a savage cry intended to apprise the beast of an enemy in its rear.

Maddened by the pain and surprised by the voice behind it, the creature evidently associated the two, instantly whirling about on the narrow ledge.

Tarzan's first impression was that in all his life he had never gazed upon such a picture of savage bestial rage as was depicted upon the snarling countenance of the mighty cave bear as its fiery eyes fell upon the author of its hurt.

In quick succession three arrows sank into its chest as it charged, howling, down upon the ape-man.

For an instant longer Tarzan held his ground. Poising his heavy spear he carried his spear hand far back behind his right shoulder, and then with all the force of those giant muscles, backed by the weight of his great body, he launched the weapon.

At the instant that it left his hand the bear was almost upon him and he did not wait to note the effect of his throw, but turned and leaped swiftly down the trail; while close behind him the savage growling and the ponderous footfalls of the carnivore proved the wisdom of his strategy.

He was sure that upon this narrow, rocky ledge, if no obstacle interposed itself, he could outdistance the bear, for only Ara, the lightning, is swifter than Tarzan of the Apes.

There was the possibility that he might meet the bear's mate coming up to their den, and in that event his position would be highly critical, but that, of course, was only a remote possibility and in the meantime he was sure that he had inflicted sufficiently severe wounds upon the great beast to sap its strength and eventually to prove its total undoing. That it possessed an immense reserve of vitality was evidenced by the strength and savagery of its pursuit. The creature seemed tireless and although Tarzan was equally so he found fleeing from an antagonist peculiarly irksome and to a considerable degree obnoxious to his self esteem. And so he cast about him for some means of terminating the flight and to that end he watched particularly the cliff walls rising above the trail down which he sped, and at last he saw that for which he had hoped—a jutting granite projection protruding from the cliff about twenty-five feet above the trail.

His coiled rope was ready in his left hand, the noose in his right, and as he came within throwing distance of the projection, he unerringly tossed the latter about it. The bear tore down the trail behind him. The ape-man pulled heavily once upon the end of the rope to assure himself that it was safely caught above, and then with the agility of Manu, the monkey, he clambered upward.

X

ONLY A MAN MAY GO

IT REQUIRED no Sherlockian instinct to deduce that Jana was angry, and Jason was not so dense as to be unaware of the cause of her displeasure, which he attributed to natural feminine vexation induced by the knowledge that she had been mistaken in assuming that her charms had effected the conquest of his heart. He judged Jana by his own imagined knowledge of feminine psychology. He knew that she was beautiful and he knew that she knew it, too. She had told him of the many men of Zoram who had wanted to take her as their mate, and he had saved her from one suitor, who had pursued her across the terrible Mountains of the Thipdars, putting his life constantly in jeopardy to win her. He felt that it was only natural, therefore, that Jana should place a high valuation upon her charms and believe that any man might fall a victim to their spell, but he saw no reason why she should be angry because she had not succeeded in enthralling him. They had been very happy together. He could not recall when ever before he had been for so long a time in the company of any girl, or so enjoyed the companionship of one of her sex. He was sorry that anything had occurred to mar the even tenor of their friendship and he quickly decided that the manly thing to do was to ignore her tantrum and go on with her as he had before, until she came to her senses. Nor was there anything else that he might do for he certainly could not permit Jana to continue her journey to Zoram without protection. Of course it was not very nice of her to have called him a jalok, which he knew to be a Pellucidarian epithet of high insult, but he would overlook that for the present and eventually she would relent and ask his forgiveness.

And so he followed her, but he had taken scarcely a dozen steps when she wheeled upon him like a young tiger, whipping her stone knife from its sheath. "I told you to go your way," she cried. "I do not want to see you again. If you follow me I shall kill you."

"I cannot let you go on alone, Jana," he said quietly.

"The Red Flower of Zoram wants no protection from such as you," she replied haughtily.

"We have been such good friends, Jana," he pleaded. "Let us go on together as we have in the past. I cannot help it if—" He hesitated and stopped.

"I do not care that you do not love me," she said. "I hate you. I hate you because your eyes lie. Sometimes lips lie and we are not hurt because we have learned to expect that from lips, but when eyes lie then the heart lies and the whole man is false. I cannot trust you. I do not want your friendship. I want nothing more of you. Go away."

"You do not understand, Jana," he insisted.

"I understand that if you try to follow me I will kill you," she said.

"Then you will have to kill me," he replied, "for I shall follow you. I cannot let you go on alone, no matter whether you hate me or not," and as he ceased speaking he advanced toward her.

Jana stood facing him, her little feet firmly planted, her crude stone dagger grasped in her right hand, her eyes flashing angrily.

His hands at his sides, Jason Gridley walked slowly up to her as though offering his breast as a target for her weapon. The stone blade flashed upward. It poised a moment above her shoulder and then The Red Flower of Zoram turned and fled along the rim of the rift.

She ran very swiftly and was soon far ahead of Jason, who was weighted down by clothes, heavy weapons and ammunition. He called after her once or twice, begging her to stop, but she did not heed him and he continued doggedly along her trail, making the best time that he could. He felt hurt and angry, but after all the emotion which dominated him was one of regret that their sweet friendship had been thus wantonly blasted.

Slowly the realization was borne in upon him that he had been very happy with Jana and that she had occupied his thoughts almost to the exclusion of every other consideration of the past or future. Even the memory of his lost comrades had been relegated to the hazy oblivion of temporary forgetfulness in the presence of the responsibility which he had assumed for the safe conduct of the girl to her home land.

"Why, she has made a regular monkey out of me," he mused. "Odysseus never met a more potent Circe. Nor one half so lovely," he added, as he regretfully recalled the charms of the little barbarian.

And what a barbarian she had proven herself—whipping out her stone knife and threatening to kill him. But he could not help but smile when he realized how in the final extremity she had proven herself so wholly feminine. With a sigh he shook his head and plodded on after The Red Flower of Zoram.

Occasionally Jason caught a glimpse of Jana as she crossed a ridge ahead of him and though she did not seem to be travelling as fast as at first, yet he could not gain upon her. His mind was constantly harassed by the fear that she might be attacked by some savage beast and destroyed before he could come to her rescue with his rifle. He knew that sooner or later she would have to stop and rest and then he was hopeful of overtaking her, when he might persuade her to forget her anger and resume their former friendly comradeship.

But it seemed that The Red Flower of Zoram had no intention of resting, though the American had long since reached a state of fatigue that momentarily threatened to force him to relinquish the pursuit until outraged nature could recuperate. Yet he plodded on doggedly across the rough ground, while the weight of his arms and ammunition seemed to increase until his rifle assumed the ponderous proportions of a field gun. Determined not to give up, he staggered down one hill and struggled up the next, his legs seeming to move mechanically as though they were some detached engine of torture over which he had no control and which were bearing him relentlessly onward, while every fiber of his being cried out for rest.

Added to the physical torture of fatigue, were hunger and thirst, and knowing that only thus might time be measured, he was confident that he had covered a great distance since they had last rested and then he topped the summit of a low rise and saw Jana directly ahead of him.

She was standing on the edge of the rift where it opened into a mighty gorge that descended from the mountains and it was evident that she was undecided what course to pursue. The course which she wished to pursue was blocked by the rift and gorge. To her left the way led back down into the valley in a direction opposite to that in which lay Zoram, while to retrace her steps would entail another encounter with Jason.

She was looking over the edge of the precipice, evidently searching for some avenue of descent when she became aware of Jason's approach.

She wheeled upon him angrily. "Go back," she cried, "or I shall jump."

"Please, Jana," he pleaded, "let me go with you. I shall not annoy you. I shall not even speak to you unless you wish it, but let me go with you to protect you from the beasts."

The girl laughed. "You protect me!" she exclaimed, her tone caustic with sarcasm. "You do not even know the dangers which beset the way. Without your strange spear, which spits fire and death, you would be helpless before the attack of even one of the lesser beasts, and in the high Mountains of the Thipdars there are beasts so large and so terrible that they would devour you and your fire spear in a single gulp. Go back to your own people, man of another world; go back to the soft women of which you have told me. Only a man may go where The Red Flower of Zoram goes."

"You half convince me," said Jason with a rueful smile, "that I am only a caterpillar, but nevertheless even a caterpillar must have guts of some sort and so I am going to follow you, Red Flower of Zoram, until some goggle-eyed monstrosity of the Jurassic snatches me from this vale of tears."

"I do not know what you are talking about," snapped Jana; "but if you follow me you will be killed. Remember what I told you—only a man may go where goes The Red Flower of Zoram," and as though to prove her assertion she turned and slid quickly over the edge of the precipice, disappearing from his view.

Running quickly forward to the edge of the chasm, Jason Gridley looked down and there, a few yards below him, clinging to the perpendicular face of the cliff, Jana was working her way slowly downward. Jason held his breath. It seemed incredible that any creature could find hand or foothold upon that dizzy escarpment. He shuddered and cold sweat broke out upon him as he watched the girl.

Foot by foot she worked her way downward, while the man, lying upon his belly, his head projecting over the edge of the cliff, watched her in silence. He dared not speak to her for fear of distracting her attention and when, after what seemed an eternity, she reached the bottom, he fell to trembling like a leaf and for the first time realized the extent of the nervous strain he had been undergoing.

"God!" he murmured. "What a magnificent display of nerve and courage and skill!"

The Red Flower of Zoram did not look back or upward once as she resumed her way, following the gorge upward, searching for some point where she might clamber out of it above the rift.

Jason Gridley looked down into the terrible abyss.

" 'Only a man may go where goes The Red Flower of Zoram,' " he mused.

He watched the girl until she disappeared behind a mass of fallen rock, where the gorge curved to the right, and he knew that unless he could descend into the gorge she had passed out of his life forever.

"Only a man may go where goes The Red Flower of Zoram!"

Jason Gridley arose to his feet. He readjusted the leather sling upon his rifle so that he could carry the weapon hanging down the center of his back. He slipped the holsters of both of his six-guns to the rear so that they, too, were entirely behind him. He removed his boots and dropped them over the edge of the cliff. Then he lay upon his belly and lowered his body slowly downward, and from a short distance up the gorge two eyes watched him from behind a pile of tumbled granite. There was anger in them at first, then skepticism, then surprise, and then terror.

As gropingly the man sought for some tiny foothold and then lowered himself slowly a few inches at a time, the eyes of the girl, wide in horror, never left him for an instant.

"Only a man may go where goes The Red Flower of Zoram!"

Cautiously, Jason Gridley groped for each handhold and foothold—each precarious support from which it seemed that even his breathing might dislodge him. Hunger, thirst and fatigue were forgotten as he marshalled every faculty to do the bidding of his iron nerve.

Hugging close to the face of the cliff he did not dare turn his head sufficiently to look downward and though it seemed he had clung there, lowering himself inch by inch, for an eternity, yet he had no idea how much further he had to descend. And so impossible of accomplishment did the task that he had set himself appear that never for an instant did he dare to hope for a successful conclusion. Never for an instant did any new hold impart to him a feeling of security, but each one seemed, if possible, more precarious than its predecessor, and then he reached a point where, grope as he would, he could find no foothold. He could not move to right or left; nor could he ascend. Apparently he had reached the end of his resources, but still he did not give up. Replacing his torn and bleeding feet upon the last, slight hold that they had found, he cautiously sought for new handholds lower down, and when he had found them—mere protuberances of rough granite—he let his feet slip slowly from their support as gradually he lowered his body to its full length, supported only by his fingers, where they clutched at the tiny projections that were his sole support.

As he clung there, desperately searching about with his feet for some slight projection, he reproached himself for not having discarded his heavy weapons and ammunition. And why? Because his life was in jeopardy and he feared to die? No, his only thought was that because of them he would be unable to cling much longer to the cliff and that when his hands slipped from their holds and he was dashed into eternity, his last, slender hope of ever again seeing The Red Flower of Zoram would be gone. It is remarkable, perhaps, that as he clung thus literally upon the brink of eternity, no visions of Cynthia Furnois or Barbara Green impinged themselves upon his consciousness.

He felt his fingers weakening and slipping from their hold. The end came suddenly. The weight of his body dragged one hand loose and instantly the other slipped from the tiny knob it had been clutching, and Jason Gridley dropped downward, perhaps eighteen inches, to the bottom of the cliff.

As he came to a stop, his feet on solid rock, Jason could not readily conceive the good fortune that had befallen him. Almost afraid to look, he glanced downward and then the truth dawned upon him—he had made the descent in

127

safety. His knees sagged beneath him and as he sank to the ground, a girl, watching him from up the gorge, burst into tears.

A short distance below him a spring bubbled from the canyon side, forming a little brooklet which leaped downward in the sunlight toward the bottom of the canyon and the valley, and after he had regained his composure he found his boots and hobbled down to the water. Here he satisfied his thirst and washed his feet, cleansing the cuts as best he could, bandaged them crudely with strips torn from his handkerchief, pulled his boots on once more and started up the canyon after Jana.

Far above, near the summit of the stupendous range, he saw ominous clouds gathering. They were the first clouds that he had seen in Pellucidar, but only for this reason did they seem remarkable or important. That they presaged rain, he could well imagine; but how could he dream of the catastrophic proportions of their menace.

Far ahead of him The Red Flower of Zoram was clambering upward along a precarious trail that gave promise of leading eventually over the rim of the gorge to the upper reaches that she wished to gain. When she had seen Jason's life in imminent jeopardy, she had been filled with terror and remorse, but when he had safely completed the descent her mood changed, and with the perversity of her sex she still sought to elude him. She had almost gained the summit of the escarpment when the storm broke and with it came a realization that the man behind her was ignorant of the danger which now more surely menaced him than had the descent of the cliff.

Without an instant's hesitation The Red Flower of Zoram turned and fled swiftly down the steep trail she had just so laboriously ascended. She must reach him before the waters reached him. She must guide him to some high place upon the canyon's wall, for she knew that the bottom of this great gorge would soon be a foaming, boiling torrent, spreading from side to side, its waters, perhaps, two hundred feet in depth. Already the water was running deep in the canyon far below her and spilling over the rim above her, racing downward in torrents and cataracts and waterfalls that carried earth and stone with them. Never in her life had Jana witnessed a storm so terrible. The thunder roared and the lightning flashed; the wind howled and the water fell in blinding sheets, and yet constantly menaced by instant death the girl groped her way blindly downward upon her hopeless errand of mercy. How hopeless it was she was soon to see, for the waters in the gorge had risen, she saw them just below her now, nor was the end in sight. Nothing down there could have survived. The man must long since have been washed away.

Jason was dead! The Red Flower of Zoram stood for an instant looking at the rising waters below her. There came to her an urge to throw herself into them. She did not want to live, but something stayed her; perhaps it was the instinct of primeval man, whose whole existence was a battle against death, who knew no other state and might not conceive voluntary surrender to the enemy, and so she turned and fought her way upward as the waters rising below her climbed to overtake her and the waters from above sought to hurl her backward to destruction.

Jason Gridley had witnessed cloudbursts in California and Arizona and he knew how quickly gulleys and ravines may be transformed into raging torrents. He had seen a river a mile wide formed in a few hours in the San Simon Flats, and when he saw the sudden rush of waters in the bottom of the gorge below him and realized that no storm that he had ever previously witnessed could compare in magnitude with this, he lost no time in seeking higher ground; but the sides of the canyon were steep and his upward progress discouragingly slow, as he saw the waters rising rapidly behind him. Yet there was hope, for just ahead and above him he saw a gentle acclivity rising toward the summit of the canyon rim.

As he struggled toward safety the boiling torrent rose and lapped his feet, while from above the torrential rain thundered down upon him, beating him backward so that often for a full minute at a time he could make no headway.

The raging waters that were filling the gorge reached

129

his knees and for an instant he was swept from his footing. Clutching at the ground above him with his hands, he lost his rifle, but as it slid into the turgid waters he clambered swiftly upward and regained momentary safety.

Onward and upward he fought until at last he reached a spot above which he was confident the flood could not reach and there he crouched in the partial shelter of an over-hanging granite ledge as Tarzan and Thoar and Tar-gash were crouching in another part of the mountains, waiting in dumb misery for the storm to spend its wrath.

He wondered if Jana had escaped the flood and so much confidence did he have in her masterful ability to cope with the vagaries of savage Pellucidarian life that he harbored few fears for her upon the score of the storm.

In the cold and the dark and the wet he tried to plan for the future. What chance had he to find The Red Flower of Zoram in this savage chaos of stupendous peaks when he did not even know the direction in which her country lay and where there were no roads or trails and where even the few tracks that she might have left must have been wholly obliterated by the torrents of water that had covered the whole surface of the ground?"

To stumble blindly on, then, seemed the only course left open to him, since he knew neither the direction of Zoram, other than in a most general way, nor had any idea as to the whereabouts of his fellow members of the O-220 expedition.

At last the rain ceased; the sun burst forth upon a steaming world and beneath the benign influence of its warm rays Jason felt the cold ashes of hope rekindled within his breast. Revivified, he took up the search that but now had seemed so hopeless.

Trying to bear in mind the general direction in which Jana had told him Zoram lay, he set his face toward what appeared to be a low saddle between two lofty peaks, which appeared to surmount the summit of the range. Thirst no longer afflicted him and the pangs of hunger had become deadened. Nor did it seem at all likely that he might soon find food since the storm seemed to have driven all animal life from the higher hills, but fortune smiled upon him. In a water worn rocky hollow he found a nest of eggs that had withstood the onslaught of the elements. The nature of the creature that had laid them he did not know; nor whether they were the eggs of fowl or reptile did he care. They were fresh and they were food and so large were they that the contents of two of them satisfied his hunger.

A short distance from the spot where he had found them grew a low stunted tree, and having eaten he carried the three remaining eggs to this meager protection from the prying eyes of soaring reptiles and birds of prey. Here he removed his clothing, hanging it upon the branches of the tree where the sunlight might dry it, and then he lay down beneath the tree to sleep, and in the warmth of Pellucidar's eternal noon he found no discomfort.

How long a time he slept he had no means of estimating, but when he awoke he was completely rested and refreshed. He was imbued with a new sense of self-confidence as he arose, stretching luxuriously, to don his clothes. His stretch half completed, he froze with consternation—his clothes were gone! He looked hastily about for them or for some sign of the creature that had purloined them, but never again did he see the one, nor ever the other.

Upon the ground beneath the tree lay a shirt that, having fallen, evidently escaped the eye of the marauder. That, his revolvers and belts of ammunition, which had lain close to him while he slept, were all that remained to him.

The temperature of Pellucidar is such that clothing is rather a burden than a necessity, but so accustomed is civilized man to the strange apparel with which he has encumbered himself for generations that, bereft of it, his efficiency, self-reliance and resourcefulness are reduced to a plane approximating the vanishing point.

Never in his life had Jason Gridley felt so helpless and futile as he did this instant as he contemplated the necessity which stared him in the face of going forth into this world clothed only in a torn shirt and an ammunition belt. Yet he realized that with the exception of his boots he had lost nothing that was essential either to his comfort or his efficiency, but perhaps he was appalled most by the realization of the effect that this misfortune would have upon the pursuit of the main object of his quest—how could he prosecute the search for The Red Flower of Zoram thus scantily appareled?

Of course The Red Flower had not been overburdened with wearing apparel; yet in her case this seemed no reflection upon her modesty, but the anticipation of finding her was now dampened by a realization of the ridiculousness of the figure he would cut, and already the mere contemplation of such a meeting caused a flush to overspread him.

In his dreams he had sometimes imagined himself walking abroad in some ridiculous state of undress, but now that such a dream had become an actuality he appreciated that in the figment of the subconscious mind he had never fully realized such complete embarrassment and loss of self-confidence as the actuality entailed.

Ruefully he tore his shirt into strips and devised a G-string; then he buckled his ammunition belt around him and stepped forth into the world, an Adam armed with two Colts.

As he proceeded upon his search for Zoram he found that the greatest hardship which the loss of his clothing entailed was the pain and discomfort attendant upon travelling barefoot on soles already lacerated by his descent of the rough granite cliff. This discomfort, however, he eventually partially overcame when with the return of the game to the mountains he was able to shoot a small reptile, from the hide of which he fashioned two crude sandals.

The sun, beating down upon his naked body, had no such effect upon his skin as would the sun of the outer world under like conditions, but it did impart to him a golden bronze color, which gave him a new confidence similar to that which he would have felt had he been able to retrieve his lost apparel, and in this fact he saw what he believed to be the real cause of his first embarrassment at his nakedness—it had been the whiteness of his skin that had made him seem so naked by contrast with other creatures, for this whiteness had suggested softness and weakness, arousing within him a disturbing sensation of inferiority; but now as he took on his heavy coat of tan and his feet became hardened and accustomed to the new conditions, he walked no longer in constant realization of his nakedness.

He slept and ate many times and was conscious, therefore, that considerable outer earthly time had passed since he had been separated from Jana. As yet he had seen no sign of her or any other human being, though he was often menaced by savage beasts and reptiles, but experience had taught him how best to elude these without recourse to his weapons, which he was determined to use only in extreme emergencies for he could not but anticipate with misgivings the time, which must sometime come, when the last of his ammunition would have been exhausted.

He had crossed the summit of the range and found a fairer country beyond. It was still wild and tumbled and rocky, but the vegetation grew more luxuriantly and in many places the mountain slopes were clothed in forests that reached far upward toward the higher peaks. There were more streams and a greater abundance of smaller game, which afforded him relief from any anxiety upon the score of food.

For the purpose of economizing his precious ammunition he had fashioned other weapons; the influence of his association with Jana being reflected in his spear, while to Tarzan of the Apes and the Waziri he owed his crude bow and arrows. Before he had mastered the intricacies of either of his new weapons he might have died of starvation had it not been for his Colts; but eventually he achieved a sufficient degree of adeptness to insure him a full larder at all times.

Jason Gridley had long since given up all hope of finding his ship or his companions and had accepted with what philosophy he could command the future lot from which there seemed no escape in which he visioned a lifetime spent in Pellucidar, battling with his primitive weapons for survival amongst the savage creatures of the inner world.

Most of all he missed human companionship and he looked forward to the day that he might find a tribe of men with which he could cast his lot. Although he was quite aware from the information that he had gleaned from Jana that it might be extremely difficult, if not impossible, for him to win either the confidence or the friendship of any Pellucidarian tribe whose attitude towards strangers was one of habitual enmity; yet he did not abandon hope and his eyes were always on the alert for a sign of man; nor was he now to have long to wait.

He had lost all sense of direction in so far as the location of Zoram was concerned and was wandering aimlessly from camp to camp in the idle hope that some day he would stumble upon Zoram, when a breeze coming from below brought to his nostrils the acrid scent of smoke. Instantly his whole being was surcharged with excitement, for smoke meant fire and fire meant man.

Moving cautiously down the mountain in the direction from which the wind was blowing, his eager, searching eyes were presently rewarded by sight of a thin wisp of smoke arising from a canyon just ahead. It was a rocky canyon with precipitous walls, those upon the opposite side from him being lofty, while that which he was approaching was much lower and in many places so broken down by erosion or other natural causes as to give ready ingress to the canyon bottom below.

Creeping stealthily to the rim Jason Gridley peered downward into the canyon. Along the center of its grassy floor tumbled a mountain torrent. Giant trees grew at intervals, lending a park-like appearance to the scene; a similarity which was further accentuated by the gorgeous blooms which starred the sward or blossomed in the trees themselves.

Beside a small fire at the edge of a brook squatted a bronzed warrior, his attention centered upon a fowl which he was roasting above the fire. Jason, watching the warrior, deliberated upon the best method of approaching him, that he might convince him of his friendly intentions and overcome the natural suspicion of strangers that he knew to be inherent in these savage tribesmen. He had decided that the best plan would be to walk boldly down to the stranger, his hands empty of weapons, and he was upon the point of putting his plan into action when his attention was attracted to the summit of the cliff upon the opposite side of the narrow canyon.

There had been no sound that had been appreciable to his ears and the top of the opposite cliff had not been within the field of his vision while he had been watching the man in the bottom of the canyon. So what had attracted his attention he did not know, unless it had been the delicate powers of perception inherent in that mysterious attribute of the mind which we are sometimes pleased to call a sixth sense.

But be that as it may, his eyes moved directly to a spot upon the summit of the opposite cliff where stood such a creature as no living man upon the outer crust had ever looked upon before—a giant armored dinosaur it was, a huge reptile that appeared to be between sixty and seventy feet in length, standing at the rump, which was its highest point, fully twenty-five feet above the ground. Its relatively small, pointed head resembled that of a lizard. Along its spine were thin, horny plates arranged alternately, the largest of which were almost three feet high and equally as long, but with a thickness of little more than an inch. The stout tail, which terminated in a long, horny spine, was equipped with two other such spines upon the upper side and toward the tip. Each of these spines was about three feet in length. The creature walked upon four lizard-like feet, its short, front legs bringing its nose close to the ground, imparting to it an awkward and ungainly appearance.

It appeared to be watching the man in the canyon, and suddenly, to Jason's amazement, it gathered its gigantic hind legs beneath it and launched itself straight from the top of the lofty cliff.

Jason's first thought was that the gigantic creature would be dashed to pieces upon the ground in the canyon bottom, but to his vast astonishment he saw that it was not falling but was gliding swiftly through the air, supported by its huge spinal plates, which it had dropped to a horizontal position, transforming itself into a gigantic animate glider.

The swish of its passage through the air attracted the attention of the warrior squatting over his fire. The man leaped to his feet, snatching up his spear as he did so, and

135

simultaneously Jason Gridley sprang over the edge of the cliff and leaped down the rough declivity toward the lone warrior, at the same time whipping both his six-guns from their holsters.

XI

THE CAVERN OF CLOVI

As Tarzan swarmed up the rope the bear, almost upon his heels and running swiftly, squatted upon its haunches to overcome its momentum and came to a stop directly beneath him. And then it was that there occurred one of those unforeseen accidents which no one might have guarded against.

It chanced that the granite projection across which Tarzan had cast his noose was at a single point of knife-like sharpness upon its upper edge, and with the weight of the man dragging down upon it the rope parted where it rested upon this sharp bit of granite, and the Lord of the Jungle was precipitated upon the back of the cave bear.

With such rapidity had these events transpired it is a matter of question as to whether the bear or Tarzan was the more surprised, but primitive creatures who would survive cannot permit surprise to disconcert them. In this instance both of the creatures accepted the happening as though it had been planned and expected.

The bear reared up and shook itself in an effort to dislodge the man-thing from its back, while Tarzan slipped a bronzed arm around the shaggy neck and clung desperately to his hold while he dragged his hunting knife from its sheath. It was a precarious place in which to stage a struggle for life. On one side the cliff rose far above them, and upon the other it dropped away dizzily into the depth of a gloomy gorge, and here the efforts of the cave bear to dislodge its antagonist momentarily bade fair to plunge them both into eternity.

The growls and roars of the quadruped reverberated among the mighty peaks of the Mountains of the Thipdars, but the ape-man battled silently, driving his blade repeatedly into the back of the lunging beast, which was seeking by every means at its command to dislodge him, though ever wary against precipitating itself over the brink into the chasm.

But the battle could not go on forever and at last the blade found the spinal cord. The creature stiffened spasmodically and Tarzan slipped quickly from its back. He found safe footing upon the ledge as the mighty carcass stumbled forward and rolled over the edge to hurtle downward to the gorge's bottom, carrying with it four of Tarzan's arrows and his spear.

The ape-man found his rope lying upon the ledge where it had fallen, and gathering it up he started back along the trail in search of the bow that he had been forced to discard in his flight, as well as to find the boy.

He had taken only a few steps when, upon rounding the shoulder of a crag, he came face to face with the youth. At sight of him the latter stopped, his spear ready, his stone knife loosened in its sheath. He had been carrying Tarzan's bow, but at sight of the ape-man he dropped it at his feet, the better to defend himself in the event that he was attacked by the stranger.

"I am Tarzan of the Apes," said the Lord of the Jungle. "I come as a friend, and not to kill."

"I am Ovan," said the boy. "If you did not come to our country to kill, then you came to steal a mate, and thus it is the duty of every warrior of Clovi to kill you."

"Tarzan seeks no mate," said the ape-man.

"Then why is he in Clovi?" demanded the youth.

"He is lost," replied the ape-man. "Tarzan comes from another world that is beyond Pellucidar. He has become separated from his friends and he cannot find his way back to them. He would be friend with the people of Clovi."

137

"Why did you attack the bear?" demanded Ovan, suddenly.

"If I had not attacked it it would have killed you," replied the ape-man.

Ovan scratched his head. "It seemed to me," he said presently, "that there could be no other reason. It is what one of the men of my own tribe would have done, but you are not of my tribe. You are an enemy and so I could not understand why you did it. Do you tell me that though I am not of your tribe you would have saved my life?"

"Certainly," replied Tarzan.

Ovan looked long and steadily at the handsome giant standing before him. "I believe you," he said presently, "although I do not understand. I never heard of such a thing before, but I do not know that the men of my tribe will believe. Even after I have told them what you have done for me they may still wish to kill you, for they believe that it is never safe to trust an enemy."

"Where is your village?" asked Tarzan.

"It is not at a great distance," replied Ovan.

"I will go there with you," said Tarzan, "and talk with your chief."

"Very well," said the boy. "You may talk with Avan the chief. He is my father. And if they decide to kill you I shall try to help you, for you saved my life when the ryth would have destroyed me."

"Why were you in the cave?" demanded Tarzan. "It was plainly apparent that it was the den of a wild beast."

"You, too, were upon the same trail," said the boy, "while you chanced to be behind the ryth. It was my misfortune that I was in front of it."

"I did not know where the trail led," said the ape-man.

"Neither did I," said Ovan. "I have never hunted before except in the company of older men, but now I have reached an age when I would be a warrior myself, and so I have come out of the caves of my people to make my first kill alone, for only thus may a man hope to become a warrior. I saw this trail and, though I did not know where it led, I followed it; nor had I been long upon it when I heard the footsteps of the ryth behind me and when I came to the cave and saw that the trail ended there, I knew that I should never again see the caves of my people, that I should never become a warrior. When the great ryth came and saw me standing there he was very angry, but I should have fought him. Perhaps I might have killed him, though I do not believe that that is at all likely.

"And then you came and with this bent stick cast a little spear into the back of the ryth, which so enraged him that he forgot me and turned to pursue you as you knew that he would. They must indeed be brave warriors who come from the land from·which you come. Tell me about your country. Where is it? Are your warriors great hunters and is your chief powerful in the land?"

Tarzan tried to explain that his country was not in Pellucidar, but that was beyond Ovan's powers of conception, and so Tarzan turned the conversation from himself to the youth and as they followed a winding trail toward Clovi, Ovan discoursed upon the bravery of the men of his tribe and the beauty of its women.

"Avan, my father, is a great chief," he said, "and the men of my tribe are mighty warriors. Often we battle with the men of Zoram and we have even gone as far as Daroz, which lies beyond Zoram, for always there are more men than women in our tribe and the warriors must seek their mates in Zoram and Daroz. Even now Carb has gone to Zoram with twenty warriors to steal women. The women of Zoram are very beautiful. When I am a little larger I shall go to Zoram and steal a mate."

"How far is it from Clovi to Zoram?" asked Tarzan.

"Some say that it is not so far, and others that it is farther," replied Ovan. "I have heard it said that going to Zoram is much farther than returning inasmuch as the warriors usually eat six times on the journey from Clovi to Zoram, but returning a strong man may make the journey eating only twice and still retain his strength."

"But why should the distance be shorter returning than going?" demanded the ape-man.

"Because when they are returning they are usually pursued by the warriors of Zoram," replied Ovan.

Inwardly Tarzan smiled at the naïveté of Ovan's reasoning, while it again impressed upon him the impossibility of measuring distances or computing time under the anomalous condition obtaining in Pellucidar.

As the two made their way toward Clovi, the boy gradually abandoned his suspicious attitude toward Tarzan and presently seemed to accept him quite as he would have a member of his own tribe. He noticed the wound made by the talons of the thipdar on Tarzan's back and shoulders and when he had wormed the story from his companion he marvelled at the courage, resourcefulness and strength that had won escape for this stranger from what a Pellucidarian would have considered an utterly hopeless situation.

Ovan saw that the wounds were inflamed and realized that they must be causing Tarzan considerable pain and discomfort, and so when first their way led near a brook he insisted upon cleansing them thoroughly, and collecting the leaves of a particular shrub he crushed them and applied the juices to the open wounds.

The pain of the inflammation had been as nothing compared to the acute agony caused by the application thus made by Ovan and yet the boy noticed that not even by the tremor of a single muscle did the stranger evidence the agony that Ovan well knew he was enduring, and once again his admiration for his new-found companion was increased.

"It may hurt," he said, "but it will keep the wounds from rotting and afterward they will heal quickly."

For a short time after they resumed their march the pain continued to be excruciating, but it lessened gradually until it finally disappeared, and thereafter the ape-man felt no discomfort.

The way led to a forest where there were straight, tough, young saplings, and here Tarzan tarried long enough to fashion a new spear and to split and scrape half a dozen additional arrows.

Ovan was much interested in Tarzan's steel-bladed knife

and in his bow and arrows, although secretly he looked with contempt upon the latter, which he referred to as little spears for young children. But when they became hungry and Tarzan bowled over a mountain sheep with a single shaft, the lad's contempt was changed to admiration and thereafter he not only evinced great respect for the bow and arrows, but begged to be taught how to make and to use them.

The little Clovian was a lad after the heart of the ape-man and the two became fast friends as they made their way toward the land of Clovi, for Ovan possessed the quiet dignity of the wild beast; nor was he given to that garrulity which is at once the pride and the curse of civilized man—there were no boy orators in the peaceful Pliocene.

"We are almost there," announced Ovan, halting at the brink of a canyon. "Below lie the caves of the Clovi. I hope that Avan, the chief, will receive you as a friend, but that I cannot promise. Perhaps it might be better for you to go your way and not come to the caves of the Clovi. I do not want you to be killed."

"They will not kill me," said Tarzan. "I come as a friend." But in his heart he knew that the chances were that these primitive savages might never accept a stranger among them upon an equal or a friendly footing.

"Come, then," said Ovan, as he started the descent into the canyon. Part way down the trail turned up along the canyon side in the direction of the head of the gorge. It was a level trail here, well kept and much used, with indications that no little engineering skill had entered into its construction. It was by no means the haphazard trail of beasts, but rather the work of intelligent, even though savage and primitive men.

They had proceeded no great distance along the trail when Ovan sounded a low whistle, which, a moment later, was answered from around the bend in the trail ahead, and when the two had passed this turn Tarzan saw before him a wide, natural ledge of rock entirely overhung by beetling cliffs and in the depth of the recess thus formed in the cliffside he saw the dark mouth of a cavern.

Upon the flat surface of the ledge, which comprised some

two acres, were congregated fully a hundred men, women and children.

All eyes were turned in their direction as they came into view and on sight of Tarzan the warriors sprang to their feet, seizing spears and knives. The women called their children to them and moved quickly toward the entrance to the cavern.

"Do not fear," cried the boy. "It is only Ovan and his friend, Tarzan."

"We kill," growled some of the warriors.

"Where is Avan the chief?" demanded the boy.

"Here is Avan the chief," announced a deep gruff voice, and Tarzan shifted his gaze to the figure of a stalwart, brawny savage emerging from the mouth of the cavern.

"What have you there, Ovan?" demanded the chief. "If you have brought a prisoner of war, you should have disarmed him first."

"He is no prisoner," replied Ovan. "He is a stranger in Pellucidar and he comes as a friend and not as an enemy."

"He is a stranger," replied Avan, "and you should have killed him. He has learned the way to the caverns of Clovi and if we do not kill him he will return to his people and lead them against us."

"He has no people and he does not know how to return to his own country," said the boy.

"Then he does not speak true words, for that is not possible," said Avan. "There can be no man who does not know the way to his own country. Come! Stand aside, Ovan, while I destroy him."

The lad drew himself stiffly erect in front of Tarzan. "Who would kill the friend of Ovan," he said, "must first kill Ovan."

A tall warrior, standing near the chief, laid his hand upon Avan's arm. "Ovan has always been a good boy," he said. "There is none in Clovi near his age whose words are as full of wisdom as his. If he says that this stranger is his friend and if he does not wish us to kill him, he must have a reason and we should listen to him before we decide to destroy the stranger."

"Very well," said the chief; "perhaps you are right, Ulan.

We shall see. Speak, boy, and tell us why we should not kill the stranger."

"Because at the risk of his life he saved mine. Hand to hand he fought with a great ryth from which I could not have escaped had it not been for him; nor did he offer to harm me, and what enemy of the Clovi is there, even among the people of Zoram or Daroz who are of our own blood, that would not slay a Clovi youth who was so soon to become a warrior? Not only is he very brave, but he is a great hunter. It would be well for the tribe of Clovi if he came to live with us as a friend."

Avan bowed his head in thought. "When Carb returns we shall call a council and decide what to do," he said. "In the meantime the stranger must remain here as a prisoner."

"I shall not remain as a prisoner," said Tarzan. "I came as a friend and I shall remain as a friend, or I shall not remain at all."

"Let him stay as a friend," said Ulan. "He has marched with Ovan and has not harmed him. Why should we think that he will harm us when we are many and he only one?"

"Perhaps he has come to steal a woman," suggested Avan.

"No," said Ovan, "that is not so. Let him remain and with my life I will guarantee that he will harm no one."

"Let him stay," said some of the other warriors, for Ovan had long been the pet of the tribe so that they were accustomed to humoring him and so unspoiled was he that they still found pleasure in doing so.

"Very well," said Avan. "Let him remain. But Ovan and Ulan shall be responsible for his conduct."

There were only a few of the Clovians who accepted Tarzan without suspicion, and among these was Maral, the mother of Ovan, and Rela, his sister. These two accepted him without question because Ovan had accepted him. Ulan's friendship, too, had been apparent from the first; nor was it without great value for Ulan, because of his intelligence, courage and ability was a force in the councils of the Clovi.

Tarzan, accustomed to the tribal life of primitive people, took his place naturally among them, paying no attention to those who paid no attention to him, observing scrupulously

the ethics of tribal life and conforming to the customs of
the Clovi in every detail of his relations with them. He liked
to talk with Maral because of her sunny disposition and her
marked intelligence. She told him that she was from Zoram,
having been captured by Avan when, as a young warrior, he
had decided to take a mate. And to her nativity he attributed
her great beauty, for it seemed to be an accepted fact
among the Clovis that the women of Zoram were the most
beautiful of all women.

Ulan he had liked from the first, being naturally attracted
to him because he had been the first of the Clovians to
champion his cause. In many ways Ulan differed from his
fellows. He seemed to have been the first among his people
to discover that a brain may be used for purposes other
than securing the bare necessities of existence. He had
learned to dream and to exercise his brain along pleasant
paths that gave entertainment to himself and others—fantas-
tic stories that sometimes amused and sometimes awed his
eager audiences; and, too, he was a maker of pictures and
these he exhibited to Tarzan with no small measure of pride.
Leading the ape-man into the rocky cavern that was the shelter, the storehouse and the citadel of the tribe, he lighted a
crude torch which illuminated the walls, revealing the pictures that Ulan had drawn there. Mammoth and saber-tooth
and cave bear were depicted, with the red deer, the hyaenodon and other familiar beasts, and in addition thereto
were some with which Tarzan was unfamiliar and one that
he had never seen elsewhere than in Pal-ul-don, where it had
been known as a gryf. Ulan told him that it was a gyor and
that it was found upon the Gyor Cors, or Gyor Plains,
which lie at the end of the range of the Mountains of the
Thipdars beyond Clovi.

The drawings were in outline and were well executed.
The other members of the tribe thought they were very
wonderful for Ulan was the first ever to have made them
and they could not understand how he did it. Perhaps if he
had been a weakling he would have lost caste among them
because of this gift, but inasmuch as he was also a noted

hunter and warrior his talents but added to his fame and the esteem in which he was held by all.

But though these and a few others were friendly toward him, the majority of the tribe looked upon Tarzan with suspicion, for never within the memory of one of them had a strange warrior entered their village other than as an enemy. They were waiting for the return of Carb and the warriors who had accompanied him, when, the majority of them hoped, the council would sentence the stranger to death.

As they became better acquainted with Tarzan, however, others among them were being constantly won to his cause and this was particularly true when he accompanied them upon their hunts, his skill and his prowess winning their admiration, and his strange weapons which they had at first viewed with contempt, soon commanding their unqualified respect.

And so it was that the longer that Carb remained away the better Tarzan's chances became of being accepted into the tribe upon an equal footing with its other members; a contingency for which he hoped since it would afford him a base from which to prosecute his search for his fellows and allies familiar with the country, whose friendly services he could enlist to aid him in his search.

He was confident that Jason Gridley, if he still lived, was lost somewhere among these stupdendous mountains and if he could but find him they might eventually, with the assistance of the Clovians, locate the camp of the O-220.

He had eaten and slept with the Clovi many times and had accompanied them upon several hunts. It had been noon when he arrived and it was still noon, so whether a day or a month had passed he did not know. He was squatting by the cook-fire of Maral, talking with her and with Ulan, when from down the gorge there sounded the whistled signal of the Clovians announcing the approach of a friendly party and an instant later a youth rounded the shoulder of the cliff and entered the village.

"It is Tomar," announced Maral. "Perhaps he brings news of Carb."

The youth ran to the center of the ledge upon which the

145

village stood and halted. For a moment he stood there dramatically with upraised hand, commanding silence, and then he spoke. "Carb is returning," he cried. "The victorious warriors of Clovi are returning with the most beautiful woman of Zoram. Great is Carb! Great are the warriors of Clovi!"

Cook fires and the routine occupations of the moment were abandoned as the tribe advanced to await the coming of the victorious war party.

Presently it came into sight, rounding the shoulder of the cliff and filing on to the ledge—twenty warriors led by Carb and among them a girl, her wrists bound behind her back, a rawhide leash around her neck, the free end held by a brawny warrior.

The ape-man's greatest interest lay in Carb, for his position in the tribe, perhaps even his life itself might rest with the decision of this man, whose influence, he had learned, was great in the councils of his people.

Carb was evidently a man of great physical strength; his regular features imparted to him much of the physical beauty that is an attribute of his people, but an otherwise handsome countenance was marred by thin, cruel lips and cold, unsympathetic eyes.

From contemplation of Carb the ape-man's eyes wandered to the face of the prisoner, and there they were arrested by the startling beauty of the girl. Well, indeed, thought Tarzan, might she be acclaimed the most beautiful woman of Zoram, for it was doubtful that there existed many in this world or the outer who might lay claim to greater pulchritude than she.

Avan, the chief, standing in the center of the ledge, received the returning warriors. He looked with favor upon the prize and listened attentively while Carb narrated the more important details of the expedition.

"We shall hold the council at once," announced Avan, "to decide who shall possess the prisoner, and at the same time we may settle another matter that has been awaiting the return of Carb and his warriors."

"What is that?" demanded Carb.

Avan pointed at Tarzan. "There is a stranger who would come into the tribe and be as one of us."

Carb turned his cold eyes in the direction of the ape-man and his face clouded. "Why has he not been destroyed?" he asked. "Let us do away with him at once."

"That is not for you to decide," said Avan, the chief. "The warriors in council alone may say what shall be done."

Carb shrugged. "If the council does not destroy him, I shall kill him myself," he said. "I, Carb, will have no enemy living in the village where I live."

"Let us hold the council at once, then," said Ulan, "for if Carb is greater than the council of the warriors we should know it." There was a note of sarcasm in his voice.

"We have marched for a long time without food or sleep." said Carb. "Let us eat and rest before the council is held, for matters may arise in the council which will demand all of our strength," and he looked pointedly at Ulan.

The other warriors, who had accompanied Carb, also wished to eat and rest before the council was held, and Avan, the chief, acceded to their just demands.

The girl captive had not spoken since she had arrived in the village and she was now turned over to Maral, who was instructed to feed her and permit her to sleep. The bonds were removed from her wrists and she was brought to the cook-fire of the chief's mate, where she stood with an expression of haughty disdain upon her beautiful face.

None of the women revealed any inclination to abuse the prisoner—an attitude which rather surprised Tarzan until the reason for it had been explained to him, for he had upon more than one occasion witnessed the cruelties inflicted upon female prisoners by the women of native African tribes into whose hands the poor creatures had fallen.

Maral, in particular, was kind to the girl. "Why should I be otherwise?" she asked when Tarzan commented upon the fact. "Our daughters, or even anyone of us, may at any time be captured by the warriors of another tribe, and if it were known that we had been cruel to their women, they would doubtless repay us in kind; nor, aside from this, is there any reason why we should be other than kind to a woman who will live among us for the rest of her life. We are few in numbers and we are constantly together. If we harbored enmities and if we quarreled our lives would be less happy. Since you have been here you have never seen quarreling among the women of Clovi; nor would you if you remained here for the rest of your life. There have been quarrelsome women among us, just as at some time there have been crippled children, but as we destroy the one for the good of the tribe we destroy the others."

She turned to the girl. "Sit down," she said pleasantly. "There is meat in the pot. Eat, and then you may sleep. Do not be afraid; you are among friends. I, too, am from Zoram."

At that the girl turned her eyes upon the speaker. "You are from Zoram?" she asked. "Then you must have felt as I feel. I want to go back to Zoram. I would rather die than live elsewhere."

"You will get over that," said Maral. "I felt the same way, but when I became acquainted I found that the people of Clovi are much like the people of Zoram. They have been kind to me; they will be kind to you, and you will be happy as I have been. When they have given you a mate you will look upon life very differently."

"I shall not mate with one of them," cried the girl, stamping her sandaled foot. "I am Jana, The Red Flower of Zoram, and I choose my own mate."

Maral shook her head sadly. "Thus spoke I once," she said; "but I have changed, and so will you."

"Not I," said the girl. "I have seen but one man with whom I would mate and I shall never mate with another."

"You are Jana," asked Tarzan, "the sister of Thoar?"

The girl looked at him in surprise, and as though she had noticed him now for the first time her eyes quickly investigated him. "Ah," she said, "you are the stranger whom Carb would destroy."

"Yes," replied the ape-man.

"What do you know of Thoar, my brother?"

"We hunted together. We were travelling back to Zoram when I became separated from him. We were following the tracks made by you and a man who was with you when a storm came and obliterated them. Your companion was the man whom I was seeking."

"What do you know of the man who was with me?" demanded the girl.

"He is my friend," replied Tarzan. "What has become of him?"

"He was caught in a canyon during the storm and he must have been drowned," replied Jana sadly. "You are from his country?"

"Yes."

"How did you know he was with me?" she demanded.

"I recognized his tracks and Thoar recognized yours."

"He was a great warrior," she said, "and a very brave man."

"Are you sure that he is dead?" asked Tarzan.

"I am sure," replied The Red Flower of Zoram.

For a time they were silent, both occupied with thoughts of Jason Gridley. "You were his friend," said Jana. She had moved close to him and had seated herself at his side. Now she leaned still closer. "They are going to kill you," she whispered. "I know the people of these tribes better than you and I know Carb. He will have his way. You were Jason's friend and so was I. If we can escape I can lead the way back to Zoram, and if you are Thoar's friend and mine the people of Zoram will have to accept you."

"Why do you whisper?" asked a gruff voice behind them, and turning they saw Avan, the chief. Without waiting for a reply, he turned to Maral. "Take the woman to the cavern," he said. "She will remain there until the council has decided who shall have her as mate, and in the meantime I will place warriors at the entrance to the cavern to see that she does not escape."

As Maral motioned Jana toward the cavern, the latter arose, and as she did so she cast an appealing glance at Tarzan. The ape-man, who was already upon his feet, looked quickly about him. Perhaps a hundred members of the tribe were scattered about the ledge, while near the opening to the trail which led down the canyon and which afforded the only avenue of escape, fully a dozen warriors loitered. Alone he might have won his way through, but with the girl it would have been impossible. He shook his head and his lips, which were turned away from Avan, formed the word, "Wait," and a moment later The Red Flower of Zoram had entered the dark cavern of the Clovians.

"And as for you, man of another country," said Avan, addressing Tarzan, "until the council has decided upon your fate, you are a prisoner. Go, therefore, into the cavern and remain there until the council of warriors has spoken."

A dozen warriors barred his way to freedom now, but they were lolling idly, expecting no emergency. A bold dash for freedom might carry him beyond them before they could realize that he was attempting escape. He was confident that the voice of the council would be adverse to him and when its decision was announced he would be surrounded by all the warriors of Clovi, alert and ready to prevent his escape. Now, therefore, was the most propitious moment; but Tarzan of the Apes made no break for liberty; instead he turned and strode toward the entrance to the cavern, for The Red Flower of Zoram had appealed to him for aid and he would not desert the sister of Thoar and the friend of Jason.

XII

THE PHELIAN SWAMP

As Jason Gridley leaped down the canyon side toward the lone warrior who stood facing the attack of the tremendous reptile gliding swiftly through the air from the top of the opposite cliff side, there flashed upon the screen of his recollection the picture of a restoration of a similar extinct reptile and he recognized the creature as a stegosaurus of the Jurassic; but how inadequately had the picture that he had seen carried to his mind the colossal proportions of the creature, or but remotely suggested its terrifying aspect.

Jason saw the lone warrior standing there facing inevitable

doom, but in his attitude there was no outward sign of fear. In his right hand he held his puny spear, and in his left his crude stone knife. He would die, but he would give a good account of himself. There was no panic of terror, no futile flight.

The distance between Jason and the stegosaurus was over great for a revolver shot, but the American hoped that he might at least divert the attention of the reptile from its prey and even, perhaps, frighten it away by the unaccustomed sound of the report of the weapon, and so he fired twice in rapid succession as he leaped downward toward the bottom of the canyon. That at least one of the shots struck the reptile was evidenced by the fact that it veered from its course, simultaneously emitting a loud, screaming sound.

Attracted to Jason by the report of the revolver and evidently attributing its hurt to this new enemy, the reptile, using its tail as a rudder and tilting its spine plates up on one side, veered in the direction of the American.

As the two shots shattered the silence of the canyon, the warrior turned his eyes in the direction of the man leaping down the declivity toward him, and then he saw the reptile veer in the direction of the newcomer.

Heredity and training, coupled with experience, had taught this primitive savage that every man's hand was against him, unless that man was a member of his own tribe. Only upon a single occasion in his life had experience controverted these teachings, and so it seemed inconceivable that this stranger, whom he immediately recognized as such, was deliberately risking his life in an effort to succor him; yet there seemed no other explanation, and so the perplexed warrior, instead of seeking to escape now that the attention of the reptile was diverted from him, ran swiftly toward Jason to join forces with him in combatting the attack of the creature.

From the instant that the stegosaurus had leaped from the summit of the cliff, it had hurtled through the air with a speed which seemed entirely out of proportion to its tremendous bulk, so that all that had transpired in the meantime had occupied but a few moments of time, and Jason Gridley found himself facing this onrushing death almost before he had had time to speculate upon the possible re-sults of his venturesome interference.

With wide distended jaws and uttering piercing shrieks, the terrifying creature shot toward him, but now at last it pre-sented an easy target and Jason Gridley was entirely com-petent to take advantage of the altered situation.

He fired rapidly with both weapons, trying to reach the tiny brain, at the location of which he could only guess and for which his bullets were searching through the roof of the opened mouth. His greatest hope, however, was that the beast could not for long face that terrific fusillade of shots, and in this he was right. The strange and terrifying sound and the pain and shock of the bullets tearing into its skull proved too much for the stegosaurus. Scarcely half a dozen feet from Gridley it swerved upward and passed over his head, receiving two or three bullets in its belly as it did so.

Still shrieking with rage and pain it glided to the ground beyond him.

Almost immediately it turned to renew the attack. This time it came upon its four feet, and Jason saw that it was likely to prove fully as formidable upon the ground as it had been in the air, for considering its tremendous bulk it moved with great agility and speed.

As he stood facing the returning creature, the warrior reached his side.

"Get on that side of him," said the warrior, "and I will attack him on this. Keep out of the way of his tail. Use your spear; you cannot frighten a dyrodor away by making a noise."

Jason Gridley leaped quickly to one side to obey the sug-gestions of the warrior, smiling inwardly at the naive sug-gestion of the other that his Colt had been used solely to frighten the creature.

The warrior took his place upon the opposite side of the approaching reptile, but before he had time to cast his spear or Jason to fire again the creature stumbled forward, its nose dug into the ground and it rolled over upon its side dead.

"It is dead!" said the warrior in a surprised tone. "What could have killed it? Neither one of us has cast a spear."

Jason slipped his Colts into their holsters. "These killed it," he said, tapping them.

"Noises do not kill," said the warrior skeptically. "It is not the bark of the jalok or the growl of the ryth that rends the flesh of man. The hiss of the thipdar kills no one."

"It was not the noise that killed it," said Jason, "but if you will examine its head and especially the roof of its mouth you will see what happened when my weapons spoke."

Following Jason's suggestion the warrior examined the head and mouth of the dyrodor and when he had seen the gaping wounds he looked at Jason with a new respect. "Who are you," he asked, "and what are you doing in the land of Zoram?"

"My God!" exclaimed Jason. "Am I in Zoram?"

"You are."

"And you are one of the men of Zoram?" demanded the American.

"I am; but who are you?"

"Tell me, do you know Jana, The Red Flower of Zoram?" insisted Jason.

"What do you know of The Red Flower of Zoram, stranger?" demanded the other. And then suddenly his eyes widened to a new thought. "Tell me," he cried, "by what name do they call you in the country from which you come?"

"My name is Gridley," replied the American; "Jason Gridley."

"Jason!" exclaimed the other; "yes, Jason Gridley, that is it. Tell me, man, where is The Red Flower of Zoram? What did you with her?"

"That is what I am asking you," said Jason. "We became separated and I have been searching for her. But what do you know of me?"

"I followed you for a long time," replied the other, "but the waters fell and obliterated your tracks."

"Why did you follow me?" asked Jason.

"I followed because you were with The Red Flower of Zoram," replied the other. "I followed to kill you, but he said you would not harm her; he said that she went with you willingly. Is that true?"

"She came with me willingly for a while," replied Jason, "and then she left me; but I did not harm her."

"Perhaps he was right then," said the warrior. "I shall wait until I find her and if you have not harmed her, I shall not kill you."

"Whom do you mean by 'he'?" asked Jason. "There is no one in Pellucidar who could possibly know anything about me, except Jana."

"Do you not know Tarzan?" asked the warrior.

"Tarzan!" exclaimed Jason. "You have seen Tarzan? He is alive?"

"I saw him. We hunted together and we followed you and Jana, but he is not alive now; he is dead."

"Dead! You are sure that he is dead?"

"Yes, he is dead."

"How did it happen?"

"We were crossing the summit of the mountains when he was seized by a thipdar and carried away."

Tarzan dead! He had feared as much and yet now that he had proof it seemed unbelievable. His mind could scarcely grasp the significance of the words that he had heard as he recalled the strength and vitality of that man of steel. It seemed incredible that that giant frame should cease to pulsate with life; that those mighty muscles no longer rolled beneath the sleek, bronzed hide; that that courageous heart no longer beat.

"You were very fond of him?" asked the warrior, noticing the silence and dejection of the other.

"Yes," said Jason.

"So was I," said the warrior; "but neither Tar-gash nor I could save him, the thipdar struck so swiftly and was gone before we could cast a weapon."

"Who is Tar-gash?" asked Jason.

"A Sagoth—one of the hairy men," replied the warrior. "They live in the forest and are often used as warriors by the Mahars."

"And he was with you and Tarzan?" inquired Jason.

"Yes. They were together when I first saw them, but now Tarzan is dead and Tar-gash has gone back to his own country and I must proceed upon my search for The Red Flower of Zoram. You have saved my life, man from another country, but I do not know that you have not harmed Jana. Perhaps you have slain her. How am I to know? I do not know what I should do."

"I, too, am looking for Jana," said Jason. "Let us look for her together."

"Then if we find her, she shall tell me whether or not I shall kill you," said the warrior.

Jason could not but recall how angry Jana had been with him. She had almost killed him herself. Perhaps she would find it easier to permit this warrior to kill him. Doubtless the man was her sweetheart and if he knew the truth he would need no urging to destroy a rival, but neither by look nor word did he reveal any apprehension as he replied.

"I will go with you," he said, "and if I have harmed The Red Flower of Zoram you may kill me. What is your name?"

"Thoar," replied the warrior.

Jana had spoken of her brother to Jason, but if she had ever mentioned his name, the American had forgotten it, and so he continued to think that Thoar was the sweetheart and possibly the mate of The Red Flower and his reaction to this belief was unpleasant; yet why it should have been he could not have explained. The more he thought of the matter the more certain he was that Thoar was Jana's mate, for who was there who might more naturally desire to kill one who had wronged her. Yes, he was sure that the man was Jana's mate. The thought made him angry for she had certainly led him to believe that she was not mated. That was just like a woman, he meditated; they were all flirts; they would make a fool of a man merely to pass an idle hour, but she had not made a fool of him. He had not fallen victim to her lures, that is why she had been so angry—her vanity had been piqued—and being a very primitive young person the first thought that had come to her mind had been to kill him. What a little devil she was to try to get him to make love to her when she already had a mate, and thus Jason almost succeeded in working himself into a rage until his sense of humor came to his rescue; yet even though he smiled, way down deep within him something hurt and he wondered why.

"Where did you last see Jana?" asked Thoar. "We can return there and try and locate her tracks."

"I do not know that I can explain," replied Jason. "It is very difficult for me to locate myself or anything else where there are no points of compass."

"We can start together at the point where we found your tracks with Jana's," said Thoar.

"Perhaps that will not be necessary if you are familiar with the country on the other side of the range," said Jason. "Returning toward the mountains from the spot where I first saw Jana, there was a tremendous gorge upon our left. It was toward this gorge that the two men of the four that had been pursuing her ran after I had killed two of their number. Jana tried to find a way to the summit, far to the right of this gorge, but our path was blocked by a deep rift which paralleled the base of the mountains, so that she was compelled to turn back again toward the gorge, into which she descended. The last I saw of her she was going up the gorge, so that if you know where this gorge lies it will not be necessary for us to go all the way back to the point at which I first met her."

"I know the gorge," said Thoar, "and if the two Phelians entered it it is possible that they captured her. We will search in the direction of the gorge then and if we do not find any trace of her, we shall drop down to the country of the Phelians in the lowland."

Through a maze of jagged peaks Thoar led the way. To him time meant nothing; to Jason Gridley it was little more than a memory. When they found food they ate; when they were tired they slept, and always just ahead there were perilous crags to skirt and stupendous cliffs to scale. To the American it would have seemed incredible that a girl ever could find her way here had he not had occasion to follow where The Red Flower of Zoram led.

Occasionally they were forced to take a lower route which led into the forests that climbed high along the slopes of the mountains, and here they found more game and with Thoar's assistance Jason fashioned a garment from the hide of a mountain goat. It was at best but a sketchy garment; yet it sufficed for the purpose for which it was intended and left his arms and legs free. Nor was it long before he realized its advantages and wondered why civilized man of the outer crust should so encumber himself with useless clothing, when the demands of temperature did not require it.

As Jason became better acquainted with Thoar he found his regard for him changing from suspicion to admiration, and finally to a genuine liking for the savage Pellucidarian, in spite of the fact that this sentiment was tinged with a feeling that, while not positive animosity, was yet akin to it. It was difficult for Jason to fathom the sentiment which seemed to animate him. There could be no rivalry between him and this primitive warrior and yet Jason's whole demeanor and attitude toward Thoar was such as might be scrupulously observed by any honorable man toward an honorable opponent or rival.

They seldom, if ever, spoke of Jana; yet thoughts of her were uppermost in the mind of each of them. Jason often found himself reviewing every detail of his association with her; every little characteristic gesture and expression was indelibly imprinted upon his memory, as were the contours of her perfect figure and the radiant loveliness of her face. Not even the bitter words with which she had parted with him could erase the memory of her joyous comradeship. Never before in his life had he missed the companionship of any woman. At times he tried to crowd her from his thoughts by recalling incidents of his friendship with Cynthia Furnois or Barbara Green, but the vision of The Red Flower of Zoram remained persistently in the foreground, while that of Cynthia and Barbara always faded gradually into forgetfulness.

This state of mental subjugation to the personality of an untutored savage, however beautiful, annoyed his ego and he tried to escape it by dwelling upon the sorrow entailed by the death of Tarzan; but somehow he never could convince himself that Tarzan was dead. It was one of those things that it was simply impossible to conceive.

Failing in this, he would seek to occupy his mind with conjectures concerning the fate of Von Horst, Muviro and the

Waziri warriors, or upon what was transpiring aboard the great dirigible in search of which his eyes were often scanning the cloudless Pellucidarian sky. But travel where it would, even to his remote Tarzana hills in far off California, it would always return to hover around the girlish figure of The Red Flower of Zoram.

Thoar, upon his part, found in the American a companion after his own heart—a dependable man of quiet ways, always ready to assume his share of the burden and responsibilities of the savage trail they trod.

So the two came at last to the rim of the great gorge and though they followed it up and down for a great distance in each direction they found no trace of Jana, nor any sign that she had passed that way.

"We shall go down to the lowlands," said Thoar, "to the country that is called Pheli and even though we may not find her, we shall avenge her."

The idea of primitive justice suggested by Thoar's decision aroused no opposing question of ethics in the mind of the civilized American; in fact, it seemed quite the most natural thing in the world that he and Thoar should constitute themselves a court of justice as well as the instrument of its punishment, for thus easily does man slough off the thin veneer of civilization, which alone differentiates him from his primitive ancestors.

Thus a gap of perhaps a hundred thousand years which yawned between Thoar of Zoram, and Jason Gridley of Tarzana was closed. Imbued with the same hatred, they descended the slopes of the Mountains of the Thipdars toward the land of Pheli, and the heart of each was hot with the lust to kill. No greedy munitions manufacturer was needed here to start a war.

Down through stately forests and across rolling foothills went Thoar and Jason toward the land of Pheli. The country teemed with game of all descriptions and their way was beset by fierce carnivores, by stupid, irritable herbivores of ponderous weight and short tempers or by gigantic reptiles beneath whose charging feet the earth trembled. It was by the exercise of the superior intelligence of man combined with

158

a considerable share of luck that they passed unscathed to the swamp land where Pheli lies. Here the world seemed dedicated to the reptilia. They swarmed in countless thousands and in all sizes and infinite varieties. Aquatic and amphibious, carnivorous and herbivorous, they hissed and screamed and fought and devoured one another constantly, so that Jason wondered in what intervals they found the time to propagate their kind and he marvelled that the herbivores among them could exist at all. A terific orgy of extermination seemed to constitute the entire existence of a large proportion of the species and yet the tremendous size of many of them, including several varieties of the herbivores, furnished ample evidence that considerable numbers of them lived to a great age, for unlike mammals, reptiles never cease to grow while they are living.

The swamp, in which Thoar believed the villages of the Phelians were to be found, supported a tremendous forest of gigantic trees and so interlaced were their branches that oftentimes the two men found it expedient to travel among them rather than upon the treacherous, boggy ground. Here, too, the reptiles were smaller, though scarcely less numerous. Among these, however, there were exceptions, and those which caused them the greatest anxiety were snakes of such titanic proportions that when he first encountered one Jason could not believe the testimony of his own eyes. They came upon the creature suddenly as it was in the act of swallowing a trachodon that was almost as large as an elephant. The huge herbivorous dinosaur was still alive and battling bravely to extricate itself from the jaws of the serpent, but not even its giant strength nor its terrific armament of teeth, which included a reserve supply of over four hundred in the lower jaw alone, availed it in its unequal struggle with the colossal creature that was slowly swallowing it alive.

Perhaps it was their diminutive size as much as their brains or luck that saved the two men from the jaws of these horrid creatures. Or, again, it may have been the dense stupidity of the reptiles themselves, which made it comparatively easy for the men to elude them.

Here in this dismal swamp of horrors not even the giant

tarags or the equally ferocious lions and leopards of Pellucidar dared venture, and how man existed there it was beyond the power of Jason to conceive. In fact he doubted that the Phelians or any other race of men made their homes here. "Men could not exist in such a place," he said to Thoar. "Pheli must lie elsewhere."

"No," said his companion, "members of my tribe have come down here more than once in the memory of man to avenge the stealing of a woman and the stories that they have brought back have familiarized us all with the conditions existing in the land of Pheli. This is indeed it."

"You may be right," said Jason, "but, like these snakes that we have seen, I shall have to see the villages of the Phelians before I will believe that they exist here and even then I won't know whether to believe it or not."

"It will not be long now," said Thoar, "before you shall see the Phelians in their own village."

"What makes you think so?" asked Jason.

"Look down below you and you will see what I have been searching for," replied Thoar, pointing.

Jason did as he was bid and discovered a small stream meandering through the swamp. "I see nothing but a brook," he said.

"That is what I have been searching for," replied Thoar. "All of my people who have been here say that Phelians live upon the banks of a river that runs through the swamp. In places the land is high and upon these hills the Phelians build their homes. They do not live in caverns as do we, but they make houses of great trees so strong that not even the largest reptiles can break into them."

"But why should anyone choose to live in such a place?" demanded the American.

"To eat and to breed in comparative peace and contentment," replied Thoar. "The Phelians, unlike the mountain people, are not a race of warriors. They do not like to fight and so they have hidden their villages away in this swamp where no man would care to come and thus they are practically free from human enemies. Also, here, meat abounds in such quantities that food lies always at their doors. For them then the conditions are ideal and here, more than elsewhere in Pellucidar, may they find contentment."

As they advanced now they exercised the greatest caution, knowing that any moment they might come within sight of a Phelian village. Nor was it long before Thoar halted and drew back behind the bole of a tree through which they were passing, then he pointed forward. Jason, looking, saw a bare hill before them, just a portion of which was visible through the trees. It was evident that the hill had been cleared by man, for many stumps remained. Within the range of his vision was but a single house, if such it might be called.

It was constructed of logs, a foot or two in diameter. Three or four of these logs, placed horizontally and lying one upon the other, formed the wall that was presented to Jason's view. The other side wall paralleled it at a distance of five or six feet, and across the top of the upper logs were laid sections of smaller trees, about six inches in diameter, and placed not more than a foot apart. These supported the roof, which consisted of several logs, a little longer than the logs constituting the walls. The roof logs were laid close together, the interstices being filled with mud. The front of the building was formed by shorter logs set upright in the ground, a single small aperture being left to form a doorway. But the most noticeable feature of Phelian architecture consisted of long pointed stakes, which protruded diagonally from the ground at an angle of about forty-five degrees, pointing outward from the base of the walls entirely around the building at intervals of about eighteen inches. The stakes themselves were six or eight inches in diameter and about ten feet long, being sharpened at the upper end, and forming a barrier against which few creatures, however brainless they might be, would venture to hurl themselves.

Drawing closer the two men had a better view of the village, which contained upon that side of the hill they were approaching and upon the top four buildings similar to that which they had first discovered. Close about the base of the hill grew the dense forest, but the hill itself had been entirely denuded of vegetation so that nothing, either large or small, could approach the habitation of the Phelians without being discovered.

No one was in sight about the village, but that did not deceive Thoar, who guessed that anything which transpired upon the hillside would be witnessed by many eyes peering through the openings between the wall logs from the dim interiors of the long buildings, beneath whose low ceilings Phelians must spend their lives either squatting or lying down, since there was not sufficient headroom to permit an adult to stand erect.

"Well," said Jason, "here we are. Now, what are we going to do?"

Thoar looked longingly at Jason's two Colts. "You have refused to use those for fear of wasting the deaths which they spit from their blue mouths," he said, "but with one of those we might soon find Jana if she was here or quickly avenge her if she is not."

"Come on then," said Jason. "I would sacrifice more than my ammunition for The Red Flower of Zoram." As he spoke he descended from the tree and started toward the nearest Phelian dwelling. Close behind him was Thoar and neither saw the eyes that watched them from among the trees that grew thickly upon the river side of the hill—cruel eyes that gleamed from whiskered faces.

XIII

THE HORIBS

Avan, chief of the Clovi, had placed warriors before the entrance to the cavern and as Tarzan approached it to enter they halted him.

"Where are you going?" demanded one.

"Into the cavern," replied Tarzan.

"Why?" asked the warrior.

"I wish to sleep," replied the ape-man. "I have entered often before and no one has ever stopped me."

"Avan has issued orders that no strangers are to enter or leave the cavern until after the council of the warriors," exclaimed the guard.

At this juncture Avan approached. "Let him enter," he said. "I sent him hither, but do not let him come out again."

Without a word of comment or question the Lord of the Jungle passed into the interior of the gloomy cavern of Clovi. It was several moments before his eyes became accustomed to the subdued light within and permitted him to take account of his surroundings.

That portion of the cavern which was visible and with which he was familiar was of considerable extent. He could see the walls on either side, and, very vaguely, a portion of the rear wall, but adjoining that was utter darkness, suggesting that the cavern extended further into the mountainside. Against the walls upon pallets of dry grasses covered with hide lay many warriors and a few women and children, almost all of whom were wrapped in slumber. In the greater light near the entrance a group squatted engaged in whispered conversation as, silently, he moved about the cavern searching for the girl from Zoram. It was she who recognized him first, attracting his attention by a low whistle.

"You have a plan of escape?" she asked as Tarzan seated himself upon a skin beside her.

"No," he said, "all that we may do is to await developments and take advantage of any opportunity that may present itself."

"I should think that it would be easy for you to escape," said the girl, "they do not treat you as a prisoner; you go about among them freely and they have permitted you to retain your weapons."

"I am a prisoner now," he replied. "Avan just instructed the warriors at the entrance not to permit me to leave here until after the council of warriors had decided my fate."

"Your future does not look very bright then," said Jana,

"and as for me I already know my fate, but they shall not have me, Carb nor any other!"

They talked together in low tones with many periods of long silence, but when Jana turned the conversation upon the world from which Jason had come, the silences were few and far between. She would not let Tarzan rest, but plied him with questions, the answers to many of which were far beyond her powers to understand. Steam and electricity and all the countless activities of civilized existence which are dependent upon them were utterly beyond her powers of comprehension, as were the heavenly bodies or musical instruments or books, and yet despite what appeared to be the darkest depth of ignorance, to the very bottom of which she had plumbed, she was intelligent and when she spoke of those things pertaining to her own world with which she was familiar, she was both interesting and entertaining.

Presently a warrior near them opened his eyes, sat up and stretched. He looked about him and then he arose to his feet. He walked around the apartment awakening the other warriors.

"Awaken," he said to each, "and attend the council of the warriors."

When he approached Tarzan and Jana he recognized the former and stopped to glare down at him.

"What are you doing here?" he demanded.

Tarzan arose and faced the Clovian warrior, but he did not reply to the other's question.

"Answer me," growled Carb. "Why are you here?"

"You are not the chief," said Tarzan. "Go and ask your question of women and children."

Carb sputtered angrily. "Go!" said Tarzan, pointing toward the exit. For an instant the Clovian hesitated, then he continued on around the apartment, awakening the remaining warriors.

"Now he will see that you are killed," said the girl.

"He had determined on that before," replied Tarzan. "We are no worse off than we were."

Now they lapsed into silence, each waiting for the doom

that was to be pronounced upon them. They knew that out-side upon the ledge the warriors were sitting in a great circle and that there would be much talking and boasting and argument before any decision was reached, most of it un-necessary, for that has been the way with men who make laws from time immemorial, a great advantage, however, lying with our modern lawmakers in that they know more words than the first ape-men.

As Tarzan and Jana waited a youth entered the cavern. He bore a torch in the light of which he searched about the interior. Presently he discovered Tarzan and came swiftly toward him. It was Ovan.

"The council has reached its decision," he said. "They will kill you and the girl goes to Carb."

Tarzan of the Apes rose to his feet. "Come," he said to Jana, "now is as good a time as any. If we can cross the ledge and reach the trail only a swift warrior can overtake us. And if you are my friend," he continued, turning to Ovan, "and you have said that you are, you will remain silent and give us our chance."

"I am your friend," replied the youth; "that is why I am here, but you would never live to cross the ledge to the trail, there are too many warriors and they are all prepared. They know that you are armed and they expect that you will try to escape."

"There is no other way," said Tarzan.

"There is another way," replied the boy, "and I have come to show it to you."

"Where?" asked Jana.

"Follow me," replied Ovan, and he started back into the remote recesses of the cavern, which were fitfully illumined by his flickering torch, while behind him followed Jana and the ape-man.

The walls of the cavern narrowed, the floor rose steeply ahead of them, so that in places it was only with considerable difficulty that they ascended in the semi-darkness. At last Ovan halted and held his torch high above his head, re-vealing a small, natural chamber, at the far end of which there was a dark fissure.

"In that dark hole," he said, "lies a trail that leads to the summit of the mountains. Only the chief and the chief's first son ever know of this trail. If my father learns that I have shown it to you, he will have to kill me, but he shall never know for when next they find me I shall be asleep upon a skin in the cavern far below. The trail is steep and rough, but it is the only way. Go now. This is the return I make you for having saved my life." With that he dashed the torch to the floor, leaving them in utter darkness. He did not speak again, but Tarzan heard the soft falls of his sandaled feet groping their way back down toward the cavern of the Clovi.

The ape-man reached out through the darkness and found Jana's hand. Carefully he led her through the stygian darkness toward the mouth of the fissure. Feeling his way step by step, groping forward with his free hand, the ape-man finally discovered the entrance to the trail.

Clambering upward over broken masses of jagged granite through utter darkness, it seemed to the two fugitives that they made no progress whatever. If time could be measured by muscular effort and physical discomfort, the two might have guessed that they passed an eternity in this black fissure, but at length the darkness lessened and they knew that they were approaching the opening in the summit of the mountains; nor was it long thereafter before they emerged into the brilliant light of the noonday sun.

"And now," said Tarzan, "in which direction lies Zoram?"

The girl pointed. "But we cannot reach it by going back that way," she said, "for every trail will be guarded by Carb and his fellows. Do not think that they will let us escape so easily. Perhaps in searching for us they may even find the fissure and follow us here."

"This is your world," said Tarzan. "You are more familiar with it than I. What, then, do you suggest?"

"We should descend the mountains, going directly away from Clovi," replied Jana, "for it is in the mountains that they will look for us. When we have reached the lowland we can turn back along the foot of the range until we are below Zoram, but not until then should we come back to the mountains."

The descent of the mountains was slow because neither of them was familiar with this part of the range. Oftentimes, their way barred by yawning chasms, they were compelled to retrace their steps to find another way around. They ate many times and slept thrice and thus only could Tarzan guess that they had consumed considerable time in the descent, but what was time to them?

During the descent Tarzan had caught glimpses of a vast plain, stretching away as far as the eye could reach. The last stage of their descent was down a long, winding canyon, and when, at last, they came to its mouth they found themselves upon the edge of the plain that Tarzan had seen. It was almost treeless and from where he stood it looked as level as a lake.

"This is the Gyor Cors," said Jana, "and may we not have the bad fortune to meet a Gyor."

"And what is a Gyor?" asked Tarzan.

"Oh, it is a terrible creature," replied Jana. "I have never seen one, but some of the warriors of Zoram have been to the Gyor Cors and they have seen them. They are twice the size of a tandor and their length is more than that of four tall men, lying upon the ground. They have a curved beak and three great horns, two above their eyes and one above their nose. Standing upright at the backs of their heads is a great collar of bony substance covered with thick, horny hide, which protects them from the horns of their fellows and spears of men. Thy do not eat flesh, but they are irritable and short tempered, charging every creature that they see and thus keeping the Gyor Cors for their own use."

"Theirs is a vast domain," said Tarzan, letting his eyes sweep the illimitable expanse of pasture land that rolled on and on, curving slowly upward into the distant haze, "and your description of them suggests that they have few enemies who would care to dispute their dominion."

"Only the Horibs," replied Jana. "They hunt them for their flesh and hide."

"What are Horibs?" asked Tarzan.

The girl shuddered. "The snake people," she whispered in an awed tone.

"Snake people," repeated Tarzan, "and what are they?"

"Let us not speak of them. They are horrible. They are worse than the Gyors. Their blood is cold and men say that they have no hearts, for they do not possess any of the characteristics that men admire, knowing not friendship or sympathy or love."

Along the bottom of the canyon through which they had descended a mountain torrent had cut a deep gorge, the sides of which were so precipitous that they found it expedient to follow the stream down into the plain in order to discover an easier crossing, since the stream lay between them and Zoram.

They had proceeded for about a mile below the mouth of the canyon; around them were low, rolling hills which gradually merged with the plain below; here and there were scattered clumps of trees; to their knees grew the gently waving grasses that rendered the Gyor Cors a paradise for the huge herbivorous dinosaurs. The noonday sun shone down upon a scene of peace and quiet, yet Tarzan of the Apes was restless. The apparent absence of animal life seemed almost uncanny to one familiar with the usual teeming activity of Pellucidar; yet the ape-man knew that there were creatures about and it was the strange and unfamiliar scent spoors carried to his nostrils that aroused within him a foreboding of ill omen. Familiar odors had no such effect upon him, but here were scents that he could not place, strangely disagreeable in the nostrils of man. They suggested the scent spoor of Histah the snake, but they were not his.

For Jana's sake Tarzan wished that they might quickly find a crossing and ascend again to the higher levels on their journey to Zoram, for there the creatures would be well known to them, and the dangers which they portended familiar dangers with which they were prepared to cope, but the vertical banks of the raging torrent as yet offered no means of descent and now they saw that the appearance of flatness which distance had imparted to the great Gyor

Cors was deceptive, since it was cut by ravines and broken by depressions, some of which were of considerable extent and depth. Presently a lateral ravine, opening into the now comparatively shallow gorge of the river, necessitated a detour which took them directly away from Zoram. They had proceeded for about a mile in this direction when they discovered a crossing and as they emerged upon the opposite side the girl touched Tarzan's arm and pointed. The thing that she saw he had seen simultaneously.

"A Gyor," whispered the girl. "Let us lie down and hide in this tall grass."

"He has not seen us yet," said Tarzan, "and he may not come in this direction."

No description of the beast looming tremendously before them could convey an adequate impression of its titanic proportions or its frightful mien. At the first glance Tarzan was impressed by its remarkable likeness to the Gryfs of Pal-ul-don. It had the two large horns above the eyes, a medial horn on the nose, a horny beak and a great, horny hood or transverse crest over the neck, and its coloration was similar but more subdued, the predominant note being a slaty gray with yellowish belly and face. The blue bands around the eyes were less well marked and the red of the hood and the bony protuberances along the spine were less brilliant than in the Gryf. That it was herbivorous, a fact that he had learned from Jana, convinced him that he was looking upon an almost unaltered type of the gigantic triceratop that had, with its fellow dinosaurs, ruled the ancient Jurassic world.

Jana had thrown herself prone among the grasses and was urging Tarzan to do likewise. Crouching low, his eyes just above the grasses, Tarzan watched the huge dinosaur.

"I think he has caught our scent," he said. "He is standing with his head up, looking about him, now he is trotting around in a circle. He is very light on his feet for a beast of such enormous size. There, he has caught a scent, but it is not ours; the wind is not in the right direction. There is something approaching from our left, but it is still at a considerable distance. I can just hear it, a faint suggestion of something moving. The Gyor is looking in that direction now.

Whatever is coming is coming swiftly. I can tell by the rapidly increasing volume of sound, and there are more than one—there are many. He is moving forward now to investigate, but he will pass at a considerable distance to our left." Tarzan watched the Gyor and listened to the sound coming from the, as yet, invisible creatures that were approaching. "Whatever is approaching is coming along the bottom of the ravine we just crossed," he whispered. "They will pass directly behind us."

Jana remained hiding low in the grasses. She did not wish to tempt Fate by revealing even the top of her head to attract the attention of the Gyor. "Perhaps we had better try to crawl away while his attention is attracted elsewhere," she suggested.

"They are coming out of the ravine," whispered Tarzan. "They are coming up over the edge—a number of men—but in the name of God what is it that they are riding?"

Jana raised her eyes above the level of the grasses and looked in the direction that Tarzan was gazing. She shuddered. "They are not men," she said; "they are the Horibs and the things upon the backs of which they ride are Gorobors. If they see us we are lost. Nothing in the world can escape the Gorobors, for there is nothing in all Pellucidar so swift as they. Lie still. Our only chance is that they may not discover us."

At sight of the Horibs the Gyor emitted a terrific bellow that shook the ground and, lowering his head, he charged straight for them. Fully fifty of the Horibs on their horrid mounts had emerged from the ravine. Tarzan could see that the riders were armed with long lances—pitiful and inadequate weapons, he thought, with which to face an enraged triceratop. But it soon became apparent that the Horibs did not intend to meet that charge head-on. Wheeling to their right they formed in single file behind their leader and then for the first time Tarzan had an exhibition of the phenomenal speed of the huge lizards upon which they were mounted, which is comparable only to the lightning-like rapidity of a tiny desert lizard known as a swift.

Following tactics similar to those of the plains Indians of

western America, the Horibs were circling their prey. The bellowing Gyor, aroused to a frenzy of rage, charged first in one direction and then another, but the Gorobors darted from his path so swiftly that he never could overtake them. Panting and blowing, he presently came to bay and then the Horibs drew their circle closer, whirling dizzily about him, while Tarzan watched the amazing scene, wondering by what means they might ever hope to dispatch the ten tons of incarnate fury that wheeled first this way and then that at the center of their circle.

As swiftly as they had darted in all three wheeled and were out again, part of the racing circle, but in the sides of the Gyor they had left two lances deeply imbedded. The fury of the wounded triceratop transcended any of his previous demonstrations. His bellowing became a hoarse, coughing scream as once again he lowered his head and charged.

This time he did not turn and charge in another direction as he had in the past, but kept on in a straight line, possibly in the hope of breaking through the encircling Horibs, and to his dismay the ape-man saw that he and Jana were directly in the path of the charging beast. If the Horibs did not turn him, they were lost.

A dozen of the reptile-men darted in upon the rear of the Gyor. A dozen more lances sank deeply into its body, proving sufficient to turn him in an effort to avenge himself upon those who had inflicted these new hurts.

This charge had carried the Gyor within fifty feet of Tarzan and Jana. It had given the ape-man an uncomfortable moment, but its results were almost equally disastrous for it brought the circling Horibs close to their position.

The Gyor stood now with lowered head, breathing heavily and bleeding from more than a dozen wounds. A Horib now rode slowly toward him, approaching him directly from in front. The attention of the triceratop was centered wholly upon this single adversary as two more moved toward him diagonally from the rear, one on either side, but in such a manner that they were concealed from his view by the great transverse crest encircling his neck behind the horns and eyes. The three approached thus to within about fifty feet

171

of the brute and then those in the rear darted forward simultaneously at terrific speed, leaning well forward upon their mounts, their lances lowered. At the same instant each struck heavily upon either side of the Gyor, driving their spears far in. So close did they come to their prey that their mounts struck the shoulders of the Gyor as they turned and darted out again.

For an instant the great creature stood reeling in its tracks and then it slumped forward heavily and rolled over upon its side—the final lances had pierced its heart.

Tarzan was glad that it was over as he had momentarily feared discovery by the circling Horibs and he was congratulating himself upon their good fortune when the entire band of snake-men wheeled their mounts and raced swiftly in the direction of their hiding place. Once more they formed their circle, but this time Tarzan and Jana were at its center. Evidently the Horibs had seen them, but had temporarily ignored them until after they had dispatched the Gyor.

"We shall have to fight," said Tarzan, and as concealment was no longer possible he arose to his feet.

"Yes," said Jana, arising to stand beside him. "We shall have to fight, but the end will be the same. There are fifty of them and we are but two."

Tarzan fitted an arrow to his bow. The Horibs were circling slowly about them inspecting their new prey. Finally they came closer and halted their mounts, facing the two.

Now for the first time Tarzan was able to obtain a good view of the snake-men and their equally hideous mounts. The conformation of the Horibs was almost identical to man insofar as the torso and extremities were concerned. Their three-toed feet and five-toed hands were those of reptiles. The head and face resembled a snake, but pointed ears and two short horns gave a grotesque appearance that was at the same time hideous. The arms were better proportioned than the legs, which were quite shapeless. The entire body was covered with scales, although those upon the hands, feet and face were so minute as to give the impression of bare skin, a resemblance which was further emphasized by the fact that these portions of the body were a much lighter color, approximating the shiny dead whiteness of a snake's belly. They wore a single apronlike garment fashioned from a piece of very heavy hide, apparently that of some gigantic reptile. This garment was really a piece of armor, its sole purpose being, as Tarzan later learned, to cover the soft, white bellies of the Horibs. Upon the breast of each garment was a strange device—an eight-pronged cross with a circle in the center. Around his waist each Horib wore a leather belt, which supported a scabbard in which was inserted a bone knife. About each wrist and above each elbow was a band or bracelet. These completed their apparel and ornaments. In addition to his knife each Horib carried a long lance shod with bone. They sat on their grotesque mounts with their toes locked behind the elbows of the Gorobors, anomodont reptiles of the Triassic, known to paleontologists as Pareiasuri. Many of these creatures measured ten feet in length, though they stood low upon squat and powerful legs.

As Tarzan gazed in fascination upon the Horibs, whose "blood ran cold and who had no hearts," he realized that he might be gazing upon one of the vagaries of evolution, or possibly upon a replica of some form that had once existed upon the outer crust and that had blazed the trail that some, to us, unknown creature must have blazed from the age of reptiles to the age of man. Nor did it seem to him, after reflection, any more remarkable that a man-like reptile might evolve from reptiles than that birds should have done so or, as scientific discoveries are now demonstrating, mammals must have.

These thoughts passed quickly, almost instantaneously, through his mind as the Horibs sat there with their beady, lidless eyes fastened upon them, but if Tarzan had been astounded by the appearance of these creatures the emotion thus aroused was nothing compared with the shock he received when one of them spoke, addressing him in the common language of the gilaks of Pellucidar.

"You cannot escape," he said. "Lay down your weapons."

XIV

THROUGH THE DARK FOREST

JASON GRIDLEY ran swiftly up the hill toward the Phelian village in which he hoped to find The Red Flower of Zoram and at his side was Thoar, ready with spear and knife to rescue or avenge his sister, while behind them, concealed by the underbrush that grew beneath the trees along the river's bank, a company of swarthy, bearded men watched the two.

To Thoar's surprise no defending warriors rushed from the building they were approaching, nor did any sound come from the interior. "Be careful," he cautioned Jason, "we may be running into a trap," and the American, profiting by the advice of his companion, advanced more cautiously. To the very entrance of the building they came and as yet no opposition to their advance had manifested itself.

Jason stopped and looked through the low doorway, then, stooping, he entered with Thoar at his heels.

"There is no one here," said Jason; "the building is deserted."

"Better luck in the next one then," said Thoar; but there was no one in the next building, nor in the next, nor in any of the buildings of the Phelian village.

"They have all gone," said Jason.

"Yes," replied Thoar, "but they will return. Let us go down among the trees at the riverside and wait for them there in hiding."

Unconscious of danger, the two walked down the hillside and entered the underbrush that grew luxuriantly beneath the trees. They followed a narrow trail, worn by Phelian sandals.

Scarcely had the foliage closed about them when a dozen men sprang upon them and bore them to the ground. In an instant they were disarmed and their wrists bound behind

174

their backs; then they were jerked roughly to their feet and Jason Gridley's eyes went wide as they got the first glimpse of his captors.

"Well, for Pete's sake!" he exclaimed. "I have learned to look with comparative composure upon woolly rhinoceroses, mammoths, trachodons, pterodactyls and dinosaurs, but I never expected to see Captain Kidd, Lafitte and Sir Henry Morgan in the heart of Pellucidar."

In his surprise he reverted to his native tongue, which, of course, none of the others understood.

"What language is that?" demanded one of their captors. "Who are you and from what country do you come?"

"That is good old American, from the U.S.A.," replied Jason; "but who the devil are you and why have you captured us?" and then turning to Thoar, "these are not the Phelians, are they?"

"No," replied Thoar. "These are strange men, such as I have never before seen."

"We know who you are," said one of the bearded men. "We know the country from which you come. Do not try to deceive us."

"Very well, then, if you know, turn me loose, for you must know that we haven't a war on with anyone."

"Your country is always at war with Korsar," replied the speaker. "You are a Sarian. I know it by the weapons that you carry. The moment I saw them, I knew that you were from distant Sari. The Cid will be glad to have you and so will Bulf. Perhaps," he added, turning to one of his fellows, "this is Tanar, himself. Did you see him when he was a prisoner in Korsar?"

"No, I was away upon a cruise," replied the other. "I did not see him, but if this is indeed he we shall be well rewarded."

"We might as well return to the ship now," said the first speaker. "There is no use waiting any longer for these flat-footed natives with but one chance in a thousand of finding a good looking woman among them."

"They told us further down the river that these people

sometimes captured women from Zoram. Perhaps it would be well to wait."

"No," said the other, "I should like well enough to see one of these women from Zoram that I have heard of all my life, but the natives will not return as long as we are in the vicinity. We have been gone from the ship too long now and if I know the captain, he will be wanting to slit a few throats by the time we get back."

Moored to a tree along the shore and guarded by five other Korsars was a ship's longboat, but of a style that was reminiscent of Jason's boyhood reading as were the bearded men with their bizarre costumes, their great pistols and cutlasses and their ancient arquebuses.

The prisoners were bundled into the boat, the Korsars entered and the craft was pushed off into the stream, which here was narrow and swift.

As the current bore them rapidly along Jason had an opportunity to examine his captors. They were as villainous a looking crew as he had ever imagined outside of fiction and were more typically piratical than the fiercest pirates of his imagination. What with earrings and, in some instances, nose rings of gold, with the gay handkerchiefs bound about their heads and body sashes around their waists, they would have presented a gorgeous and colorful picture at a distance sufficiently great to transform their dirt and patches into a pleasing texture.

Although in the story of Tanar of Pellucidar that Jason had received by radio from Perry, he had become familiar with the appearance and nature of the Korsars, yet he now realized that heretofore he had accepted them more as he had accepted the pirates of history and of his boyhood reading—as fictionary or, at best, legendary—and not men of flesh and bone such as he saw before him, their mouths filled with oaths and coarse jokes, the grime and filth of reality marking them as real human beings.

In these savage Korsars, their boat, their apparel and their ancient firearms, Jason saw conclusive proof of their descent from men of the outer crust and realized how they must have carried to the mind of David Innes an overwhelming conviction of the existence of a polar opening leading from Pellucidar to the outer world.

While Thoar was disheartened by the fate that had thrown them into the hands of these strange people, Jason was not at all sure but that it might prove a stroke of fortune for himself, as from the conversation and comments that he had heard since their capture it seemed reasonable to assume that they were to be taken to Korsar, the city in which David Innes was confined and which was, therefore, the first goal of their expedition to effect the rescue of the Emperor of Pellucidar.

That he would arrive there alone and a prisoner were not in themselves causes for rejoicing; yet, on the whole, he would be no worse off than to remain wandering aimlessly through a country filled with unknown dangers without the faintest shadow of a hope of ever being able to locate his fellows. Now, at least, he was almost certain of being transported to a place that they also were attempting to reach and thus the chances of a reunion were so much the greater.

The stream down which they floated wound through a swampy forest, crossing numerous lagoons that sometimes were a size that raised them to the dignity of lakes. Everywhere the waters and the banks teemed with reptilian life, suggesting to Jason Gridley that he was reviewing a scene such as might have been enacted in a Mesozoic paradise countless ages before upon the outer crust. So numerous and oftentimes so colossal and belligerent were the savage reptiles that the descent of the river became a running fight, during which the Korsars were constantly upon the alert and frequently were compelled to discharge their arquebuses in defense of their lives. More often than not the noise of the weapons frightened off the attacking reptiles, but occasionally one would persist in its attack until it had been killed; nor was the possibility ever remote that in one of these encounters some fierce and brainless saurian might demolish their craft and with its fellows devour the crew.

Jason and Thoar had been placed in the middle of the boat, where they squatted upon the bottom, their wrists still secured behind their backs. Close to Jason was a Korsar whose fellows addressed him as Lajo. There was something about this fellow that attracted Jason's particular attention. Perhaps it was his more open countenance or a less savage and profane demeanor. He had not joined the others in the coarse jokes that were directed against their captives; in fact, he paid little attention to anything other than the business of defending the boat against the attacking monsters.

There seemed to be no one in command of the party, all matters being discussed among them and in this way a decision arrived at; yet Jason had noticed that the others listened attentively when Lajo spoke, which was seldom, though always intelligently and to the point. Guided by the result of these observations he selected Lajo as the most logical Korsar through whom to make a request. At the first opportunity, therefore, he attracted the man's attention.

"What do you want?" asked Lajo.

"Who is in command here?" asked Jason.

"No one," replied the Korsar. "Our officer was killed on the way up. Why do you ask?"

"I want the bonds removed from our wrists," replied Jason. "We cannot escape. We are unarmed and outnumbered and, therefore, cannot harm you; while in the event that the boat is destroyed or capsized by any of these reptiles we shall be helpless with our wrists tied behind our backs."

Lajo drew his knife.

"What are you going to do?" asked one of the other Korsars who had been listening to the conversation.

"I am going to cut their bonds," replied Lajo. "There is nothing to be gained by keeping them bound."

"Who are you to say that their bonds shall be cut?" demanded the other belligerently.

"Who are you to say that they shall not?" returned Lajo quietly, moving toward the prisoners.

"I'll show you who I am," shouted the other, whipping out his knife and advancing toward Lajo.

There was no hesitation. Like a panther Lajo swung upon his adversary, striking up the other's knife-hand with his left forearm and at the same time plunging his villainous looking

178

blade to the hilt in the other's breast. Voicing a single blood-curdling scream the man sank lifeless to the bottom of the boat. Lajo wrenched his knife from the corpse, wiped it upon his adversary's shirt and quietly cut the bonds that confined the wrists of Thoar and Jason. The other Korsars looked on, apparently unmoved by the killing of their fellow, except for a coarse joke or two at the expense of the dead man and a grunt of approbation for Lajo's act.

The killer removed the weapons from the body of the dead man and cast them aft out of reach of the prisoners, then he motioned to the corpse. "Throw it overboard," he commanded, addressing Jason and Thoar.

"Wait," cried another member of the crew. "I want his boots."

"His sash is mine," cried another, and presently half a dozen of them were quarreling over the belongings of the corpse like a pack of dogs over a bone. Lajo took no part in this altercation and presently the few wretched belongings that had served to cover the nakedness of the dead man were torn from his corpse and divided among them by the simple expedient of permitting the stronger to take what they could; then Jason and Thoar eased the naked body over the side, where it was immediately seized upon by voracious denizens of the river.

Interminable, to an unknown destination, seemed the journey to Jason. They ate and slept many times and still the river wound through the endless swamp. The luxuriant vegetation and flowering blooms which lined the banks long since had ceased to interest, their persistent monotony making them almost hateful to the eyes.

Jason could not but wonder at the superhuman efforts that must have been necessary to row this large, heavy boat upstream in the face of all the terrific assaults which must have been launched upon it by the reptilian hordes that contested every mile of the downward journey.

But presently the landscape changed, the river widened and the low swamp gave way to rolling hills. The forests, which still lined the banks, were freer from underbrush, suggesting that they might be the feeding grounds of droves of

179

herbivorous animals, a theory that was soon substantiated by sight of grazing herds, among which Jason recognized red deer, bison, bos and several other species of herbivorous animals. The forest upon the right bank was open and sunny and with its grazing herds presented a cheerful aspect of warmth and life, but the forest upon the left bank was dark and gloomy. The foliage of the trees, which grew to tremendous proportions, was so dense as practically to shut out the sunlight, the space between the boles giving the impression of long, dark aisles, gloomy and forbidding.

There were fewer reptiles in the stream here, but the Korsars appeared unusually nervous and apprehensive of danger after they entered this stretch of the river. Previously they had been drifting with the current, using but a single oar, scull fashion, from the stern to keep the nose of the boat pointed downstream, but now they manned the oars, pressing Jason and Thoar into service to row with the others. Loaded arquebuses lay beside the oarsmen, while in the bow and stern armed men were constantly upon watch. They paid little attention to the right bank of the river, but toward the dark and gloomy left bank they directed their nervous, watchful gaze. Jason wondered what it was that they feared, but he had no opportunity to inquire and there was no respite from the rowing, at least not for him or Thoar, though the Korsars alternated between watching and rowing.

Between oars and current they were making excellent progress, though whether they were close to the end of the danger zone or not, Jason had no means of knowing any more than he could guess the nature of the menace which must certainly threaten them if aught could be judged by the attitude of the Korsars.

The two prisoners were upon the verge of exhaustion when Lajo noticed their condition and relieved them from the oars. How long they had been rowing, Jason could not determine, although he knew that while no one had either eaten or slept, since they had entered this stretch of the river, the time must have been considerable. The distance they had come he estimated roughly at something over a hundred miles, and he and Thoar had been continuously at the oars during the entire period, without food or sleep, but they had barely thrown themselves to the bottom of the boat when a cry, vibrant with excitement, arose from the bow. "There they are!" shouted the man, and instantly all was excitement aboard the boat.

"Keep to the oars!" shouted Lajo. "Our best chance is to run through them."

Although almost too spent with fatigue to find interest even in impending death, Jasond ragged himself to a sitting position that raised his eyes above the level of the gunwales of the boat. At first he could not even vaguely classify the horde of creatures swimming out upon the bosom of the placid river with the evident intention of intercepting them, but presently he saw that they were man-like creatures riding upon the backs of hideous reptiles. They bore long lances and their scaly mounts sped through the waters at incredible speed. As the boat approached them he saw that the creatures were not men, though they had the forms of men, but were grotesque and horrid reptiles with the heads of lizards to whose naturally frightful mien, pointed ears and short horns added a certain horrid grotesquery.

"My God!" he exclaimed. "What are they?"

Thoar, who had also dragged himself to a sitting posture, shuddered. "They are the Horibs," he said. "It is better to die than to fall into their clutches."

Carried downward by the current and urged on by the long sweeps and its own terrific momentum, the heavy boat shot straight toward the hideous horde. The distance separating them was rapidly closing; the boat was almost upon the leading Horib when an arquebus in the bow spoke. Its loud report broke the menacing silence that had overhung the river like a pall. Directly in front of the boat's prow the horde of Horibs separated and a moment later they were racing along on either side of the craft. Arquebuses were belching smoke and fire, scattering the bits of iron and pebbles with which they were loaded among the hissing enemy, but for every Horib that fell there were two to take its place.

Now they withdrew to a little distance, but with apparently no effort whatever their reptilian mounts kept pace with the boat and then, one after another on either side, a rider would dart in and cast his lance; nor apparently ever did one miss its mark. So deadly was their aim that the Korsars were compelled to abandon their oars and drop down into the bottom of the boat, raising themselves above the gunwales only long enough to fire their arquebuses, when they would again drop down into concealment to reload. But even these tactics could not preserve them for long, since the Horibs, darting in still closer to the side of the boat, could reach over the edge and lance the inmates. Straight to the muzzles of the arquebuses they came, apparently entirely devoid of any conception of fear; great holes were blown entirely through the bodies of some, others were decapitated, while more than a score lost a hand or an arm, yet still they came.

Presently exhausted and without weapons to defend themselves, Jason and Thoar had remained lying upon the bottom of the boat almost past caring what fate befell them. Half covered by the corpses of the Korsars that had fallen, they lay in a pool of blood. About them arquebuses still roared amid screams and curses, and above all rose the shrill, hissing screech that seemed to be the war cry of the Horibs.

The boat was dragged to shore and the rope made fast about the bole of a tree, though three times the Korsars had cut the line and three times the Horibs had been forced to replace it.

There was only a handful of the crew who had not been killed or wounded when the Horibs left their mounts and swarmed over the gunwales to fall upon their prey. Cutlasses, knives and arquebuses did their deadly work, but still the slimy snake-men came, crawling over the bodies of their dead to fall upon the survivors until the latter were practically buried by greater numbers.

When the battle was over there were but three Korsars who had escaped death or serious wounds—Lajo was one of them. The Horibs bound their wrists and took them ashore, after which they started unloading the dead and wounded from the boat, killing the more seriously wounded with their knives. Coming at last upon Jason and Thoar and finding them unwounded, they bound them as they had the living Korsars and placed them with the other prisoners on the shore.

The battle over, the prisoners secured, the Horibs now fell upon the corpses of the dead, nor did they rest until they had devoured them all, while Jason and his fellow prisoners sat nauseated with horror during the grizzly feast. Even the Korsars, cruel and heartless as they were, shuddered at the sight.

"Why do you suppose they are saving us?" asked Jason.

Lajo shook his head. "I do not know," he said.

"Doubtless to feed us to their women and children," said Thoar. "They say that they keep their human prisoners and fatten them."

"You know what they are? You have seen them before?" Lajo asked Thoar.

"Yes, I know what they are," said Thoar, "but these are the first that I have ever seen. They are the Horibs, the snake people. They dwell between the Rela Am and the Gyor Cors."

As Jason watched the Horibs at their grizzly feast, he became suddenly conscious of a remarkable change that was taking place in their appearance. When he had first seen them and all during the battle they had been of a ghastly bluish color, the hands, feet and faces being several shades paler than the balance of the body, but as they settled down to their gory repast this hue gradually faded to be replaced by a reddish tinge, which caried in intensity in different individuals, the faces and extremities of a few of whom became almost crimson as the feast progressed.

If the appearance and blood-thirsty ferocity of the creatures appalled him, he was no less startled when he first heard them converse in the common language of the men of Pellucidar.

The general conformation of the creatures, their weapons, which consisted of long lances and stone knives, the apron-like apparel which they wore and the evident attempt at ornamentation as exemplified by the insignia upon the breasts of their garments and the armlets which they wore, all tended toward establishing a suggestion of humanity that was at once grotesque and horrible, but when to these other attributes was added human speech the likeness to man created an impression that was indescribably repulsive.

So powerful was the fascination that the creatures aroused in the mind of Jason that he could divert neither his thoughts nor his eyes from them. He noticed that while the majority of them were about six feet in height, there were many much smaller, ranging downward to about four feet, while there was one tremendous individual that must have been fully nine feet tall; yet all were proportioned identically and the difference in height did not have the appearance of being at all related to a difference in age, except that the scales upon the largest of them were considerably thicker and coarser. Later, however, he was to learn that differences in size predicated differences in age; the growth of these creatures being governed by the same law which governs the growth of reptiles, which, unlike mammals, continue to grow throughout the entire duration of their lives.

When they had gorged themselves upon the flesh of the Korsars, the Horibs lay down, but whether to sleep or not Jason never knew since their lidless eyes remained constantly staring. And now a new phenomenon occurred. Gradually the reddish tinge faded from their bodies to be replaced by a dull brownish gray, which harmonized with the ground upon which they lay.

Exhausted by his long tour at the oars and by the horrors that he had witnessed, Jason gradually drifted off into deep slumber, which was troubled by hideous dreams in which he saw Jana in the clutches of a Horib. The creature was attempting to devour The Red Flower of Zoram, while Jason struggled with the bonds that secured him.

He was awakened by a sharp pain in his shoulder and opening his eyes he saw one of the homosaurians, as he had mentally dubbed them, standing over him, prodding him with the point of his sharp lance. "Make less noise," said

184

the creature, and Jason realized that he must have been raving in his sleep.

The other Horibs were rising from the ground, voicing strange whistling hisses, and presently from the waters of the river and from the surrounding aisles of the gloomy forest their hideous mounts came trooping in answer to the summons.

"Stand up!" said the Horib who had awakened Jason. "I am going to remove your bonds," he continued. "You cannot escape. If you try to you will be killed. Follow me," he then commanded after he had removed the thongs which secured Jason's wrists.

Jason accompanied the creature into the midst of the herd of periosauri that was milling about, snapping and hissing, along the shore of the river.

Although the Gorobors all looked alike to Jason, it was evident that the Horibs differentiated between individuals among them for he who was leading Jason threaded his way through the mass of slimy bodies until he reached the side of a particular individual.

"Get up," he said, motioning Jason to mount the creature. "Sit well forward on its neck."

It was with a sensation of the utmost disgust that Jason vaulted onto the back of the Gorobor. The feel of its cold, clammy, rough hide against his naked legs sent a chilly shudder up his spine. The reptilcman mounted behind him and presently the entire company was on the march, each of the other prisoners being mounted in front of a Horib.

Into the gloomy forest the strange cavalcade marched, down dark, winding corridors overhung with dense vegetation, much of which was of a dead pale cast through lack of sunlight. A clammy chill, unusual in Pellucidar, pervaded the atmosphere and a feeling of depression weighed heavily upon all the prisoners.

"What are you going to do with us?" asked Jason after they had proceeded in silence for some distance.

"You will be fed upon eggs until you are fit to be eaten by the females and the little ones," replied the Horib. "They

185

tire of fish and Gyor flesh. It is not often that we get as much gilak meat as we have just had."

Jason relapsed into silence, discovering that, as far as he was concerned, the Horib was conversationally a total loss and for long after the horror of the creature's reply weighed upon his mind. It was not that he feared death; it was the idea of being fattened for slaughter that was peculiarly abhorrent.

As they rode between the never ending trees he tried to speculate as to the origin of these grewsome creatures. It seemed to him that they might constitute a supreme effort upon the part of Nature to reach a higher goal by a less devious route than that which evolution had pursued upon the outer crust from the age of reptiles upwards to the age of man.

During the march Jason caught occasional glimpses of Thoar and the other prisoners, though he had no opportunity to exchange words with them, and after what seemed an interminable period of time the cavalcade emerged from the forest into the sunlight and Jason saw in the distance the shimmering blue water of an inland lake. As they approached its shores he discerned throngs of Horibs, some swimming or lolling in the waters of the lake, while others lay or squatted upon the muddy bank. As the company arrived among them they showed only a cold, reptilian interest in the returning warriors, though some of the females and young evinced a suggestive interest in the prisoners.

The adult females differed but slightly from the males Aside from the fact that they were hornless and went naked Jason could discover no other distinguishing feature. He saw no signs of a village, nor any indication of arts or crafts other than those necessary to produce their crude weapons and the simple apron-like armor that the warriors wore to protect the soft skin of their bellies.

On the way they passed a number of females laying eggs which they deposited in the soft, warm mud just above the water line, covering them lightly with mud, afterwards pushing a slender stake into the ground at the spot to mark the nest. All along the shore at this point were hundreds of such stakes and further on Jason saw several tiny Horibs, evidently but just hatched, wriggling upward out of the mud. No one paid the slightest attention to them as they stumbled and reeled about trying to accustom themselves to the use of their limbs, upon all four of which they went at first, like tiny, grotesque lizards.

Arrived at the higher bank the warrior in charge of Thoar, who was in the lead, suddenly clapped his hand over the prisoner's mouth, pinching Thoar's nose tightly between his thumb and first finger, and, without other preliminaries, dove head foremost into the waters of the lake carrying his victim with him.

Jason was horrified as he saw his friend and companion disappear beneath the muddy waters, which, after a moment of violent agitation, settled down again, leaving only an ever widening circular ripple to mark the spot where the two had disappeared. An instant later another Horib dove in with Lajo and in rapid succession the other two Korsars shared a similar fate.

With a superhuman effort Jason sought to tear himself free from the clutches of his captor, but the cold, clammy hands held him tightly. One of them was suddenly clapped over his mouth and nose and an instant later he felt the warm waters of the lake close about him.

Still struggling to free himself he was conscious that the Horib was carrying him swiftly beneath the surface. Presently he felt slimy mud beneath him, along which his body was being dragged. His lungs cried out in tortured agony for air, his senses reeled and momentarily all went black before him, though no blacker than the stygian darkness of the hole into which he was being dragged, and then the hand was removed from his mouth and nose; mechanically his lungs gasped for air and as consciousness slowly returned Jason realized that he was not drowned, but that he was lying upon a bed of mud inhaling air and not water.

Total darkness surrounded him; he felt a clammy body scrape against his, and then another and another. There was a sound of splashing, gurgling water and then silence—the silence of the tomb.

187

XV

PRISONERS

STANDING UPON the edge of the great Gyor plains surrounded by armed creatures, who had but just demonstrated their ability to destroy one of the most powerful and ferocious creatures that evolution has ever succeeded in producing, Tarzan of the Apes was yet loath to lay down his weapons as he had been instructed and surrender, without resistance, to an unknown fate.

"What do you intend to do with us?" he demanded of the Horib who had ordered him to lay down his weapons.

"We shall take you to our village where you will be well fed," replied the creature. "You cannot escape us; no one escapes the Horibs."

The ape-man hesitated. The Red Flower of Zoram moved closer to his side. "Let us go with them," she whispered. "We cannot escape them now; there are too many of them. Possibly if we go with them we shall find an opportunity later."

Tarzan nodded and then he turned to the Horib. "We are ready," he said.

Mounted upon the necks of Gorobors, each in front of a Horib warrior, they were carried across a corner of the Gyor Cors to the same gloomy forest through which Jason and Thoar had been taken, though they entered it from a different direction.

Rising at the east end of the Mountains of the Thipdars, a river flows in a southeasterly direction entering upon its course the gloomy forest of the Horibs, through which it runs down to the Rela Am, or River of Darkness. It was near the confluence of these two rivers that the Korsars had been attacked by the Horibs and it was along the upper reaches of the same river that Tarzan and Jana were being conducted down stream toward the village of the lizard-men.

The lake of the Horibs lies at a considerable distance from the eastern end of the Mountains of the Thipdars, perhaps five hundred miles, and where there is no time and distances are measured by food and sleep it makes little difference whether places are separated by five miles or five hundred. One man might travel a thousand miles without mishap, while another, in attempting to go one mile, might be killed, in which event the one mile would be much further than the thousand miles, for, in fact, it would have proved an interminable distance to him who had essayed it in this instance.

As Tarzan and Jana rode through the dismal forest, hundreds of miles away Jason Gridley drew himself to a sitting position in such utter darkness that he could almost feel it. "God!" he exclaimed.

"Who spoke?" asked a voice out of the darkness, and Jason recognized the voice as Thoar's.

"It is I, Jason," replied Gridley.

"Where are we?" demanded another voice. It was Lajo.

"It is dark. I wish they had killed us," said a fourth voice.

"Don't worry," said a fifth, "we shall be killed soon enough."

"We are all here," said Jason. "I thought we were all done for when I saw them drag you into the water one by one."

"Where are we?" demanded one of the Korsars. "What sort of hole is this into which they have put us?"

"In the world from which I come," said Jason, "there are huge reptiles, called crocodiles, who build such nests or retreats in the banks of rivers, just above the water line, but the only entrance leads down below the waters of the river. It is such a hole as that into which we have been dragged."

"Why can't we swim out again?" asked Thoar.

"Perhaps we could," replied Jason, "but they would see us and bring us back again."

"Are we going to lie here in the mud and wait to be slaughtered?" demanded Lajo.

"No," said Jason; "but let us work out a reasonable plan of escape. It will gain us nothing to act rashly."

For some time the men sat in silence, which was finally broken by the American. "Do you think we are alone here?" he asked in a low tone. "I have listened carefully, but I have heard no sound other than our own breathing."

"Nor I," said Thoar.

"Come closer then," said Jason, and the five men groped through the darkness and arranged themselves in a circle, where they squatted leaning forward till their heads touched. "I have a plan," continued Jason. "When they were bringing us here I noticed that the forest grew close to the lake at this point. If we can make a tunnel into the forest, we may be able to escape."

"Which way is the forest?" asked Lajo.

"That is something that we can only guess at," replied Jason. "We may guess wrong, but we must take the chance. But I think that it is reasonable to assume that the direction of the forest is directly opposite the entrance through which we were carried into this hole."

"Let us start digging at once," exclaimed one of the Korsars.

"Wait until I locate the entrance," said Thoar.

He crawled away upon his hands and knees, groping through the darkness and the mud. Presently he announced that he had found the opening, and from the direction of his voice the others knew where to start digging.

All were filled with enthusiasm, for success seemed almost within the range of possibility, but now they were confronted with the problem of the disposal of the dirt which they excavated from their tunnel. Jason instructed Lajo to remain at the point where they intended excavating and then had the others crawl in different directions in an effort to estimate the size of the chamber in which they were confined. Each man was to crawl in a straight line in the direction assigned him and count the number of times that his knees touched the ground before he came to the end of the cavern.

By this means they discovered that the cave was long and narrow and, if they were correct in the directions they had assumed, it ran parallel to the lake shore. For twenty feet it extended in one direction and for over fifty in the other.

It was finally decided that they should distribute the earth equally over the floor of the chamber for a while and then carry it to the further end, piling it against the further wall uniformly so as not to attract unnecessary attention in the event that any of the Horibs visited them.

Digging with their fingers was slow and laborious work, but they kept steadily at it, taking turns about. The man at work would push the dirt behind him and the others would gather it up and distribute it, so that at no time was there a fresh pile of earth upon the ground to attract attention should a Horib come. Horibs did come; they brought food, but the men could hear the splash of their bodies in the water as they dove into the lake to reach the tunnel leading to the cave and being thus warned they grouped themselves in front of the entrance to their tunnel effectually hiding it from view. The Horibs who came into the chamber at no time gave any suggestion of suspicion that all was not right. While it was apparent that they could see in the dark it was also quite evident that they could not discern things clearly and thus the greatest fear that their plot might be discovered was at least partially removed.

After considerable effort they had succeeded in excavating a tunnel some three feet in diameter and about ten feet long when Jason, who was excavating at the time, unearthed a large shell, which greatly facilitated the process of excavation. From then on their advance was more rapid, yet it seemed to them all that it was an endless job; nor was there any telling at what moment the Horibs would come to take them for the feast.

It was Jason's wish to get well within the forest before turning their course upward toward the surface, but to be certain of this he knew that they must first encounter roots of trees and pass beyond them, which might necessitate a detour and delay; yet to come up prematurely would be to nullify all that they had accomplished so far and to put a definite end to all hope of escape.

And while the five men dug beneath the ground in the dark hole that was stretching slowly out beneath the dismal forest of the Horibs a great ship rode majestically high in air above the northern slopes of the Mountains of the Thipdars.

"They never passed this way," said Zuppner. "Nothing short of a mountain goat could cross this range."

"I quite agree with you, sir," said Hines. "We might as well search in some other direction now."

"God!" exclaimed Zuppner, "if I only knew in what direction to search."

Hines shook his head. "One direction is as good as another, sir," he said.

"I suppose so," said Zuppner, and, obeying his light touch upon the helm, the nose of the great dirigible swung to port. Following an easterly course she paralleled the Mountains of the Thipdars and sailed out over the Gyor Cors. A slight turn of the wheel would have carried her to the southeast, across the dismal forest through whose gloomy corridors Tarzan and Jana were being borne to a horrible fate. But Captain Zuppner did not know and so the O-220 continued on toward the east, while the Lord of the Jungle and The Red Flower of Zoram rode silently toward their doom.

From almost the moment that they had entered the forest Tarzan had known that he might escape. It would have been the work of but an instant to have leaped from the back of the Gorobor upon which he was riding to one of the lower branches of the forest, some of which barely grazed their heads as they passed beneath, and once in the trees he knew that no Horib nor any Gorobor could catch him, but he could not desert Jana; nor could he acquaint her with his plans for they were never sufficiently together for him to whisper to her unheard by the Horibs. But even had he been able to lay the whole thing before her, he doubted her ability to reach the safety of the trees before the Horibs recaptured her.

If he could but get near enough to take hold of her, he was confident that he could effect a safe escape for both of them and so he rode on in silence, hoping against hope that the opportunity he so desired would eventually develop.

They had reached the upper end of the lake and were skirting its western shore and, from remarks dropped by the Horbis in their conversations, which were far from numerous, the ape-man guessed that they were almost at their destination, and still escape seemed as remote as ever.

Chafing with impatience Tarzan was on the point of making a sudden break for liberty, trusting that the unexpectedness of his act would confuse the lizard-men for just the few seconds that would be necessary for him to throw Jana to his shoulder and swing to the lower terrace that beckoned invitingly from above.

The nerves and muscles of Tarzan of the Apes are trained to absolute obedience to his will; they are never surprised into any revelation of emotion, nor are they often permitted to reveal what is passing in the mind of the ape-man when he is in the presence of strangers or enemies, but now, for once, they were almost shocked into revealing the astonishment that filled him as a vagrant breeze carried to his nostrils a scent spoor that he had never thought to know again.

The Horbis were moving almost directly up wind so that Tarzan knew that the authors of the familiar odors that he had sensed were somewhere ahead of them. He thought quickly now, but not without weighing carefully the plan that had leaped to his mind the instant that that familiar scent spoor had impinged upon his nostrils. His major consideration was for the safety of the girl, but in order to rescue her he must protect himself. He felt that it would be impossible for them both to escape simultaneously, but there was another way now—a way which seemed to offer excellent possibilities for success. Behind him, upon the Gorobor, and so close that their bodies touched, sat a huge Horib. In one hand he carried a lance, but the other hand was free. Tarzan must move so quickly that the fellow could not touch him with his free hand before he was out of reach. To do this would require agility of an almost superhuman nature, but there are few creatures who can compare in this respect with the ape-man. Low above them swung the branches of the dismal forest; Tarzan waited, watching for the opportunity he sought. Presently he saw it—a sturdy branch with ample head room above it—a doorway in the ceiling of somber foliage. He leaned forward, his hands resting lightly upon the neck of the Gorobor. They were almost beneath the branch he had selected when he sprang lightly to his feet and almost in the same movement sprang upward into the tree. So quickly had he accomplished the feat that he was gone before the Horib that had been guarding him realized it. When he did it was too late—the prisoner had gone. With others, who had seen the escape, he raised a cry of warning to those ahead, but neither by sight nor sound could they locate the fugitive, for Tarzan travelled through the upper terrace and all the foliage beneath hid him from the eyes of his enemies.

Jana, who had been riding a little in the rear of Tarzan, saw his escape and her heart sank for in the presence of the Horibs The Red Flower of Zoram had come as near to experiencing fear as she ever had in her life. She had derived a certain sense of comfort from the presence of Tarzan and now that he was gone she felt very much alone. She did not blame him for escaping when he had the opportunity, but she was sure in her own heart that Jason would not thus have deserted her.

Following the scent spoor that was his only guide, Tarzan of the Apes moved rapidly through the trees. At first he climbed high to the upper terraces and here he found a new world—a world of sunlight and luxuriant foliage, peopled by strange birds of gorgeous plumage which darted swiftly hither and thither. There were flying reptiles, too, and great gaudy moths. Snakes coiled upon many a branch and because they were of varieties unknown to him, he did not know whether they constituted a real menace or not. It was at once a beautiful and a repulsive world, but the feature of it which attracted him most was its silence, for its denizens seemed to be voiceless. The presence of the snakes and the dense foliage rendered it an unsatisfactory world for one who wished to travel swiftly and so the ape-man dropped to a lower level, and here he found the forest more open and the scent spoor clearer in his nostrils.

Not once had he doubted the origin of that scent, although it seemed preposterously unbelievable that he should discover it here in this gloomy wood in vast Pellucidar.

He was moving very rapidly for he wished, if possible, to reach his destination ahead of the Horibs. He hoped that his escape might delay the lizard-men and this was, in fact, the case, for they had halted immediately while a number of them had climbed into the trees searching for Tarzan. There was little in their almost expressionless faces to denote their anger, but the sickly bluish cast which overspread their scales denoted their mounting rage at the ease with which this gilak prisoner had escaped them, and when, finally, thwarted in their search, they resumed their interrupted march, they were in a particularly ugly mood.

Far ahead of them now Tarzan of the Apes dropped to the lower terraces. Strong in his nostrils was the scent spoor he had been following, telling him in a language more dependable than words that he had but little further to go to find those he sought, and a moment later he dropped down into one of the gloomy aisles of the forest, dropping as from heaven into the astonished view of ten stalwart warriors.

For an instant they stood looking at him in wide-eyed amazement and then they ran forward and threw themselves upon their knees about him, kissing his hands as they shed tears of happiness. "Oh, Bwana, Bwana," they cried; "it is indeed you! Mulungu has been good to his children; he has given their Big Bwana back to them alive."

"And now I have work for you, my children," said Tarzan; "the snake people are coming and with them is a girl whom they have captured. I thank God that you are armed with rifles and I hope that you have plenty of ammunition."

"We have saved it, Bwana, using our spears and our arrows whenever we could."

"Good," said Tarzan; "we shall need it now. How far are we from the ship?"

"I do not know," said Muviro.

"You do not know?" repeated Tarzan.

"No, Bwana, we are lost. We have been lost for a long while," replied the chief of the Waziri.

"What were you doing away from the ship alone?" demanded Tarzan.

"We were sent out with Gridley and Von Horst to search for you, Bwana."

"Where are they?" asked Tarzan.

A long time ago, I do not know how long, we became separated from Gridley and never saw him again. At that time it was savage beasts that separated us, but how Von Horst became separated from us we do not know. We had found a cave and had gone into it to sleep; when we awoke Von Horst was gone; we never saw him again."

"They are coming!" warned Tarzan.

"I hear them, Bwana," replied Muviro.

"Have you seen them—the snake people?" asked Tarzan.

"No, Bwana, we have seen no people for a long time; only beasts—terrible beasts."

"You are going to see some terrible men now," Tarzan warned them; "but do not be frightened by their appearance. Your bullets will bring them down."

"When, Bwana, have you seen a Waziri frightened?" asked Muviro proudly.

The ape-man smiled. "One of you let me take his rifle," he said, "and then spread out through the forest. I do not know exactly where they will pass, but the moment that any of you makes contact with them commence shooting and shoot to kill, remembering, however, that the girl rides in front of one of them. Be careful that you do not harm her."

He had scarcely ceased speaking when the first of the Horibs rode into view. Tarzan and the Waziri made no effort to seek concealment and at sight of them the leading Horib gave voice to a shrill cry of pleasure. Then a rifle spoke and the leading Horib writhed convulsively and toppled sideways to the ground. The others in the lead, depending upon the swiftness of their mounts, darted quickly toward the Waziri and the tall, white giant who led them, but swifter than the Gorobors were the bullets of the outer world. As fast as Tarzan and the Waziri could fire the Horibs fell. Never before had they known defeat. They blazed blue with rage, which faded to a muddy gray when the bullets found their hearts and they rolled dead upon the ground.

So swiftly did the Gorobors move and so rapidly did Tarzan and the Waziri fire that the engagement was decided within a few minutes of its inception, and now the remaining Horibs, discovering that they could not hope to overcome and capture gilaks armed with these strange weapons that hit them more swiftly than they could hurl their lances, turned and scattered in an effort to pass around the enemy and continue on their way.

As yet Tarzan had not caught a glimpse of Jana, though he knew that she must be there somewhere in the rear of the remaining Horibs, and then he saw her as she flashed by in the distance, borne swiftly upon the back of a fleet Gorobor. What appeared to be the only chance to save her now was to shoot down the swift beast upon which she was being borne away. Tarzan swung his rifle to his shoulder and at the same instant a riderless Gorobor struck him in the back and sent him sprawling upon the ground. By the time he had regained his feet, Jana and her captor were out of sight, hidden by the boles of intervening trees.

Milling near the Waziri were a number of terrified, riderless Gorobors. It was from this number that the fellow had broken who had knocked Tarzan down. The beasts seemed to be lost without the guidance of their masters, but when they saw one of their number start in pursuit of the Horibs who had ridden away, the others followed and in their mad rush these savage beasts constituted as great a menace as the Horibs themselves.

Muviro and his warriors leaped nimbly behind the boles of large trees to escape them, but to the mind of the ape-man they carried a new hope, offering as they did the only means whereby he might overtake the Horib who was bearing away The Red Flower of Zoram, and then, to the horror and astonishment of the Waziri, Tarzan leaped to the back of one of the great lizards as it scuttled abreast of him. Locking his toes beneath its elbows, as he had seen the Horibs do, he was carried swiftly in the mad rush of the creature to overtake its fellows and its masters. No need to urge it on, if

197

he had known what means to employ to do so, for probably still terrified and excited by the battle it darted with incredible swiftness among the boles of the gray trees, outstripping its fellows and leaving them behind.

Presently, just ahead of him, Tarzan saw the Horib who was bearing Jana away and he saw, too, that he would soon overtake him, but so swiftly was his own mount running that it seemed quite likely that he would be carried past Jana without being able to accomplish anything toward her rescue, and with this thought came the realization that he must stop the Horib's mount.

There was just an instant in which to decide and act, but in that instant he raised his rifle and fired. Perhaps it was a wonderful bit of marksmanship, or perhaps it was just luck, but the bullet struck the Gorobor in the spine and a moment later its hind legs collapsed and it rolled over on its side, pitching Jana and the Horib heavily to the ground. Simultaneously Tarzan's mount swept by and the ape-man, risking a bad fall, slipped from its back to go tumbling head over heels against the carcass of the Horib's mount.

Leaping to his feet, he faced the lizard-man and as he did so the ground gave way beneath him and he dropped suddenly into a hole, almost to his armpits. As he was struggling to extricate himself something seized him by the ankles and dragged him downward—cold fingers that clung relentlessly to him dragging him into a dark, subterranean hole.

XVI

ESCAPE

THE O-220 cruised slowly above the Gyor Cors, watchful eyes scanning the ground below, but the only living things they saw were huge dinosaurs. Disturbed by the motors of the dirigible, the great beasts trotted angrily about in circles and occasionally an individual, sighting the ship above him, would gallop after it, bellowing angrily, or again one might charge the elliptical shadow that moved along the ground directly beneath the O-220.

"Sweet tempered little fellows," remarked Lieutenant Hines, who had been watching them from a messroom port.

"Jes' which *am* dem bad dreams, Lieutenant?" asked Robert Jones.

"Triceratops," replied the officer.

"Ah'll try most anything once, suh, but not dem babies," replied Robert.

Unknown to the bewildered navigating officer, the ship was taking a southeasterly course. Far away, on its port side, loomed a range of mountains, hazily visible in the up-curving distance, and now a river cut the plain—a river that came down from the distant mountains—and this they followed, knowing that men lost in a strange country are prone to follow the course of a river, if they are so fortunate as to find one.

They had followed the river for some distance when Lieutenant Dorf telephoned down from the observation cabin. "There is a considerable body of water ahead, sir," he reported to Captain Zuppner. "From its appearance I should say that we might be approaching the shore of a large ocean."

All eyes were now strained ahead and presently a large body of water became visible to all on board. The ship cruised slowly up and down the coast for a short distance, and as it had been some time since they had had fresh water or fresh meat, Zuppner decided to land and make camp, selecting a spot just north of the river they had been following, where it emptied into the sea. And as the great ship settled gently to rest upon a rolling, grassy meadow, Robert Jones made an entry in his little black diary.

"Arrived here at noon."

While the great ship settled down beside the shore of the silent Pellucidarian sea, Jason Gridley and his companions, hundreds of miles to the west, pushed their tunnel upward toward the surface of the ground. Jason was in front, laboriously pushing the earth backward a few handfuls at a time to those behind him. They were working frantically now because the length of the tunnel already was so great that it was with difficulty that they could return to the cavern in time to forestall discovery when they heard Horibs approaching.

As Jason scraped away at the earth above him, there broke suddenly upon his ears what sounded like the muffled reverberation of rifle shots. He could not believe that they were such, and yet what else could they be? For so long had he been separated from his fellows that it seemed impossible that any freak of circumstance had brought them to this gloomy corner of Pellucidar, and though hope ran high yet he cast this idea from his mind, substituting for it a more natural conclusion—that the shots had come from the arquebuses of Korsars, who had come up from the ship that Lajo had told him was anchored somewhere below in the Rela Am. Doubtless the captain had sent an expedition in search of the missing members of his crew, but even the prospects of falling again into the hands of the fierce Korsars appeared a heavenly one by comparison to the fate with which they were confronted.

Now Jason redoubled his efforts, working frantically to drive his narrow shaft upward toward the surface. The sound of the shots, which had lasted but a few minutes, had ceased, to be followed by the rapidly approaching thunder of many feet, as though heavy animals were racing in his direction. He heard them passing almost directly overhead and they seemed so close that he was positive he must be near the surface of the ground. Another shot sounded almost directly above him; he heard the thud of a heavy body and the earth about him shook to the impact of its fall. Jason's excitement had arisen to the highest pitch when suddenly the earth gave way above him and something dropped into the shaft upon his head.

His mind long imbued with the fear that their plan for escape would be discovered by the Horibs, Jason reacted instinctively to the urge of self-preservation, the best chance for the accomplishment of which seemed to be to drag the discoverer of their secret out of sight as quickly as possible, and with this end in view he backed quickly into the tunnel, dragging the interloper with him, and to a certain point this was not difficult, but it so happened that Tarzan had clung to his rifle. The rifle chanced to strike the ground in a horizontal position, as the ape-man was dragged into the tunnel, and the muzzle and butt lodged upon opposite sides of the opening, thus forming a rigid bar across the mouth of the aperture, to which the ape-man clung as Jason dragged frantically upon his ankles, and then slowly the steel thews of the Jungle Lord tensed and as he drew himself upward, he drew Jason Gridley with him. Strain and struggle as he would, the American could not overcome the steady pull of those giant thews. Slowly, irresistibly, he was dragged into the shaft and upward toward the surface of the ground.

By this time, of course, he knew that the creature to which he clung was no Horib, for his fingers were closed upon the smooth skin of a human being, and not upon the scaly hide of a lizard-man, but yet he felt that he must not let the fellow escape.

The Horib, who had been expecting Tarzan's attack, had seen him disappear mysteriously into the ground; nor did he wait to investigate the miracle, but seizing Jana by the wrist he hurried after his fellows, dragging the struggling girl with him.

The two were just disappearing among the boles of the trees down a gloomy aisle of the somber forest when Tarzan, emerging from the shaft, caught a single fleeting glimpse of them. It was almost the growl of an enraged beast that escaped his lips as he realized that this last calamity might have definitely precluded the possibility of effecting the girl's rescue. Chafing at the restraint of the clutching fingers clinging desperately to his ankles, the ape-man kicked violently in an effort to dislodge them and with such good effect that he sent Jason tumbling back into his tunnel, while he leaped to the solid ground and freedom to spring into pursuit of the Horib and The Red Flower of Zoram.

Calling back to his companions to hurry after him, Jason clambered swiftly to the surface of the ground just in time to see a half-naked bronzed giant before he disappeared from view behind the bole of a large tree, but that single glimpse awakened familiar memories and his heart leaped within him at the suggestion it implied. But how could it be? Had not Thoar seen the Lord of the Jungle carried to his doom? Whether the man was Tarzan or not was of less import than the reason for his haste. Was he escaping or pursuing? But in either event something seemed to tell Jason Gridley that he should not lose sight of him; at least he was not a Horib, and if not a Horib, then he must be an enemy of the lizard-men. So rapidly had events transpired that Jason was confused in his own mind as to the proper course to pursue; yet something seemed to urge him not to lose sight of the stranger and acting upon this impulse, he followed at a brisk run.

Through the dark wood ran Tarzan of the Apes, guided only by the delicate and subtle aroma that was the scent spoor of The Red Flower of Zoram and which would have been perceptible to no other human nostrils than those of the Lord of the Jungle. Strong in his nostrils, also, was the sickening scent of the Horibs and fearful less he come upon them unexpectedly in numbers, he swung lightly into the trees and, with undiminished speed, raced in the direction of his quarry; nor was it long before he saw them beneath him—a single Horib dragging the still-struggling Jana.

There was no hesitation, there was no diminution in his speed as he launched himself like a living projectile straight for the ugly back of the Horib. With such force he struck the creature that it was half stunned as he bore it to the ground. A sinewy arm encircled its neck as Tarzan arose dragging the creature up with him. Turning quickly and bending forward, Tarzan swung the body over his head and hurled it violently to the ground, still retaining his hold about its neck. Again and again he whipped the mighty body over his head and dashed it to the gray earth, while the girl, wide-eyed with astonishment at this exhibition of Herculean strength, looked on.

At last, satisfied that the creature was dead or stunned, Tarzan released it. Quickly he appropriated its stone knife and picked up its fallen lance, then he turned to Jana.

202

"Come," he said, "there is but one safe place for us," and lifting her to his shoulder he leaped to the low hanging branch of a nearby tree. "Here, at least," he said, "you will be safe from Horibs, for I doubt if any Gorobor can follow us here."

"I always thought that there were no warriors like the warriors of Zoram," said Jana, "but that was before I had known you and Jason;" nor could she, as Tarzan well knew, have voiced a more sincere appreciation of what he had done for her, for to the primitive woman there are no men like her own men. "I wish," she continued sadly after a pause, "that Jason had lived. He was a great man and a mighty warrior, but above all he was a kind man. The men of Zoram are never cruel to their women, but they are not always thoughtful and considerate. Jason seemed always to think of my comfort before everything except my safety."

"You were very fond of him, were you not?" asked Tarzan.

The Red Flower of Zoram did not answer. There were tears in her eyes and in her throat so that she could only nod her head.

Once in the trees, Tarzan had lowered Jana to her feet, presently discovering that she could travel quite without assistance, as might have been expected of one who could leap lightly from crag to crag upon the dizzy slopes of Thipdars' heights. They moved without haste back to the point where they had last seen Muviro, and his Waziri warriors, but as the way took them down wind Tarzan could not hope to pick up the scent spoor of his henchmen and so his ears were constantly upon the alert for any slightest sound that might reveal their whereabouts. Presently they were rewarded by the sound of footsteps hurrying through the forest toward them.

The ape-man drew the girl behind the bole of a large tree and waited, silent, motionless, for all footfalls are not the footfalls of friends.

They had waited for but a moment when there came into view upon the ground below them an almost naked man clothed in a bit of filthy goatskin, which was almost undistinguishable as such beneath a coating of mud, while the original color of his skin was hidden beneath a similar covering. A great mass of tousled black hair surmounted his head. He was quite the filthiest appearing creature that Tarzan had ever looked upon, but he was evidently no Horib and he was unarmed. What he was doing there alone in the grim forest, the ape-man could not imagine, so he dropped to the ground immediately in front of the surprised wayfarer.

At sight of the ape-man, the other stopped his eyes wide with astonishment and incredulity. "Tarzan!" he exclaimed. "My God, it is really you. You are not dead. Thank God you are not dead."

It was an instant before the ape-man could recognize the speaker, but not so the girl hiding in the tree above. The instant that she had heard his voice she had known him.

A slow smile overspread the features of the Lord of the Jungle. "Gridley!" he exclaimed. "Jason Gridley! Jana told me that you were dead."

"Jana!" exclaimed Jason. "You know her? You have seen her? Where is she?"

"She is here with me," replied Tarzan.

The Red Flower of Zoram had slipped to the ground upon the opposite side of the tree and now she stepped from behind its trunk.

"Jana!" cried Jason, coming eagerly toward her.

The girl drew herself to her full height and turned a shoulder toward him. "Jalok!" she cried contemptuously. "Must I tell you again to keep away from The Red Flower of Zoram?"

Jason halted in his tracks, his arms dropped limply to his sides, his attitude one of utter dejection.

Tarzan looked silently on, his brows momentarily revealing his perplexity; but it was not his way to interfere in affairs that were wholly the concern of others. "Come," he said, "we must find the Waziri."

Suddenly loud voices just ahead apprised them of the presence of other men and in the babel of excited voices Tarzan recognized the tones of his Waziri. Hurrying forward the three came upon a scene that was momentarily ludicrous, but which might soon have developed into tragedy had they not arrived in time.

Ten Waziri warriors armed with rifles had surrounded Thoar and the three Korsars and each party was jabbering volubly in a language unknown to the other.

The Pellucidarians, never before having seen human beings of the rich, deep, black color of the Waziri and assuming that all strangers were enemies, apprehended only the worst and were about to make a concerted effort to escape their captors, while Muviro, believing that these men might have some sinister connection with the disappearance of his master, was determined to hold and question them; nor would he have hesitated to kill them had they resisted him. It was, therefore, a relief to both parties when Tarzan, Jason and Jana appeared, and the Waziri saw their Big Bwana greet one of their captives with every indication of friendship.

Thoar was even more suprised to find Tarzan alive than Jason had been, and when he saw Jana the natural reserve which ordinarily marked his bearing was dissipated by the joy and relief which he felt in finding her safe and well; nor any less surprised and happy was Jana as she rushed forward and threw herself into her brother's arms.

His breast filled with emotion such as he had never experienced before, Jason Gridley stood apart, a silent witness of this loving reunion, and then, probably for the first time, there came to him an acute realization of the fact that the sentiment which he entertained for this little barbarian was nothing less than love.

It galled him even to admit it to himself and he felt that he was contemptible to harbor jealousy of Thoar, not only because Thoar was his friend, but because he was only a primitive savage, while he, Jason Gridley, was the product of ages of culture and civilization.

Thoar, Lajo and the other two Korsars were naturally delighted when they found that the strange warriors whom they had looked upon as enemies were suddenly transformed into friends and allies, and when they heard the story of the battle with the Horibs they knew that the greatest danger which threatened them was now greatly minimized because of the presence of these warriors armed with death-dealing weapons that made the ancient arquebuses of the

Korsars appear as inadequate as sling shots, and that escape from this horrible country was as good as accomplished.

Resting after their recent exertion, each party briefly narrated the recent adventures that had befallen them and attempts were made to formulate plans for the future, but here difficulties arose. Thoar wished to return to Zoram with Jana. Tarzan, Jason and the Waziri desired only to find the other members of their expedition; while Lajo and his two fellows were principally concerned with getting back to their ship.

Tarzan and Jason, realizing that it might not be expedient to acquaint the Korsars with the real purpose of their presence in Pellucidar and finding that the men were familiar with the story of Tanar, gave them to believe that they were merely searching for Sari in order to pay a friendly visit to Tanar and his people.

"Sari is a long way," said Lajo. "He who would go to Sari from here must sleep over a hundred times upon the journey, which would take him across the Korsar Az and then through strange countries filled with enemies, even as far as The Land of Awful Shadow. Maybe one would never reach it."

"Is there no way overland?" asked Tarzan.

"Yes," replied Lajo, "and if we were at Korsar, I might direct you, but that, too, would be a terrible journey, for no man knows what savage tribes and beasts beset the long marches that must lie between Korsar and Sari."

"And if we went to Korsar," said Jason, "we could not hope to be received as friends. Is this not true, Lajo?"

The Korsar nodded. "No," he said. "You would not be received as friends."

"Nevertheless," said Tarzan to Jason, "I believe that if we are ever to find the O-220 again our best chance is to look for it in the vicinity of Korsar."

Jason nodded in acquiescence. "But that will not accord with Thoar's plans," he said, "for, if I understand it correctly, we are much nearer to Zoram now than we are to Korsar and if we decide to go to Korsar, our route will lead directly away from Zoram. But unless we accompany them with the Waziri, I doubt if Thoar and Jana could live to reach Zoram if they returned by the route that he and I have followed since we left the Mountains of the Thipdars."

Tarzan turned to Thoar. "If you will come with us, we can return you very quickly to Zoram if we find our ship. If we do not find it within a reasonable time, we will accompany you back to Zoram. In either event you would have a very much better chance of reaching your own country than you would if you and Jana set out alone from here."

"We will accompany you, then," said Thoar, and then his brow clouded as some thought seemed suddenly to seize upon his mind. He looked for a moment at Jason, and then he turned to Jana. "I had almost forgotten," he said. "Before we can go with these people as friends, I must know if this man offered you any injury or harm while you were with him. If he did, I must kill him."

Jana did not look at Jason as she replied. "You need not kill him," she said. "Had that been necessary The Red Flower of Zoram would have done it herself."

"Very well," said Thoar, "I am glad because he is my friend. Now we may all go together."

"Our boat is probably in the river where the Horibs left it after they captured us," said Lajo. "If it is we can soon drop down to our ship, which is anchored in the lower waters of the Rela Am."

"And be taken prisoners by your people," said Jason. "No, Lajo, the tables are turned now and if you go with us, it is you who will be the prisoners."

The Korsar shrugged. "I do not care," he said. "We will doubtless get a hundred lashes apiece when the captain finds that we have been unsuccessful, that we have brought back nothing and that he has lost an officer and many members of his crew."

It was finally decided that they would return to the Rela Am and look for the longboat of the Korsars. If they found it they would float down in search of the ship, when they would at least make an effort to persuade the captain to receive them as friends and transport them to the vicinity of Korsar.

On the march back to the Rela Am they were not molested by the Horibs, who had evidently discovered that they had met their masters in the Waziri. During the march Jason made it a point to keep as far away from Jana as possible. The very sight of her reminded him of his hopeless and humiliating infatuation, and to be very near her constituted a form of refined agony which he could not endure. Her contempt, which she made no effort to conceal galled him bitterly, though it was no greater than his own self-contempt when he realized that in spite of every reason that he had to dislike her, he still loved her—loved her more than he had thought it was possible for him to love any woman.

The American was glad when a glimpse of the broad waters of the Rela Am ahead of them marked the end of this stage of their journey, which his own unhappy thoughts, combined with the depressing influence of the gloomy forest, had transformed into one of the saddest periods of his life.

To the relief of all, the boat was found still moored where the Horibs had left it; nor did it take them long to embark and push out upon the waters of the River of Darkness.

The river widened as they floated down toward the sea until it became possible to step a mast and set sail, after which their progress was still more rapid. Though the way was often beset by dangers in the form of angry and voracious saurians, the rifles of the Waziri proved adequate protection when other means of defense had failed.

The river became very wide so that but for the current they might have considered it an arm of the sea and at Lajo's direction they kept well in toward the left bank, near which, he said, the ship was anchored. Dimly visible in the distance was the opposite shore, but only so because the surface of Pellucidar curved upward. At the same distance upon the outer crust, it would have been hidden by the curvature of the earth.

As they neared the sea it became evident that Lajo and the two other Korsars were much concerned because they had not sighted their ship.

"We have passed the anchorage," said Lajo at last. "That wooded hill, which we just passed, was directly opposite the spot where the ship lay. I cannot be mistaken because I noted it particularly and impressed it upon my memory as a landmark against the time when we should return from our expedition up the river."

"He has sailed away and left us," growled one of the Korsars, applying a vile epithet to the captain of the departed ship.

Continuing on down to the ocean they sighted a large island directly off the mouth of the river, which Lajo told them afforded good hunting with plenty of fresh water and as they were in need of meat they landed there and made camp. It was an ideal spot inasmuch as that part of the island at which they had touched seemed to be peculiarly free from the more dangerous forms of carnivorous mammals and reptiles; nor did they see any sign of the presence of man. Game, therefore, was abundant.

Discussing their plans for the future, it was finally decided that they would push on toward Korsar in the longboat, for Lajo assured them that it lay upon the coast of the same landmass that loomed plainly from their island refuge. "What lies in that direction," he said, pointing south, "I do not know, but there lies Korsar, upon this same coast," and he pointed in a direction a little east of north. "Otherwise I am not familiar with this sea, or with this part of Pellucidar, since never before has an expedition come as far as the Rela Am."

In preparation for the long cruise to Korsar, great quantities of meat were cut into strips and dried in the sun, or smoked over slow fires, after which it was packed away in bladders that had been carefully cleaned and dried. These were stowed in the boat together with other bladders filled with fresh water, for, although it was their intention to hug the coast on the way to Korsar, it might not always be expedient to land for water or food and there was always the possibility that a storm arising they might be blown out to sea.

At length, all preparations having been made, the strangely assorted company embarked upon their hazardous journey toward distant Korsar.

Jana had worked with the others preparing the provisions and the containers and though she had upon several occasions worked side by side with Jason, she had never relaxed toward him; nor appeared to admit that she was cognizant of his presence.

"Can't we be friends, Jana?" he asked once. "I think we would both be very much happier if we were."

"I am as happy as I can be," she replied lightly, "until Thoar takes me back to Zoram."

XVII

REUNITED

As FAVORABLE winds carried the longboat and its company up the sunlit sea, the O-220, following the same route, made occasional wide circles inland upon what Zuppner now considered an almost hopeless quest for the missing members of the expedition, and not only was he hopeless upon this score, but he also shared the unvoiced hopelessness of the balance of the company with regard to the likelihood of their ever being able to find the polar opening and return again to the outer world. With them, he knew that even their tremendous reserve of fuel and oil would not last indefinitely and if they were unable to find the polar opening, while they still had sufficient in reserve to carry them back to civilization, they must resign themselves to remaining in Pellucidar for the rest of their lives.

Lieutenant Hines finally broached this subject and the two officers, after summoning Lieutenant Dorf to their conference, decided that before their fuel was entirely exhausted they would try to locate some district where they might be reasonably free from attacks by savage tribesmen, or the even more dangerous menace of the mighty carnivores of Pellucidar.

While the remaining officers of the O-220 pondered the

serious problems that confronted them, the great ship moved serenely through the warm Pellucidarian sunlight and the members of the crew went quietly and efficiently about their various duties.

Robert Jones of Alabama, however, was distressed. He seemed never to be able to accustom himself to the changed conditions of Pellucidar. He often mumbled to himself, shaking his head vehemently, and frequently he wound a battered alarm clock or took it down from the hook upon which it hung and held it to his ear.

Below the ship there unrolled a panorama of lovely sea coast, indented by many beautiful bays and inlets. There were rolling hills and plains and forests and winding rivers blue as turquoise. It was a scene to inspire the loftiest sentiments in the lowliest heart nor was it without its effect upon the members of the ship's company, which included many adventurous spirits, who would experience no regret should it develop that they must remain forever in this, to them, enchanted land. But there were others who had left loved ones at home and these were already beginning to discuss the possibilities and the probabilities of the future. With few exceptions, they were keen and intelligent men and fully as cognizant of the possible plight of the O-220 as was its commander, but they had been chosen carefully and there was not one who waivered even momentarily in loyalty to Zuppner, for they well knew that whatever fate was to be theirs, he would share it with them and, too, they had confidence that if any man could extricate them from their predicament, it was he. And so the great ship rode its majestic way between the sun and earth and each part, whether mechanical or human, functioned perfectly.

The Captain and his Lieutenant discussed the future as Robert Jones laboriously ascended the climbing shaft to the walkingway upon the ship's back, a hundred and fifty feet above his galley. He did not come entirely out of the climbing shaft onto the walkingway, but merely looked about the blue heaven and when his gaze had completed the circle, he hesitated a moment and then looked straight up, where, directly overhead, hung the eternal noonday sun of Pellucidar.

Robert Jones blinked his eyes and retreated into the shaft, closing the hatch after him. Muttering to himself, he descended carefully to the galley, crossed it, took the clock off its hook and, walking to an open port, threw it overboard.

To the occupants of the longboat dancing over the blue waves, without means of determining either time or distance, the constant expectation of nearing their journey's end lessened the monotony as did the oft recurring attacks of the frightful denizens of this Mesozoic sea. To the highly civilized American the utter timelessness of Pelluciarian existence brought a more marked nervous reaction than to the others. To a lesser degree Tarzan felt it, while the Waziri were only slightly conscious of the anomalous conditions. Upon the Pellucidarians, accustomed to no other state, it had no effect whatever. It was apparent when Tarzan and Jason discussed the matter with them that they had practically no conception of the meaning of time.

But time did elapse, leagues of ocean passed beneath them and conditions changed.

As they moved along the coast their course changed; though without instruments or heavenly bodies to guide them they were not aware of it. For a while they had moved northeast and then, for a long distance, to the east, where the coast curved gradually until they were running due north.

Instinct told the Korsars that they had come about three quarters of the distance from the island where they had outfitted to their destination. A land breeze was blowing stiffly and they were tacking briskly up the coast at a good clip. Lajo was standing erect in the bow apparently sniffing the air, as might a hunting dog searching out a scent spoor. Presently he turned to Tarzan.

"We had better put in to the coast," he said. "We are in for a stiff blow." But it was too late, the wind and the sea mounted to such proportions that finally they had to abandon the attempt and turn and flee before the storm. There was no rain nor lightning, for there were no clouds—just a terrific wind that rose to hurricane violence and stupendous seas that threatened momentarily to engulf them.

The Waziri were frankly terrified, for the sea was not their element. The mountain girl and her brother seemed awed, but if they felt fear they gave no outward indication of it. Tarzan and Jason were convinced that the boat could not live and the latter made his way to where Jana sat huddled upon a thwart. The howling of the wind made speech almost impossible, but he bent low placing his lips close to her ear.

"Jana," he said, "it is impossible for this small boat to ride out such a storm. We are going to die, but before we die, whether you hate me or not, I am going to tell you that I love you," and then before she could reply, before she could humiliate him further, he turned away and moved forward to where he had been before.

He knew that he had done wrong; he knew that he had no right to tell Thoar's sweetheart that he loved her; it had been an act of disloyalty and yet a force greater than loyalty, greater than pride, had compelled him to speak those words—he could not die with them unspoken. Perhaps it had been a little easier because he could not help but have noticed the seemingly platonic relationship which existed between Thoar and Jana and being unable to picture Jana as platonic in love, he had assumed that Thoar did not appreciate her. He was always kind to her and always pleasant, but he had never been quite as thoughtful of her as Jason thought that he should have been. He felt that perhaps it was one of the strange inflections of Pellucidarian character, but it was difficult to know either Jana or Thoar and also to believe that, for they were evidently quite as normal human beings as was he, and though they had much of the natural primitive reserve and dignity that civilized man now merely affects; yet it seemed unlikely that either one of them could have been for so long a time in close association without inadvertently, at least, having given some indication of their love. "Why," mused Jason, "they might be brother and sister from the way they act."

By some miracle of fate the boat lived through the storm,

but when the wind diminished and the seas went down there were only tumbling waters to be seen on every hand; nor any sign of land.

"Now that we have lost the coast, Lajo, how are we going to set our course for Korsar?" asked Tarzan.

"It will not be easy," replied Lajo. "The only guide that we have is the wind. We are well out on the Korsar Az and I know from which direction the wind usually blows. By keeping always on the same tack we shall eventually reach land and probably not far from Korsar."

"What is that?" asked Jana, pointing, and all eyes turned in the direction that she indicated.

"It is a sail," said Lajo presently. "We are saved."

"But suppose the ship is manned by unfriendly people?" asked Jason.

"It is not," said Lajo. "It is manned by Korsars, for no other ships sail the Korsar Az."

"There is another," exclaimed Jana. "There are many of them."

"Come about and run for it," said Tarzan; "perhaps they have not seen us yet."

"Why should we try to escape?" asked Lajo.

"Because we have not enough men to fight them," replied Tarzan. "They may not be your enemies, but they will be ours."

Lajo did as he was bid, nor had he any alternative since the Korsars aboard were only three unarmed men, while there were ten Waziri with rifles.

All eyes watched the sails in the distance and it soon became apparent that they were coming closer, for the long-boat, with its small sail, was far from fast. Little by little the distance between them and the ships decreased until it was evident that they were being pursued by a considerable fleet.

"Those are no Korsars," said Lajo. "I have never seen ships like those before."

The longboat wallowed through the sea making the best headway that it could, but the pursuing ships, stringing out as far as the eye could reach until their numbers presented the appearance of a vast armada, continued to close up rapidly upon it.

The leading ship was now closing up so swiftly upon them that the occupants of the longboat had an excellent view of it. It was short and broad of beam with rather a high bow. It had two sails and in addition was propelled by oars, which protruded through ports along each side, there being some fifty oars all told. Above the line of oars, over the sides of the ship, were hung the shields of the warriors.

"Lord!" exclaimed Jason to Tarzan; "Pellucidar not only boasts Spanish pirates, but vikings as well, for if those are not viking ships they certainly are an adaptation of them."

"Slightly modernized, however," remarked the Lord of the Jungle. "There is a gun mounted on a small deck built in the bow."

"So there is," exclaimed Jason, "and I think we had better come about. There is a fellow up there turning it on us now."

Presently another man appeared upon the elevated bow deck of the enemy. "Heave to," he cried, "or I'll blow you out of the water."

"Who are you?" demanded Jason.

"I am Ja of Anoroc," replied the man, "and this is the fleet of David I, Emperor of Pellucidar."

"Come about," said Tarzan to Lajo.

"Someone in this boat must have been born on Sunday," exclaimed Jason. "I never knew there was so much good luck in the world."

"Who are you?" demanded Ja as the longboat came slowly about.

"We are friends," replied Tarzan.

"The Emperor of Pellucidar can have no friends upon the Korsar Az," replied Ja.

"If Abner Perry is with you, we can prove that you are wrong," replied Jason.

"Abner Perry is not with us," said Ja; "but what do you know of him?"

By this time the two boats were alongside and the bronzed Mezop warriors of Ja's crew were gazing down curiously upon the occupants of the boat.

"This is Jason Gridley," said Tarzan to Ja, indicating the American. "Perhaps you have heard Abner Perry speak of him. He organized an expedition in the outer world to come here to rescue David Innes from the dungeons of the Korsars."

The three Korsars of the longboat made Ja suspicious, but when a full explanation had been made and especially when he had examined the rifles of the Waziri, he became convinced of the truth of their statements and welcomed them warmly aboard his ship, about which were now gathered a considerable number of the armada. When word was passed among them that two of the strangers were friends from the outer world who had come to assist in the rescue of David Innes, a number of the captains of other ships came aboard Ja's flagship to greet Tarzan and Jason. Among these captains were Dacor the Strong One, brother of Dian the Beautiful, Empress of Pellucidar; Kolk, son of Goork, who is chief of the Thurians; and Tanar, son of Ghak, the Hairy One, King of Sari.

From these Tarzan and Jason learned that this fleet was on its way to effect the rescue of David. It had been building for a great while, so long that they had forgotten how many times they had eaten and slept since the first keel was laid, and then they had had to find a way into the Korsar Az from the Lural Az, where the ships were built upon the island of Anoroc.

"Far down the Sojar Az beyond the Land of Awful Shadow we found a passage that led to the Korsar Az. The Thurians had heard of it and while the fleet was building they sent warriors out to see if it was true and they found the passage and soon we shall be before the city of Korsar."

"How did you expect to rescue David with only a dozen men?" asked Tanar.

"We are not all here," said Tarzan. "We became separated from our companions and have been unable to find them. However, there were not very many men in our expedition. We depended upon other means than manpower to effect the rescue of your Emperor."

At this moment a great cry arose from one of the ships.

The excitement rose and spread. The warriors were all looking into the air and pointing. Already some of them were elevating the muzzles of their cannons and all were preparing their rifles, and as Tarzan and Jason looked up they saw the O-220 far above them.

The dirigible had evidently discovered the fleet and was descending toward it in a wide spiral.

"Now I *know* someone was born on Sunday," said Jason. "That is our ship. Those are our friends," he added, turning to Ja.

All that transpired on board the flagship passed quickly from ship to ship until every member of the armada knew that the great thing hovering above them was no gigantic flying reptile, but a ship of the air in which were friends of Abner Perry and their beloved Emperor, David I.

Slowly the great ship settled toward the surface of the sea and as it did so Jason Gridley borrowed a spear from one of the warriors and tied Lajo's head handkerchief to its tip. With this improvised flag he signalled, "O-220 ahoy! This is the war fleet of David I, Emperor of Pellucidar, commanded by Ja of Anoroc; Lord Greystoke, ten Waziri and Jason Gridley aboard."

A moment later a gun boomed from the rear turret of the O-220, marking the beginning of the first international salute of twenty-one guns that had ever reverberated beneath the eternal sun of Pellucidar, and when the significance of it was explained to Ja he returned the salute with the bow gun of his flagship.

The dirigible dropped lower until it was within speaking distance of the flagship.

"Are you all well aboard?" asked Tarzan.

"Yes," came back the reassuring reply in Zuppner's booming tone.

"Is Von Horst with you?" asked Jason.

"No," replied Zuppner.

"Then he alone is missing," said Jason sadly.

"Can you drop a sling and take us aboard?" asked Tarzan.

Zuppner maneuvered the dirigible to within fifty feet of the deck of Ja's flagship, a sling was lowered and one after another the members of the party were taken on board the O-220, the Waziri first and then Jana and Thoar, followed by Jason and Tarzan, the three Korsars being left prisoners with Ja with the understanding that they were to be treated humanely.

Before Tarzan left the deck of the flagship he told Ja that if he would proceed toward Korsar, the dirigible would keep in touch with him and in the meantime they would be perfecting plans for the rescue of David Innes.

As Thoar and Jana were hoisted aboard the O-220, they were filled with a boundless amazement. To them such a creation as the giant dirigible was inconceivable. As Jana expressed it afterward: "I knew that I was dreaming, but yet at the same time I knew that I could not dream about such a thing as this because no such thing existed."

Jason introduced Jana and Thoar to Zuppner and Hines, but Lieutenant Dorf did not come to the cabin until after Tarzan had boarded the ship, and it was the latter who introduced them to Dorf.

He presented Lieutenant Dorf to Jana and then, indicating Thoar, "This is Thoar, the brother of The Red Flower of Zoram."

As those words broke upon the ears of Jason Gridley he reacted almost as to the shock of a physical blow. He was glad that no one chanced to be looking at him at the time and instantly he regained his composure, but it left him with a distinct feeling of injury. They had all known it and none of them had told him. He was almost angry at them until it occurred to him that they had all probably assumed that he had known it too, and yet try as he would he could not quite forgive Jana. But, really, what difference did it make, for, whether sister or mate of Thoar or another, he knew that The Red Flower of Zoram was not for him. She had made that definitely clear in her attitude toward him, which had convinced him even more definitely than had her bitter words.

The reunited officers of the expedition had much to discuss and many reminiscences to narrate as the O-220 followed above the slowly moving fleet. It was a happy reunion, clouded only by the absence of Von Horst.

As the dirigible moved slowly above the waters of the Korsar Az, Zuppner dropped occasionally to within speaking distance of Ja of Anoroc, and when the distant coast of Korsar was sighted a sling was lowered and Ja was taken aboard the O-220, where plans for the rescue of David were discussed, and when they were perfected Ja was returned to his ship, and Lajo and the two other Korsars were taken aboard the dirigible.

The three prisoners were filled with awe and consternation as Jason and Tarzan personally conducted them throughout the giant craft. They were shown the armament, which was carefully explained to them, special stress being laid upon the destructive power of the bombs which the O-220 carried.

"One of these," said Jason to Lajo, "would blow The Cid's palace a thousand feet into the air and, as you see, we have many of them. We could destroy all of Korsar and all the Korsar ships."

While Ja's fleet was still a considerable distance off the coast, the O-220 raced ahead at full speed toward Korsar, for the plan which they had evolved was such that, if successful, David's release would be effected without the shedding of blood—a plan which was especially desirable since if it was necessary to attack Korsar either from the sea or the air, the Emperor's life would be placed in jeopardy from the bombs and cannons of his friends, as well as from a possible spirit of vengeance which might animate The Cid.

As the dirigible glided almost silently over the city of Korsar, the streets and courtyards filled with people staring upward in awe-struck wonder.

Three thousand feet above the city the ship stopped and Tarzan sent for the three Korsar prisoners.

"As you know," he said to them, "we are in a position to destroy Korsar. You have seen the great fleet coming to the rescue of the Emperor of Pellucidar. You know that every warrior manning those ships is armed with a weapon far more effective than your best; even with their knives and spears and their bows and arrows they might take Korsar without their rifles, but they have the rifles and they have better ammunition than yours and in each ship of the fleet cannons are mounted. Alone the fleet could reduce Korsar, but in addition to the fleet there is this airship. Your shots could never reach it as it sailed back and forth above Korsar, dropping bombs upon the city. Do you think, Lajo, that we can take Korsar?"

"I know it," replied the Korsar.

"Very well," said Tarzan. "I am going to send you with a message to The Cid. Will you tell him the truth?"

"I will," replied Lajo.

"The message is simple," continued Tarzan. "You may tell him that we have come to effect the release of the Emperor of Pellucidar. You may explain to him that the means that we have to enforce our demands, and then you may say to him that if he will place the Emperor upon a ship and take him out to our fleet and deliver him unharmed to Ja of Anoroc, we will return to Sari without firing a shot. Do you understand?"

"I do," said Lajo.

"Very well, then," said Tarzan. He turned to Dorf, "Lieutenant, will you take him now?" he asked.

Dorf approached with a bundle in his hand. "Slip into this," he said.

"What is it?" asked Lajo.

"It is a parachute," said Dorf.

"What is that?" demanded Lajo.

"Here," said Dorf, "put your arms through here." A moment later he had the parachute adjusted upon the Korsar.

"Now," said Jason, "a great distinction is going to be conferred upon you—you are going to make the first parachute jump that has ever been witnessed in Pellucidar."

"I don't understand what you mean," said Lajo.

"You will presently," said Jason. "You are going to take Lord Greystoke's message to The Cid."

"But you will have to bring the ship down to the ground before I can," objected Lajo.

"On the contrary we are going to stay right where we are," said Jason; "you are going to jump overboard."

"What?" exclaimed Lajo. "You are going to kill me?"

"No," said Jason with a laugh. "Listen carefully to what I tell you and you will land safely. You have seen some wonderful things on board this ship so you must have some conception of what we of the outer world can do. Now you are going to have a demonstration of another very wonderful invention and you may take my word for it that no harm will befall you if you do precisely as I tell you to. Here is an iron ring," and he touched the ring opposite Lajo's left breast; "take hold of it with your right hand. After you jump from the ship, pull it; give it a good jerk and you will float down to the ground as lightly as a feather."

"I will be killed," objected Lajo.

"If you are a coward," said Jason, "perhaps one of these other men is braver than you. I tell you that you will not be hurt."

"I am not afraid," said Lajo. "I will jump."

"Tell The Cid," said Tarzan, "that if we do not presently see a ship sail out alone to meet the fleet, we shall start dropping bombs upon the city."

Dorf led Lajo to a door in the cabin and flung it open. The man hesitated.

"Do not forget to jerk the ring," said Dorf, and at the same time he gave Lajo a violent push that sent him headlong through the doorway and a moment later the watchers in the cabin saw the white folds of the parachute streaming in the air. They saw it open and they knew that the message of Tarzan would be delivered to The Cid.

What went on in the city below we may not know, but presently a great crowd was seen to move from the palace down toward the river, where the ships were anchored, and a little later one of the ships weighed anchor and as it drifted slowly with the current its sails were set and presently it was moving directly out to sea toward the fleet from Sari.

The O-220 followed above it and Ja's flagship moved forward to meet it, and thus David Innes, Emperor of Pelluci-dar, was returned to his people.

As the Korsar ship turned back to port the dirigible dropped low above the flagship of the Sarian fleet and greet-ings were exchanged between David and his rescuers—men from another world whom he had never seen.

The Emperor was half starved and very thin and weak from his long period of confinement, but otherwise he had been unharmed, and great was the rejoicing aboard the ships of Sari as they turned back to cross the Korsar Az toward their own land.

Tarzan was afraid to accompany the fleet back to Sari for fear that their rapidly diminishing store of fuel would not be sufficient to complete the trip and carry them back to the outer world. He followed the fleet only long enough to obtain from David explicit directions for reaching the polar opening from the city of Korsar.

"We have another errand to fulfill first," said Jason to Tarzan. "We must return Thoar and Jana to Zoram."

"Yes," said the ape-man, "and drop these two Korsars off near their city. I have thought of all that and we shall have fuel enough for that purpose."

"I am not going to return with you," said Jason. "I wish to be put aboard Ja's flagship."

"What?" exclaimed Tarzan. "You are going to remain here?"

"This expedition was undertaken at my suggestion. I feel responsible for the life and safety of every man in it and I shall never return to the outer world while the fate of Lieu-tenant Von Horst remains a mystery."

"But how can you find Von Horst if you go back to Sari with the fleet?" asked Tarzan.

"I shall ask David Innes to equip an expedition to go in search of him," replied Jason, "and with such an expedition made up of native Pellucidarians I shall stand a very much better chance of finding him than we would in the O-220."

"I quite agree with you," said Tarzan, "and if you are un-alterably determined to carry out your project, we will lower you to Ja's ship immediately."

As the O-220 dropped toward Ja's flagship and signalled

it to heave to, Jason gathered what belongings he wished to take with him, including rifles and revolvers and plenty of ammunition. These were lowered first to Ja's ship, while Jason bid farewell to his companions of the expedition.

"Good-bye, Jana," he said, after he had shaken hands with the others.

The girl made no reply, but instead turned to her brother.

"Good-bye, Thoar," she said.

"Good-bye?" he asked. "What do you mean?"

"I am going to Sari with the man I love," replied The Red Flower of Zoram.